# PROJECT HERO

BRIAR PRESCOTT

# ABOUT THIS BOOK

*What if you accidentally fell in love with the right guy?*

**Andy:**

If my life was a movie, I would be the sidekick. Not an especially promising start when my plan is to finally let my best friend know I have a crush on him. No worries, though. I have a plan. I just need a complete makeover. Change everything about myself so that when Falcon returns from his summer vacation, he can finally see I'm the love of his life. I totally know what I'm doing here.

Well, not really.

If I knew what I was doing, I wouldn't look like every nerd cliché wrapped into one awkward package.

In short, I'm screwed.

But then Law Anderson enters the picture...

**Law:**

It's all very simple. I need somebody to tutor my hockey team, and Andy needs somebody to help him with his crush. Sounds like a match made in heaven.

Only the more time I spend with Andy, the more I like this quirky guy who makes me laugh, and pretty soon *I'm* the one who's tutoring Andy in way more than we initially agreed upon.

It's fine.

I have it all under control.

But as weeks pass and the chemistry between us turns explosive, I'm starting to think that I might be in way over my head with Andy.

If only I could make Andy realize that he doesn't need to change himself for love. If only I could make Andy see that he just needs to be with somebody who has considered him perfect all along…

Cover by: Black Jazz Design

Editing by: Louisa Keller at LesCourt Author Services

Proofreading by: Jill Wexler at LesCourt Author Services

Formatting by: Leslie Copeland at LesCourt Author Services

# PROLOGUE

## ANDY

I was sixteen years old when I realized something life changing about myself—I was the sidekick.

In hindsight, I'm forced to admit there were signs. I'm unremarkable in every aspect of my life. Okay, fine, I'm decent with numbers. Throw some physics at me, and I can chew my way through it. It's the reason I routinely exchanged the illusion of friendship for help with homework while I was in high school.

Everything else, though? Mediocre city, population me. I'm not particularly tall, nor am I noticeably short. I'm not fit. No six packs or V-shapes have ever graced my body with their presence. My hair is a very average brown and my eyes are an equally ordinary gray. I don't look repulsive, but there's nothing about me that would catch anybody's attention.

I'm the guy who looks like the boring neighbor that lives across the hall from you and later turns out to be a cannibal with a freezer full of body parts in his spare bedroom. All the neighbors would be completely surprised once the police came to arrest me, and they'd say things like, *but he was so ordinary*. The old lady from upstairs would wax poetic about how I helped her carry her grocery bags to her apartment every Sunday, and to that I say, "That's how they get you, Mirna. That's how they get you."

So...

That's me. Minus the people-eating part. I'm too average to be a psycho.

I have no talents. My singing sounds like somebody is trying to stuff a litter of angry cats into a wet bag. My drawings are at a preschool level at best.

I once drew a bunny for my niece. She started crying when she saw the result. My sister was pissed and refused to listen to my explanation that I was not trying to scar her kid for life with my rendition of mutant rabbits but rather, I was trying to educate Lily and show her which rabbits to avoid should there ever be a nuclear disaster. That's what I get for trying to make the best of a bad situation and turn a disaster of a drawing into a teaching moment.

As for other talents, I can't dance, and I'm very much opposed to public speaking, proven by the vomiting-onstage incident at the seventh-grade debate. The accompanying stage fright was so bad that I couldn't even walk across the stage at my high school graduation. I had an honest-to-God panic attack five minutes before the principal called my name. My mom had to step in and claim my diploma for me. Needless to say, acting, politics, and even teaching are not viable career options for me.

I have glasses that are an absolute must, since otherwise, I'm blind as a bat and walk into a lot of walls. I've tried not wearing them in hopes of walking into a hot guy instead. Didn't happen. I *did* stumble into an angry janitor once, who sprayed me with a bottle of Windex and yelled at me. It wasn't a love match.

I wear sweats a lot. And I do mean *a lot*. I was actively campaigning for wearing sweats to my high school graduation because those suckers are just that comfortable and nobody would have even seen them under the robe. Unfortunately, I was downvoted by every single member of my extended family. Even my great-grandpa, the traitor. My closet holds a wide variety of physics-themed T-shirts, and I can proudly say that I wore socks with sandals before it was cool.

My hair is a curly mess, and when passing on genes, my dad bestowed upon me the gift of multiple cowlicks. On a good day, I look like I do not own a hairbrush. On a bad day, I look like the lovechild of Albert Einstein and Edward Scissorhands. There are more bad days than good ones.

The only remarkable thing about me is my best friend. Falcon Asola. Even his name sounds like he'd be a good protagonist in any story. He's everything I'm not. Tall, handsome as hell, ridiculously in shape. He's the captain of Baril University's basketball team, which is a big deal, since they tend to win a lot. I mean, we're a hockey school, but Falcon has single-handedly brought basketball back to everyone's attention in Baril. They even renovated the courts last year because winners get special perks like that.

Falcon is popular and there are no vomit-related episodes in *his* past. Instead, he's quick with a comeback, funny and smart. It would be annoying as hell if he wasn't my best friend since the summer before ninth grade, and the coolest, nicest human being on planet Earth.

He's the Wayne to my Garth. Wallace to my Gromit. Shrek to my Donkey. Batman to my Robin.

And sure, I guess you could argue that without Watson's help, Sherlock would be a neurotic mess who couldn't even solve the case half the time, but let's face it, nobody would go see a film about Dr. Watson. He's not charismatic enough, hence, the position as a sidekick.

Ever since Falcon's family moved in next door the summer before ninth grade, we've been best friends. He doesn't mind that I'm awkward and dress like a cross between a nerd and the thirty-five-year-old whose parents just can't seem to get him to move out of their basement.

I had been deathly afraid my less-than-stellar situation in school would make him drop me like a hot potato once he realized he'd chained himself to his unpopular nerd of a neighbor by accident. But Falcon had stuck by me. He'd also put a stop to the nickname hurl-

master, which had taken off like a rocket when one of the jocks had yelled it out after the debate that shall not be talked about.

The thing about sidekicks is, they are usually left in the hero's shadow. See, when I made my big, life changing discovery about being a sidekick, it took me a while to come to terms with it. Everybody wants to be a hero in their story. It's human nature. But like my grandma used to say, life is not a wish factory. If you want something, you've got to be willing to work for it. And so, with those words of wisdom in mind, I took a good, hard look at myself at the end of my junior year of college. The results were disappointing, but I had a quick fix—I decided to drown all my sorrows in alcohol.

The next morning, while battling the mother of all hangovers, I came up with a plan. I'm a problem-solver at heart, so the way I saw it, if I didn't like myself that much, I could just change everything about myself. My goal was to turn the sidekick into a hero. And that's how Project Hero was born. It was a brilliant stroke of genius.

It would have been better if I'd done it just because I wanted to be a better, more accomplished version of myself. Unfortunately, I had a bit of a different goal in mind. Namely, I was in love with Falcon Asola, and I would finally make him notice me.

# 1

# ANDY

I, like a lot of people, am a creature of habit. I eat oatmeal for breakfast every morning. I take an eighteen-minute nap every afternoon. When I go to the library, I sit in a certain spot.

Some people don't like the routine. Me? I love it. It helps me concentrate and makes my brain less crowded if I have all the everyday decisions made beforehand. Which is why it throws me for a loop when I get to the library on a sunny Friday afternoon, only to find that my usual seat has already been taken.

I come to a complete standstill and stare at the behemoth of a guy who occupies the corner that usually belongs to me. It's not like there's a sign with my name on the desk, but damn, not many people even step foot into the science wing. Most students in my department know each other. If not by name, then by face and also by where we like to sit.

Rebecca, the biology major, likes to sit by the window that faces the lake. Tyson, another physicist, prefers the desk that is an equal distance from the physics shelves and the rows dedicated to math. He's a double major and coincidentally also a major overachiever. The redheaded freshman likes to be close to the information desk. Lots of questions and awkward flirting with the help desk lady for that one.

And I like the back corner of the library because it's quiet and very few people venture this way, so I can concentrate better while studying.

Baril U is a small university in the state of Vermont. The physics department is tiny, one of those everybody-knows-everybody type of deals. It's a decent program. It's not the best in the world, but it's far from the worst. Definitely the best Vermont has to offer, and since my parents have six kids, with me in the fourth position, there isn't exactly money to spare for college. Am I a tiny bit bitter about not attending MIT? I guess a minuscule part of me had dreamed about going, but there's always a chance I'll go for my PhD. At least that's the plan right now. Anyway, what matters is here and now, and right now, out-of-state schools are a definite no. Besides, Baril offered me a generous scholarship, so long story short, here I am.

And here is also this other dude I've never seen before, sitting in my chair, in my corner, like he owns the place. Unfortunately, a sign with my name hasn't magically appeared out of thin air, so first, I make a mental note to create a sign.

Right now, I have to come to terms with the fact that, technically, it's a free country, and the dude can sit wherever he wants. I huff under my breath as I find a free seat. I make sure to keep *my* seat in my line of sight. The goal is to observe and when baseball cap here leaves, I'll be on it like cream cheese on a bagel, before some other idiot with bad manners seizes the opportunity to snatch the best desk in the library. Not that there is exactly a line out the door, but you never know. I didn't expect Mr. I've-Got-An-Incredibly-Firm-Ass over there either, and yet, here we are...

I take out my laptop and my books and notes and lay them out on the desk in front of me, all the while throwing icy glances at the guy. He doesn't even seem to register that somebody else has entered the room. He's hunched over, but his back is so wide that it's impossible to say what he's doing. I glare at the massive shoulders. Nothing happens. Guess I can cross off freezing people with my eyeballs from my potential list of superpowers. Bummer.

The unexpected seating complication has thrown me off my game, but I open the research proposal I have to perfect and get to work. It takes a while to get going, and I'm not concentrating as well as I usually do because I'm busy glaring at the intruder and swearing under my breath. There's no way I'll finish the task I've set for myself on time, which means I'll have to cut my eighteen-minute nap from my schedule, and it annoys me to no end.

I grumble and huff like I'm the big, bad wolf, ready to blow down the straw house. The guy straightens himself and I'm pretty certain he's heard me, but he only adjusts his headphones and leans forward on his elbows. There's some space left between the elbow and his side, and fuck it, it looks like he's not studying at all. I have no idea what possesses me to do it, but I get up from my chair and move closer until I'm standing right behind the guy. I look over his shoulder, and just as I suspected, he's scrolling through his phone. There are no books, no pens, no laptop, not even a smell of a notecard anywhere in his vicinity. The bastard is occupying my seat to waste time on social media. Fucking perfect.

I grit my teeth and turn around, but before I can go back to my seat, I reconsider. This is supposed to be the new me. I'm not supposed to blend into the tapestry any longer. A hero has a can-do attitude, and he fights injustice, so that's exactly what I'm going to do. With epic tunes playing in my mind as an encouraging soundtrack for my act of bravery, I straighten my shoulders and prepare myself to stand up for my rights.

"Excuse me," I say. I'm louder than I should be, considering it's a library. Already I'm getting annoyed looks thrown my way. The seat stealer doesn't react at all. He has his music turned up so high I can hear the aggressive guitar riffs floating around him.

I tap on his shoulder and bark, "Hey!" with a firm voice that would make a drill sergeant proud.

The guy jumps, tears his earbuds out, and slams them on the desk in front of him. "What the hell?" he snaps and glares at me.

He takes off his baseball cap and drags his hand through his dark hair, and I wince. The guy sitting in front of me is none other than

Law Anderson. He's my nemesis. Well, as much of a nemesis as someone can be when they don't even know you exist.

Law used to be the star of the hockey team, and since the hockey team and the basketball team don't like each other because of some stupid prank from freshman year, I'm forced to dislike the guy too. Falcon claims it's the bro code, and so far, it hasn't been a challenge to honor it, since I've never actually talked to Law. I've seen him at a couple of parties Falcon has dragged me to, but Law has never noticed me. He's usually busy with being in the spotlight with people scrambling to get his attention.

Now that Law has quit the team, I should probably ask Falcon if the feud still stands. As of last season, Law is the assistant coach and not a player anymore, so that might change the situation a bit. I make a mental note to check. Just in case. Putting all those technicalities aside, though, if Law doesn't get out of my seat, I'll have to start a whole separate feud for a completely different reason.

I channel my best Sheldon Cooper impression as I stare at Law. "You're in my seat."

He frowns. "I didn't know there was assigned seating."

"There isn't," I reply with as much dignity as I can muster.

"This is my regular seat, and you're not using it for its intended purpose anyway, so I figure you might as well 'study' your phone somewhere else." I add finger quotes around the word study to fully express my disdain.

Law leans back in his seat and looks at me.

"Is that so?" he asks. Law is fighting a smile, and I make a valiant effort to not let it get to me. I'm supposed to be authoritative and resolute, but so far, Law only looks amused at my tentative display of alpha-maleness and shows no sign that he's planning to move anywhere. Even so, I persevere.

"There's an unwritten understanding that there are some seats that are always taken." I point to the one Law is using. "That's one of them."

Law's smile widens. "That seems unfair. How am I supposed to know about this nonverbal, non-written agreement?"

"You're not. What you are supposed to do is free the seat when the official owner shows up."

"The library?" he asks. He's full-on laughing at me now, and if I felt indifferent toward him before, I now fully support Falcon in his hate for the guy.

"Me," I snap.

He cocks his head to the side and studies me like I'm a fascinating creature on display in a circus. "Nah," he finally says. "I don't feel like it."

"But... you're not even using it for its intended purpose," I sputter. "You can notify your followers or stalkers or whoever of your whereabouts from anywhere. You don't need to be in this particular seat for it. I'm sure they'd be happy to murder you in a place that has fewer witnesses."

"There are available seats all around here. I don't see why *you* need that specific seat either," he reasons. My hackles rise because he's so calm, and I'm teetering on the edge of losing it.

"But it's my seat," I grit out, well aware that my argument is as thin as a layer of graphene but not ready to give up yet either.

Law leans back in his chair with a calculating look in his eyes. "What is this seat worth to you?" he asks.

I'm not an idiot. I guess I have above-average intelligence in some areas of my life, but most of that pertains to science. That intelligence, however, is counterbalanced by my complete and total lack of understanding when it comes to social situations. Like right now. What does Law mean? Does he want me to offer him money for the seat? Is this a thinly veiled threat and I'm supposed to start running so I don't get beaten up? Or is he...

"Are you coming on to me?" I blurt out the most ridiculous option that comes to mind and immediately wish the library floor would open up and suck me into a black hole because the guy loses it. There's no other word to describe what is happening to him. He laughs so hard there are actual tears running down his cheeks. If there ever was a time to carry out seppuku, this is it. If only I had something sharp within reach.

"Okay. Thanks for the humiliation," I say. "This should last me a good while."

I turn around to flee the premises, and jump in a lake while I'm at it, but Law stops me with a hand. "Don't leave. I'm very sorry. I didn't mean to laugh or insinuate that the idea is ridiculous. It was just unexpected. You surprised me. Not many people manage to do that. Let's just say that your guess was the opposite of what I was planning."

I squint. His fingers are wrapped around my wrist, and although I'm now officially a first-class passenger on the Law Anderson hate train, it's hard not to get sidetracked by how freaking handsome the guy is.

His black hair is messy like he's in the habit of combing through it with his fingers. He has that whole square jaw, high cheekbones look going on, which is my kryptonite. And as if that wasn't enough, he has the most piercing, emerald-green eyes I've ever seen on a person. There must be some Irish somewhere in his gene pool because he definitely looks the part.

I frown. Good looks will not sway me. I'm not that shallow of a person. I pull my hand free and glare at Law.

"What exactly were you planning, then?" I ask because, damn it, I'm curious.

"You're Andy Carter," he says. He doesn't ask it. He's stating a fact.

I stare at him. It's my turn to be surprised. Law Anderson knows my name? How? Why? Since when? And, oh yeah, how?

Immediately, my brain decides that over-the-top paranoia is the way to go. Has he been following me? Did he know it was my seat before he took it? Why is Law Anderson even here, talking to *me*? It could be an elaborate prank. Why on earth he'd want to prank me is a mystery on its own, but thanks to my sisters, I've seen a lot of romantic comedies set in high school, so I'm willing to entertain outlandish scenarios. Of course, pretending to be interested in me just to humiliate me later doesn't seem like it would serve any purpose. There's nothing interesting about me. I did get some fascinating results in my experiment on lattice vibration last week, but I doubt Law is here for that information.

Unless he's doing it to find out something about Falcon. Why would he, though? It's not like he's a spy and Falcon is some kind of secret agent with classified information hidden in a briefcase under his bed.

Or is he?

I force my errant mind to stop throwing idiotic thoughts at me because it's getting ridiculous even for my standards. Coming for me because of Falcon still seems plausible, though. Granted, it seems farfetched and like a waste of time on his part. Then again, what the hell do I know about feuds? The whole not-liking-a-person-because-he-plays-a-different-sport thing is pretty stupid, to be honest. Not that I would ever tell that to Falcon. Go Wildcats.

While I'm busy reeling in the crazy, Law starts to look unsure of himself. Whether it's because he's questioning if he has the right person or if he is realizing the right person is a head case is anybody's guess.

"I am," I finally say.

He nods, still weary, but I can't really blame him. "Good. Okay. This is going to sound weird, but I would like to offer you a job."

He's right. It does sound weird. And my brain is off again, conjuring up another set of ideas that are way too out there for even the most dedicated conspiracy theorists.

What a great day it is turning out to be.

## 2

---

# LAW

The guy stares at me like jobs are a foreign concept. It goes on for a long time, but eventually, he snorts and rolls his eyes. "Hah. Good one. And now, would you please be so kind as to get the hell out of my seat?"

What is this weird obsession he has with this damn chair? I have no idea, but it seems like it's the bargaining chip I have for this exchange, so I stay put. I do stand up, though. To even the playing field. I plant my hands on the back of the chair and lean forward.

"I need help," I say.

He snorts again. "Do I look like somebody who's good at sports?" he asks.

"No," I say way too quickly and immediately wish I could take it back. I should be buttering up the guy, not insulting him.

He doesn't seem to be that bothered, though, as he nods and says, "Exactly." He moves to his desk, which is right behind the one I've been using for the past hour and a half while I waited for him to show up. I've gone full-on stalker on the dude. I have a picture of him, taken at some kind of a party, and I'm armed with the knowledge that I've gathered over the last few days.

Andy Carter. Twenty-two. Majors in physics. Can be found in the library every day, even though it's the end of the semester, and we're heading for the summer break. I've been trying to track Andy down for three days. It hasn't been smooth sailing. I'm volunteering at a hockey camp this summer, and the meetings and preparations have taken up a lot of my time. Still, I've been in the library every day, waiting for Andy.

It seems like a lot of trouble to go through for one guy, but there's a reason for that. Baril University prides itself on giving all the students a well-rounded education, which is not a bad thing at all. Baril has prerequisites for math and science, and there are several core subjects everybody has to take. It's not exactly stuff for beginners most of the time and bad news for those who hoped they could leave physics and chemistry behind them once high school was over. Most people can deal with it because Baril U is a good school, and you need a certain amount of gray matter to even get in.

There have always been people who need a little extra help, and it's generally easy enough to find tutors. That is to say, it *was* easy enough until the appointment of Professor Robert Shaw last year. He teaches physics, and he's the sole reason every one of our rookies flunked physics this spring term. All seven of them. Rumor has it the dean forced Shaw's hand so he would take on the class in the first place, which is why he's failing people as revenge.

I'm not sure if it's that, or if he's just a mean old bastard, and the reason doesn't really matter. What matters is that he's failed a good number of people on my team, and if they don't get their shit together, come fall, we'll fail on ice because I won't have players. The rule is, you can't play when your GPA is lower than 3.0, and a failing grade in physics brings some of those guys dangerously close.

So far, I've found them a couple of different tutors, but they've all been more or less useless. I was getting desperate until I went to the physics department in person and started harassing people. It turns out Shaw has a student who helps him in the lab, and who Shaw seems to like. Every person I talked to said that Andy Carter is essentially the Holy Grail and the solution to all my problems.

And that's the short version of how I ended up stalking Andy

Carter. The way I see it, Andy is my last hope. He knows Shaw. Knows his demands. He has never failed Shaw's class, and I'm hoping he can explain the material so that the guys will get it. He's my Hail Mary.

I sound dramatic, but there's a reason for that, too. I need the team to be successful because my career depends on it. If I'm ever going to coach an NHL team, I need a fantastic track record. I'm already at a disadvantage because I'm twenty-four and was forced to quit playing before I ever got to set skate on NHL ice, but I'll be damned if I let that stop me. I will fight, and I will succeed, and the first step on that journey is to get Andy Carter to help me.

Now that I'm face to face with Andy, I have to admit, there's something vaguely familiar about him. I'm about seventy percent sure I've seen him before, but for the life of me, I can't remember where.

He looks pretty... scruffy, for lack of a better word. He's wearing sweats and a T-shirt that has a large picture of Beyoncé with the words *Who run the world? Physicists!* on it.

He has a lot of hair. And I do mean a lot. It's around his head like a lion's mane, only darker, and I don't think any self-respecting lion would keep it that messy. He's kind of skinny, although it's hard to tell because of the large T-shirt, but if there's any muscle mass under the clothes, it's well hidden. He's shorter than me by a few inches, so he has to lift his head a bit to look at me. The move makes the hair fall back and gives me the opportunity to see that eyes are definitely Andy Carter's best characteristic. They're silvery gray. Lighter than most eyes that color, piercing and intense. They're mesmerizing, and due to the glasses, the eyes only seem that much bigger.

He's scowling at me, which reminds me, I should explain my offer before he takes off. "I need a physics tutor," I say, hoping there's some kind of magic in the air that would make Andy smile and go all, *Sure, dude. When and where? I'm your guy.*

Alas, that does not happen, and Andy scowls harder. "I'm not a tutor," he says instead and tries to leave. Again.

I stop him. Again. At this point, we're pretty much holding hands. "I don't need just any tutor," I say. "People tell me you're the best, so I want you."

There was a TA who told me Andy is working for Shaw and possesses a magical ability to, and I quote, *dumb things down to an extent that everybody gets them*. From what I've seen so far with the tutoring sessions, I'm in desperate need of that exact quality.

I have no idea how I'll get this guy to agree to help me, but for starters, I figure a little flattery goes a long way. It seems to work because Andy flushes and blinks, but just as quickly, the scowl is back, bigger and meaner than ever.

He shakes his hand loose and glares at me. "That's not possible. People don't know who I am."

The weird way he phrases it stumps me for a second, but I wave it off and persevere. I need him, damn it, and I'm going to get him.

Andy marches to his desk and starts stuffing his belongings in his backpack. I follow him there. "Hear me out. Let's get a coffee and I'll explain the situation."

Andy finishes stuffing his laptop into his bag and hikes the battered, black backpack over his shoulders.

"I'll pay you, of course," I hurry to add, and that makes him stutter in his steps. I almost feel disappointed that, once again, money will help me solve this problem. Without even realizing it, I had kind of wanted Andy to differ from other people.

*Should he do it out of the goodness of his heart?* My brain is a snarky dick sometimes.

Meanwhile, Andy's jaw twitches as he seems to reconsider my offer. He doesn't look at me, instead concentrating on some point over my shoulder.

"How much?" he asks, voice strained.

I can almost taste the victory. Now I just need to make the dollar amount enticing enough to seal the deal. Since there are multiple people in need of tutoring, I can be generous with money, so I say, "A hundred bucks an hour."

Andy's shoulders fall as he meets my gaze. There's reluctant interest there. It's clear as day. "How many hours per week?"

I scratch the back of my head. *Enough for them to pass* doesn't seem like a good answer, but I figure *a lot* is definitely the way to go. Once a month will not cut it, even though some of the guys would definitely go for it.

"Two?" I suggest.

Andy seems even more conflicted as he pulls out a chair and sits back down. "What do you need tutoring in again?" he asks.

I let out a breath. I've done it. Not that it's exactly a surprise. When I put my mind to something, I usually succeed. It's that simple. Still, for a moment there, I thought I would have to waste a lot more time to convince Andy. It's a relief this whole process is going this smoothly.

"Well, I don't need tutoring," I explain as I pull a chair and sit down on the other side of the desk. "My team does."

"Your team," Andy says while blinking at me like an owl through his glasses and all that hair.

"The hockey team," I explain. "Some of them flunked Freshman Physics with Shaw, so they're retaking it this summer."

"Shaw," Andy repeats with understanding dawning in his eyes.

"Yeah. I mean, you're a physics major. You know the material, right?"

He gives me an annoyed look. "Of course I know Freshman Physics. It's the easiest class there is," he scoffs as I try to hide my smile at the wounded pride.

"Great. So I'll tell the guys you agreed. We'll do it at the house they're renting. The living room has plenty of space for it. Or do you prefer a classroom?" I ask.

"A classroom?" he all but squeaks.

"I'm sure I could arrange something," I go on, determined not to give him a chance to refuse. "You should also give me a list of things you might need. Like a whiteboard or something like that? I don't have desks and such, but if that's something you need tell me, and I'll find them. Also—"

"Whoa!" Andy's voice is loud, and he raises his hands like I'm a spooked horse, even though he's the one that looks alarmed and ready to bolt. I stop talking. He looks overwhelmed, so I wait him out.

"How... how many people are there exactly?" he asks.

I scratch my head. "Seven. Two of them are scraping by, but five need serious help because Shaw is not great at simplifying concepts, and physics is not their strongest subject."

"Seven," he repeats to himself. "Seven."

And then he's out of his seat like a bolt of lightning. I'm honestly shocked he can even move that fast. "Can't do it," he declares and all but runs off. I take off after him, but I've left my jacket, my phone, and my earbuds on Andy's desk and with the time it takes me to retrieve them, Andy is gone.

"Fuck me," I mutter as I stuff my things into my jacket pockets. I throw the thing on, and just as I'm about to leave, I see something under Andy's desk. He's dropped his wallet. I pick it up.

It looks like recruiting Andy Carter will take more effort than I thought. Now, a decent person might take to the information desk, but the way I see it, I've gained myself a bit of an advantage here, and I'd be an idiot not to use it. After all, there's a good chance Andy will be a lot more receptive to my offer if he's feeling grateful.

I cram Andy's wallet into my pocket and leave the library.

Game on, Andy Carter. Game on.

3

ANDY

Jesus Christ, seven people! I hurry down the library stairs and head toward my apartment at a brisk walk. Seven people is ridiculous. That's not tutoring, for fuck's sakes. That's like teaching a class, and there is no way I can do it.

As far as experience goes, it's much more likely Law's hockey players will learn what I had for breakfast that day from the contents of my stomach than any actual physics. If I could teach a class, I would have taken that TA position Shaw has repeatedly tried to talk me into. It would have been a good addition to my resume, and I considered it for a moment, but as if on cue, I remembered what it felt like to have everybody point their fingers at me and laugh as I spewed my lunch all over the floor for the whole school to see. The desire to say yes was put out quicker than a burning candle facing down a bucketful of water.

When Law told me a couple of people on the hockey team needed tutoring, I'd figured two at the most, and I'd still been hesitant. Even one person was iffy, but the money had been really enticing. My job at the lab with Shaw pays the rent for my room in the apartment I share with Falcon and two of his teammates. I've spent the last two summers on campus working for Shaw. The job is interesting, and it'll look good on my application for MIT. The pay is lousy, but I don't spend much, and it's enough to put a little something in my savings account, which will make the rest of the year somewhat easier.

My tuition and books are covered by different scholarships, but that still leaves everyday expenses like food and shampoo and every kind of unforeseeable addition to my budget that is already stretched thin. Like the time I had to pay for dry cleaning when I wasn't paying attention to where I was going, walked into some girl and spilled my coffee all over her shirt.

My parents help me some, so I'm not exactly starving, but I try my hardest to manage on my own. They still have Landon and Ryan to put through college, so the more they can save, the easier it will be. Those two hundred bucks a week would be a nice supplement to my income. Then again, seven people is a crowd, and I don't do crowds. One public humiliation was enough, thank you very much.

I reach my apartment and let out a relieved sigh. It's not that I expected Law to follow me home, but that didn't stop me from looking over my shoulder the entire time that I was walking.

Falcon is in the living room with our other roommates, Rory and Paul. They're watching game tape, which is par for the course in our apartment. That's the beauty of living with three dedicated basketball players—there's no shortage of basketball-related activities. There are game tapes to review, strategies to discuss, and opponents to trash talk. And if they find themselves in need of a little light entertainment, they play basketball on the game console. It's a never-ending cycle.

I drop my bag on the floor and say hi to the guys, but I'm not sure they even notice me. They're all staring at the TV like they're a part of a cult, and the screen is broadcasting their supreme leader. North Koreans would be proud of their dedication. Unbothered, I turn toward the kitchen to find something to eat. Right now, not being noticed is a good thing.

"Dinner's in the fridge," Falcon says without taking his eyes off the screen. So he did hear me, which feels nice. He's the one person who seems to notice me, even in all my mediocre glory.

"Great," I holler over my shoulder and retreat to the kitchen.

I open the fridge, and sure enough, there's a Tupperware container. I take a moment to pray to the food gods before I open it.

"Please don't be spinach. Please don't be spinach," I repeat like a mantra.

I pull the lid off and take another deep breath before I look at the contents and groan. It's worse. Quinoa with broccoli.

I lift my eyes to the ceiling and mutter, "Thanks a lot."

I slam the lid on the container and stuff it back in the fridge like the thing is laced with cyanide. It's a shame we now have to burn the fridge to get rid of its offensive contents. I place my palm on the door and lower my head.

"You shall be remembered fondly," I say.

Done paying my respects, I walk to the living room and glance toward my roommates. They're still zombified by the TV. I tiptoe back to the kitchen and open the cabinet next to the fridge. I sneak my hand behind the bags of brown rice and oatmeal.

"Come on," I mutter as I rummage around trying to get my hands on the contraband. It should be right here. Back left corner. I stuff my hand back there until my fingers touch the back wall of the cabinet. "Where the hell are you hiding?"

"Looking for something?" The voice is so unexpected that I jump back and ram the back of my head into the corner of the fridge.

"Fuck! Ow!" I curse as I rub my head and glare at my smirking former best friend.

He has his hands behind his back as he strolls into the kitchen. "Dinner's in the fridge," he says.

"Yes," I say with a polite smile. "It looked delicious. Can't wait to taste it."

"Then why are you rummaging around in the cabinet?"

I wrack my brain for a good cover story. "I was looking for salt."

"Salt?" Falcon has the bad cop routine down pat with his expressionless face and stoic tone of voice.

"Well, I tasted the quinoa. Great choice, by the way. There's nothing I enjoy more for dinner than a bit of quinoa. And broccoli too. Awesome," I say as I sneak covert glances toward the cabinet.

There's no way he found my stash. I've hidden it behind a ton of brown rice, and I buy a new packet every time I go to the store so that there will never be a sudden rice shortage, meaning nobody should ever have a reason to go digging in the back.

"You tasted it?" Falcon asks, an affable smile on his face, which immediately makes me suspicious because it looks fake as fuck. "But I thought you said you couldn't wait to eat it? Which one is it, Andy?" he asks, and that smile is really creeping me out now.

Shit. "It looked like it could use some salt." Words rush out, and Falcon raises his brows. I brace myself, grabbing the Tupperware from the fridge and a fork from a drawer. "I was going to sit down and enjoy this delicious meal, but I didn't want to get up to go looking for salt should I need it. Wouldn't want to interrupt the moment, you know? It's a preemptive salt collection."

Falcon cocks his head to the side so that his blond hair falls over his forehead, making him look boyish and oh so handsome. "Well, go on. Taste it then. If you need salt, I'll get it for you."

I force a smile as I open the container and pretend to smell the food. "Mm-hmm," I say, trying to look appreciative. I shudder as I look at the contents. So much grainy stuff with bits of green mixed in it. It reminds me of frog spawn, and I can already picture myself spending the next two hours trying to get the taste out of my mouth.

I take a bite. If quinoa's taste had a color, it would be the bland beige of hospital corridors. It's just there. No excitement or anything that would make it remotely interesting. It has a slight nutty taste, but if I liked that, I would eat actual nuts. There aren't enough words to describe how much I hate quinoa. Why does everything healthy have to taste so blah?

"So?" Falcon asks. "What's the verdict? Should I get you some salt?" And with those words he uncovers the thing he's been holding behind his back and places the container of potato chips on the counter in front of me.

"Damn it," I mutter as I look longingly at the container. "Did you toss them?" I ask, even though I already know the answer.

Falcon shakes his head in exasperation. "I keep finding junk food hidden in the craziest places. It's like living with an alcoholic, so I'm warning you now, the moment I find Cheetos in the toilet tank, you're going to rehab." He taps at the now-empty potato chip container. "These things will kill you." He says something else about trans fats and chemicals that cause cancer, but I'm mourning my loss and don't pay attention.

It's the one drawback of living with Falcon. He's a health nut, and he's been trying to turn me into one as well. It's been a real challenge to accept him the way he is. I've already given up sweets, and by given up I mean, I won't eat them at home. Instead I stuff my face with Snickers bars from the vending machine while I'm studying at the library. But now he's coming after my potato chips, and I've got to be honest, I'm not appreciating this development. I'm already on thin ice in the library because of my snacking habit. I'm pretty sure the help desk lady thinks I'm doing drugs under my desk the way I'm sitting all crouched over as I try to sneak mini chocolate bars into my mouth. No way will I be able to do that with chips. They crunch too loudly.

"They're *potato* chips," I point out. "A potato is a vegetable."

"Please," Falcon scoffs. "*I'm* more potato than those things." He points to my dinner. "Eat. It's good for you."

"Yes, Mom," I mutter as I stuff quinoa in my mouth, hoping against hope that not chewing will somehow minimize the taste.

Falcon takes a seat at the counter because he seems to think I need a chaperone. I guess tossing the food out of the window is a no go. Falcon picks up an infinity cube and starts toying with it. He's always been fidgety, but it has never bothered me that he taps his foot or snaps his fingers when he's forced to sit still.

When he was younger it drove his teachers mad. One Christmas I got him a Rubik's Cube. After that, whenever Falcon had to sit still, he would solve that, and peace was restored. Now, we have all sorts of toys strewn everywhere in the apartment, and all of us, Rory and Paul included, have gotten into a habit of finding puzzles and brain teasers for Falcon. He, of course, solves them all in no time because he's smart, but he keeps them around for when he needs something to do with his hands.

"How was your day?" he asks. I almost choke on the quinoa. The whole scene is way too domestic for my liking. I'm afraid my imagination will run wild and I'll do something stupid because while, for Falcon, I'm just his best friend, for me, Falcon is way more than that.

"It was fine," I mumble through a mouthful of food. "Somebody took my seat in the library."

"The horror," he deadpans. "Let me guess, you took a seat somewhere else and stewed in your anger until the person left? Dude, I keep telling you you've got to stand up for yourself."

"I didn't have a leg to stand on," I say. "It's not exactly *my* seat, as in, it doesn't belong to me, so I have no right to ask anybody to take a hike."

Falcon steals my fork and takes a bite of the quinoa. He doesn't seem to register what he's doing, and I don't stop him because if he wants to help me finish that sorry excuse for a dinner, I'm not going to complain.

He rolls his eyes at me. "It's the science section of the library. Don't you all have assigned seating or something?"

"Or something," I agree.

"So then, next time say something, otherwise some newbie is going to hijack that spot from right under your nose. Want me to scare the living crap out of them?"

I snort, which makes Falcon throw me a questioning look. I shake my head. "It's nothing."

I doubt Falcon could scare Law off. Maybe I should mention that the person responsible for the hijacking isn't exactly a stranger to Falcon? Then again, I've heard Falcon, Rory, and Paul trash talk hockey players for years now, and I don't feel like I should give them any more ammunition for their—let's face it—stupid feud.

"I actually did say something." I lean back in my chair and brush my hair out of my face.

Falcon blinks in surprise. "You did?"

I bristle at Falcon's astonishment. I *can* stand up for myself. Most times I just choose not to because it doesn't seem worth the trouble.

What does it matter if somebody cuts a line in the cafeteria or blasts loud music while I'm trying to sleep?

"And did you get your seat back?" he asks.

"Well, not exactly." My face heats. "We... came to a mutual decision to both leave," I say with as much dignity as I can.

Falcon snorts. "Next time, will you just call me?" he asks with fond exasperation. He stands up and tousles my hair. "You know I'll take care of you. You're like my baby brother, so it's my job to protect you from the big, bad world," he jokes as he stands up to leave the kitchen so he can get back to his game. "I'm already hesitant about going away for the summer. How will you ever deal without me?"

"Asola. Get your ass back here, you've got to see this guy," Paul yells from the other room. Falcon hurries back to whatever team the three of them are studying right now, but my mood has plummeted at the mention of summer.

Falcon is leaving town at the beginning of June. He's going back home to work for his dad. The Asola family owns a couple of bed and breakfasts and they offer guided hiking tours and fishing and boating and all sorts of other outdoor activities. Falcon loves it and is planning to take over the business one day.

He's leaving in two weeks, and he'll be gone until September, which sucks because I'll miss him. The summer after my freshman year I went home too, but then the next year I got the job with Shaw, and now Falcon and I spend our summers apart. I'm being overdramatic. I drive up there every few weeks, so we see enough of each other, but I'm used to seeing him every day, so every year, it's an adjustment, and the first few days of summer always suck.

I know. I'm a cliché. I'm the nerdy sidekick in love with his cool best friend, but if all goes according to plan, I will make Falcon realize that we are perfect for each other. For one thing, we already know each other through and through, so there will be no nasty surprises in store for either of us. He doesn't mind my awkwardness and isn't embarrassed to be seen with me, and I don't mind the constant basketball chatter and his nervous habits. We just fit.

Too bad it's obvious only to me and not to Falcon.

I stare at the remains of my dinner. My mood has soured at the mention of summer, and the little brother comment makes it even worse. *That.* How the fuck have I managed to turn this situation into such a mess? Falcon shouldn't be seeing me as his little bro. I want to wow him with my confidence and quick wit, not be a damsel in distress who needs saving all the time.

Ever since realizing how average I am, I've been planning my eventual transformation into a new Andy. The cool Andy. The Andy who Falcon would be able to see in a new light. I thought I was doing a decent job. I stood up for myself in the library, didn't I? I mean, I didn't get to sit in my usual seat because I escaped before that could happen, but I didn't leave without standing up for myself.

Sort of.

Maybe what happened in the library isn't the best example, but I also...

And I've got nothing. I've got absolutely nothing else to put on that list. I try to wrack my brain for some kind of achievement, a milestone in my personal growth. I come up empty.

The realization slams into me. I've done shit all. Project Hero is in a rut even before it has begun. Somehow I've been making all these plans and haven't actually executed any of them.

I straighten myself. Right. That's got to change. I need a strong start to get this thing off the ground. I suppose some of the trouble I'm having with shaking my sidekick persona is that I still look like the old me. Falcon is used to me looking like the same nerd from the ninth grade. Maybe he would be able to see the changes in my personality better if I shook things up a little with a new look? Make the package more appealing, so to speak.

And Falcon's leaving for the summer...

For the first time, it dawns on me that the fact that Falcon is going home for three months might actually be beneficial for me. I straighten myself, feeling excited. I can already see it. Falcon will leave behind the old Andy, the average dude who looks like he's homeless half the time, and then, when he returns, *bam!* He'll see the new, improved Andy. One who doesn't look like an awkward octopus. And

Falcon will realize that he likes this new guy way more than he could ever imagine. Cue a happy ending.

I have to start planning. A haircut would be a good start. Some new clothes. Nothing too drastic. I still want to look like me, only better. An improved version of me. Andy 2.0.

I glance down at my trusty combo of sweats and a T-shirt and sigh. How the fuck will I pull this off?

# 4

## LAW

I have to face the facts. I've turned into a stalker. I can already see the restraining order in my future. Still, I've come this far, so it would be a shame to quit now.

Mind made up, I push open the door of the small Italian restaurant and enter. It's a little after three in the afternoon, so the lunch rush is already over, and the place is quiet. Only a couple of people occupy the tables near the windows.

It's a sunny afternoon. For a while there, it seemed that summer would never arrive, but over the last week or so the sun has decided that it might as well make an appearance. Most people are sitting outside, soaking up the warmth and enjoying the fresh air. Not Andy. The guy is parked inside and he's wearing a sweatshirt like he doesn't trust that the weather will stay warm.

He's got his nose in a thick book and his unruly hair is, once again, all over the place. His glasses have slid down his nose, and I watch as he pushes them back up with his pinky finger. There's a pencil between his lips, which he's methodically destroying as he chews on it like he's a beaver.

He doesn't notice as I approach him, so I figure payback is a bitch and snatch the pencil from between his teeth to save the poor thing.

Andy looks up with the kind of confused expression that people get when they've been completely in their own little bubble and it takes them a while to remember where they are and why.

He frowns and plucks his pencil back. "Are you trying to make taking my things a habit?" he asks. "Because if so, I should get a vote, and I'm gonna go with a firm no on that one."

I smile and take a seat. For whatever reason, I enjoy the exchanges with this smart-mouthed guy. I like how genuine he is. People aren't usually that honest in how they present themselves to the world. We all have masks we put on when dealing with each other. Not Andy. He's as authentic as they come. Right now, for example, he's annoyed with me. It's written all over his face. Not many people get annoyed with me, or if they do, they sure as hell don't show it, so it's a definite change to be in the presence of somebody who is not that thrilled to see me.

"Speaking of taking your things," I say and place Andy's wallet on the table in front of him.

He stares at the thing for a moment before he lifts his eyes to me again and frowns. "Did you steal my wallet?" he asks. The outrage is strong with this one.

"I rescued your wallet," I correct him.

He gapes at me like he can't believe what he's hearing. "From my pocket?" he asks with one eyebrow in an impressive arch. Supermodels get paid the big bucks to master that expression.

No one has ever accused me of stealing, so that's another first and not a very enjoyable one. Andy reaches out his hand and pulls his phone, his book, and his empty plate away from me, glaring at my hands the whole time like he's expecting me to snatch one of those items any moment now. He's not even trying to be subtle about it.

I cross my arms over my chest. "Really? The plate too? What kind of thief do you think I am?"

"Not a very good one. Here's a free tip: it's more profitable to steal from the rich."

I shake my head. I should get down to business and get Andy to agree to tutor the team instead of shooting the shit. I don't have much time. The one class I promised my parents I'd take this summer starts in a half an hour, but instead of heading there, I take a seat. It seems I'll have to skip Financial Management. What a shame.

"That's a good idea in theory," I agree, "but since stealing a wallet is usually something you do without going all *Ocean's Eleven* about it, pickpockets have to cross their fingers and hope that they get lucky. Maybe the mark has been to the ATM recently and has taken out a thousand bucks."

Andy laughs at that. "It must be karma that you chose me as your victim. My bank account has about forty dollars in it. Better luck next time." He regards me, head cocked to the side. "Is that why you brought the wallet back? Not enough money in there for you?"

"It was pitiful." I shake my head and paste an expression of sorrow on my face.

"Huh. It seems being poor has its advantages."

"Indeed."

I tap my finger on the table in front of me. "You dropped it in the library," I say. "I thought about keeping it hostage to convince you to tutor the team, but then I changed my mind." I gesture around the restaurant. "Good thing too. If I hadn't returned it to you, you would have had to make a run for it when it came time to pay for your lunch. Now that I think about it, you owe me one. Thanks to my efforts, you don't have to start a life of crime."

Andy isn't convinced. Instead, he frowns. "How did you even know where to find me?" His eyes go wide. "I have a feeling I'm not going to like it. Did you stalk me? Plant a bug in my laptop? Steal my phone and download a tracker app onto it?"

"Yes, I also downloaded the whole Spice Girls' music catalogue for you in honor of their billionth reunion."

He snorts, and I smile at the sound. "You give me way too much credit. I went to the physics department, and some guy told me you'd be here. So, the way I see it, I've rescued your wallet. I've protected it overnight. *And* I've taken time out of my very busy schedule to hand-deliver it to you, allowing you to pay for your food and not have to work as a dishwasher to compensate for it. Huh. Might be just me, but it seems you owe me one."

Andy laughs at that. "This is gonna be good. Did you look inside it?"

Now I'm confused. "Is that a trick question? No, I did not rummage through your stuff."

He pushes the leather square toward me. "Go on, then."

I narrow my eyes at Andy, but for the life of me, I can't figure out what kind of game he's playing, so I take the wallet and open it.

There's pretty much nothing there. Five bucks in the cash compartment. A bus pass. That's it.

I close the wallet. "It's... very minimalist."

"Yeah. I lose my wallet about once a month, so I always have cash on my person. There's five bucks in my pocket, a couple of dollars in my backpack and for real emergencies, I have a fiver under the insole of my sneaker. Sooo... about that whole you-owe-me deal? I already paid for lunch." He shrugs, lips twitching. "Sorry, you can't trick your way into tutoring, since I wouldn't even have noticed the missing wallet for at least another week." He plucks the wallet out of my fingers and stuffs it into his backpack. "Listen, I'd help you if I could, but as I keep telling you, I'm not the right fit for this job."

I lean back in my chair. Until he said that, I'd almost forgotten that I had a purpose for being here. It's enjoyable to banter with Andy. I'm not sure what I expected Andy to be like, but I was definitely leaning toward somebody much less... interesting. Yeah, that seems about right. Andy is smart, quick with a comeback, and witty. Even though he seems unsure about the tutoring gig, I'm getting more and more convinced that fate has pointed me in the right direction, and Andy Carter is going to be my saving grace.

I'm about to continue when a shadow falls over our table. I look up and wince. Falcon Asola. The guy despises me, and all because of a teensy-weensy little prank the hockey team played on the basketball team once upon a time.

We filled the basketball court with plastic cups of water. I admit, not the most sophisticated prank out there, but it worked well as a team-building exercise since it took a hell of a lot of planning not to get caught, and the whole team needed to work together for several hours to pull the whole thing off. It wouldn't have caused so much animosity between the basketball and hockey teams if it weren't for the fact that the basketball team retaliated, but unlike us, they got caught. Somehow Asola seems to think it's my fault they scored themselves punishment. Needless to say, neither of us is going to start any fan clubs for each other anytime soon.

"Anderson." Asola's tone is icy.

Mine isn't much warmer, as I reply, "Asola."

I admit, I don't especially like the guy, but the same can't be said about Andy because he seems to have lit up as soon as he noticed the dude.

"Hey," Andy says and smiles.

I blink in surprise. I can see his gums. That is one hell of a warm greeting and isn't even in the same universe with the suspicious look I got from Andy when I arrived.

Asola frowns at me but then seems to decide ignoring me is the best tactic, so he concentrates all his attention on Andy. He pulls something out of his back pocket and taps it against Andy's shoulder.

"You forgot this again," he says and—what do you know—places another wallet in front of Andy. Andy throws me a quick glance before he grabs the thing and flashes another one of those gum-bearing smiles at Asola.

"Dude, thanks. I didn't even notice. I don't know what I would have done without it." Andy chuckles, more strained this time, as his eyes flitter over me again. "I would have had to wash the dishes to pay for my lunch or something."

I cross my arms on my chest and fight back a smile. This is getting very, very interesting.

Asola reaches out his hand and ruffles Andy's hair like somebody would his ten-year-old brother. "You know I would have come and saved you—again—if you'd called. What are friends for? I should sew that thing on you. One of these days you're going to lose it, and then you'll have to replace all of your documents and stuff, and you know how much you hate the DMV."

Andy rubs the back of his neck and looks at everywhere but at me. The tips of his ears are bright red. "Hah. Yeah. I definitely owe you one," is all he has to say about that.

Asola chuckles and pats Andy on the back, and I swear to God, Andy leans into the touch like a cat, starved for attention.

"Listen, I've gotta run. I have some last-minute shopping to do. Mom wants some kind of a crazy new cookbook, and I promised to get it for her." Asola gives me another one of those patented suspicious glares that he seems to keep at hand just for me. "Want me to give you a ride home?" he asks Andy.

Andy glances at me and flushes, and I can't help but grin because I've found my angle for approaching the tutoring gig.

"Actually," I interrupt and make them both look at me with similar expressions of suspicion. "Andy was helping me with something."

"Helping?" Falcon asks, confused now. "With what?" He looks between me and Andy, and frowns. "Andy sucks at sports."

Andy's face falls at that, and I raise my brows because even if Andy doesn't happen to be as athletic as Asola and I are, I wouldn't dismiss everything else Andy has to offer.

"Whatever." Asola ignores me. "You should come. I'll be leaving tomorrow, and there's this thing with the basketball team. You could tag along."

Andy seems to have checked out, though. He's staring at a point on the wall, deep in thought, and whatever is going on in his mind, he doesn't seem happy about it.

Andy takes a moment to realize that both Falcon and I are looking at him.

"What?" he asks.

Falcon stares at Andy as if checking if the guy hasn't been replaced by a body double. "I asked you if you want me to give you a ride home."

Andy's eyes move between me and Falcon. He seems unsure, but

I'm not going to take any chances and let Andy's loyalty to Falcon win. "We're not done talking yet," I say.

Falcon snorts. "What have you two got to talk about?" I hold back a smug smile because even though Asola doesn't seem to realize it, he has lost.

A defiant look appears in Andy's eyes. "Just... stuff," he says.

"Stuff." Falcon repeats. He's skeptical, and Andy lifts his chin as he stares Falcon down.

"I've got stuff," he says, and it finally seems to register with Asola that he has put his foot in his mouth.

He raises his hands. "I believe you."

"Well... good," Andy says.

"Good," Asola repeats.

They stare at each other, Asola's gaze curious and Andy's defiant.

"This is riveting stuff," I interrupt. "Hey! Stuff!" I hold back a smirk as I high-five myself. Asola looks like he's got confirmation of my douchiness, as he's always suspected. "But Andy and I do have things to discuss, so you can run along and go do your errands now."

Asola's jaw clenches, but when Andy doesn't make a move to go with him, he says goodbye and gets out of there.

Andy looks after him until he disappears behind the door. He doesn't look lovesick or anything, but I would bet my car he's over-thinking it all in his head, contemplating if he made the wrong choice and will regret it later.

"I'm feeling hungry," I say and grin, drawing Andy's attention back to me. "Pizza?" I ask.

"I've already eaten." Andy points to his empty plate.

I shrug. "Suit yourself." It only takes me a moment to catch the attention of the waitress.

"So, you and Falcon Asola, huh?" I ask once I've placed my order, and the waitress has left.

Andy is in the middle of drinking, and he almost chokes on his water. "What?" he squeaks.

I reach over and pat him on the back. "Easy there. You two seemed... friendly."

Andy eyes me over his half-empty glass. "We've known each other since middle school. He moved in to the house next to mine, and we've been friends ever since."

"That's nice," I say mildly, and Andy's shoulders relax a fraction. "And how long have you had a crush on him?"

Andy chokes on air this time. Huh. I didn't know you could do that. I reach over and tap him on the back. "What's with all the choking? I thought *you* of all people knew about your crush."

"Yeah, and I thought it was a well-kept secret." He scowls at me.

I purse my lips. "Ooh, I wouldn't bet on that one."

Andy slams his head against the table so hard that the glasses rattle. "Kill me now. End my misery with a pizza cutter."

"Sorry, we don't have one." It's getting hard to hide my amusement, but I do my best. I don't think Andy would appreciate me laughing in the middle of his crisis.

"Break the glass, then. Use your creativity. I'm mortified here and need a friend's help."

"Oh, so we're friends?" I ask.

"Not if you refuse to help a guy out."

"Fine, fine," I sigh. "I guess I can strangle you if you insist."

He lifts his head and scrunches his nose, and I'm caught unawares by how adorable it looks. "I don't think that's how I want to go."

"Oh, but a pizza cutter would be fine."

"I like the gore factor. I presume you're not very skilled at murder, so it'd be a bloodbath. People would forever remember me as the slaughtered-pizza-place guy. They would come here and see the bloodstains on the floor, and I'd get a pizza named after me. I'd prefer Andy's Assassination to have pineapple, ham, blue cheese, and potato chips on it. Be a pal and let the owners know, m'kay?"

"The level of thought you've put into this is disturbing."

He places his palm on his heart and gasps. "You haven't made plans for how you're going to die? I'm not sure I can be friends with somebody so careless about the important things in life."

"I prefer to be spontaneous," I say. "Potato chips on a pizza. Really?"

He raises his index finger in warning. "Do not even go there. I already have Falcon to give me a hard time about my eating habits, so you and I are going to be the kind of friends who don't nag about junk food and sweets and don't try to poison each other by serving kale."

He shudders in disgust.

"Not a fan?" I ask with a grin that is getting wider and wider by second.

"It's the devil's food, and since it's super trendy people force themselves to ignore the fact that it tastes like old newspaper garnished with sweat from socks that have been forgotten in the bottom of someone's gym bag for a week."

I raise my glass and nod solemnly. "I'll drink to that."

We clink our glasses together and then the waitress appears with my pizza. I grab myself a big slice and wave the plate in front of Andy's nose. "Come on, you know you want to." He rolls his eyes, but takes a slice. For a few moments we just eat.

I study Andy. I need to play this smart. I don't think I'll get another shot to convince Andy to help me. Let's face it, I'm already flirting with a restraining order here, so somehow, I have to make Andy think he needs me just as much as I need him.

This should be interesting.

# 5

## ANDY

"So why haven't you told Asola how you feel?" Law asks.

The pleasant feeling inside me disappears with a snap, replaced by the nervous, jittery worry that always accompanies thoughts of Falcon and my crush on him.

I tinker with the edge of the coaster. "It's complicated."

Law leans back in his chair. "You're scared."

I scoff. "You'd be a lousy detective. I'm not scared. Besides, didn't you insinuate a moment ago that my feelings are so obvious that everybody knows? Falcon has said nothing, so maybe he's not into me."

"I didn't say Asola knows. I'm about ninety-nine percent certain he lives in his safe friend bubble, and you know it." He looks smug. "So it's up to you to pop that bubble for him, and yet you've said nothing. Your words say tough guy, but your actions say coward."

I roll my eyes so hard that, for a moment, it feels like I can see the inside of my head. "Fine. I'm not afraid *yet*," I amend.

Law's face is a stellar representation of a question mark.

"I'm not going to say anything to Falcon until I've made some changes," I explain. "First, I need to… to present myself in a way that would make him see me as a potential boyfriend."

The question mark is still there. I sigh as I try to think of the best way to explain the predicament that has stopped me from professing my undying love for my best friend.

"It's like you said, we've known each other for so long that I don't think Falcon is able to see me as anything other than the Andy he met the summer before ninth grade. You think I'm a dork now? You should have seen that dude. Let's just say that I had a lot in common with Martin Prince."

"The nerdy kid from *The Simpsons?*"

"Oh yeah. I mean, there was less bullying because my sisters threatened to beat up anybody who was mean to me, but it took me a while in elementary school to learn to curb my teacher's pet tendencies, so I wasn't exactly popular."

Law mulls that over for a minute. "So what's the plan, then?"

"Isn't it obvious? I'm going to need to change," I say.

Law's eyebrows almost disappear into his hairline. "Hasn't anybody ever told you that's a bad idea? You can't alter your personality to fit somebody else's. It's a recipe for disaster."

"I'm not talking about a complete overhaul of my personality," I say, even though some changes are definitely in order. I don't say that to Law because he seems determined to talk me out of it. It's nice of him, but let's be realistic, the guy's known me for a minute. He hasn't seen all the annoying, uncool parts that have been packed into me and that have got to go.

The encounter with Falcon, and now sitting here with Law, only reinforces my realization that Project Hero needs a serious jolt to get started. Based on Falcon's disbelief when he saw me with Law, I must be sidekickier than ever, and that will not fly. At all.

This is depressing, so I concentrate back on Law. "I figure, for starters, I need to do something about how I look."

Law's eyes measure me from head to, well, not toe because he can't see those, but to somewhere above my belly button. He doesn't say anything for a long while as he keeps looking at me. I've never been regarded so blatantly before. It would be flattering if the look came from, say, a hot guy across the bar, but all I can think right now is, *What does Law see that is wrong?*

But then I shrug. I have had a thorough look-over already, so I doubt he'll find anything new. The hair must go and the T-shirts must go and my comfy, comfy sweats must go. Yadda, yadda, yadda.

But Law surprises me. "What's wrong with how you look?" he asks.

"I'm too sexy," I deadpan. "People find it hard to resist me, which let me tell you, makes walking down the street a real challenge."

"I feel for you," Law says drily, but let's face it, unlike me, for him that's probably a real issue. A six-foot-three hockey god with a fit body, emerald-green eyes, and black hair isn't exactly what most people consider repulsive.

It's not that I walk around all day in despair about how I look. Frankly, it hardly ever crosses my mind, but the thing is, aside from getting Falcon's attention, it has crossed my mind that I'll be graduating sometime next year, which means I'll either be going to grad school, or getting a job. Looking at myself right now, I highly doubt I'm what prospective employers look for. Not to mention the people at MIT.

The tough part about changing things about myself is that I'm so used to how I look and the things I wear that whenever I buy new clothes, I automatically gravitate toward what has made me feel comfortable so far. Hence the nerdy T-shirts, which I have worn practically my whole life. I don't even own a suit.

I went to my sister's wedding in clothes I borrowed from my brother. I'd left mentioning my lack of suit until the last possible moment, so there had been no time to buy anything. The fact that Ian is five inches taller and twenty pounds heavier didn't help the look. Mom has placed the frame with that particular family picture so that the side where I am is strategically hidden behind a photograph of Mom and Dad after they went bungee jumping.

I don't blame her.

I could ask my sisters, Cecilia and Emily, for help, but they'd ask too many questions, and I don't want to explain to them why I've suddenly changed my mind about *looking more polished*, as Cecilia puts it. I could also do without the comments and jokes they would most definitely throw into the mix should I ask my sisters for help.

Law takes a sip of his soda. "So a makeover, huh? You probably have a plan for what you're going to do?"

I scratch my cheek and knock my glasses in the process so that they almost slip off my nose. I adjust the frames and look at anywhere but Law. "Sure. I have extensive knowledge about makeovers."

"You sure about that?"

"Yes," I say, but it sounds more like a question than an answer.

Law calls me out on it immediately. "You don't sound like it."

"Fine," I say, throwing my hands in the air dramatically. "I know nothing. I'm a fraud. I'll probably go to a hair salon and let them give me a buzz cut and color what little hair is left turquoise. And don't even get me started on the clothes I plan to buy. Hammer pants are still in style, right?"

I admit, I excel at sarcasm, but there's a very strong possibility that's exactly how it'll all play out. My only consolation is that Hammer pants look almost as comfortable as sweats, so at least there's that.

"I could help with that," Law offers.

I'm immediately suspicious. It's what growing up with siblings who love pranks does to you. "Why would you do that?"

He grins. "I'm a nice person. And as you said, we're friends, and I don't know about you, but as far as my experience goes, friends help each other out."

*He just wants you to work for him.*

But that's not all it is. He looks laidback. It doesn't feel like he's here, suffering through every minute spent in my presence. His pose is casual, feet stretched out and whole body relaxed. Spending time with me doesn't seem to be a chore for him. I could be wrong, but it almost feels like Law Anderson might enjoy my company.

Maybe.

I think.

Man, I really wish I was better at reading people.

It's not like I haven't tried. Once, in high school, I even took an online course on body language. The instructor sent us all these pictures and video clips with explanations about how to interpret things like blinking and arm-crossing and so on, and for a while, I thought I was getting it.

But then things became super uncomfortable when, based on my newfound knowledge, I drew the conclusion that Mrs. Diaz, my seventy-year-old Spanish teacher, was flirting with me. She kept eye contact and had her toes pointed at me and her pupils were enlarged. Of course, the eye contact and the toes turned out to be because she was standing in front of me, talking to me, and the enlarged pupils were the side effect of taking Atropine. I quit the class after that. It was not a well-spent six hundred bucks, and my parents were not happy with me when the principal called them in for a meeting to discuss my behavior. So much for trying to subtly hint to Mrs. Diaz that I wasn't interested.

So yeah, I'm not that comfortable trying to read body language, but Law's smile doesn't feel fake like he's forcing himself to tolerate me and will bolt the first chance he gets.

"So, what do you say?" Law prompts.

"I don't know?" I say, because apparently I'm now only capable of speaking in sentences that have question marks tacked at the end of them.

"Can you do it yourself?" Law asks point-blank.

I slump in my chair because, no, no I definitely can't.

"Then let me help," Law says.

"How exactly would you help?"

Law leans forward, excitement shining in his eyes. He seems awfully confident that he has something that will change my mind about this whole tutoring ordeal.

"I'll pay for a stylist to help you with your makeover," he says.

I blink. Okay. Did not expect that.

Already I'm tempted to abandon all common sense. It doesn't take a genius to do the math and figure out that I will never be able to transform myself like a professional stylist would.

"But wait, there's more," Law says in a voice that is eerily similar to the guy from the shopping channel who my grandma stalks on Facebook. "I'll also lend you my expertise on how to deal with Asola." Law continues his sales pitch. "You want him? I'll help you get him."

I'm envious of his easy confidence as he says the words. I'd never be able to make promises like that. I mean, I could say the words, but the moment they were out of my mouth, I'd start to doubt myself and try to take them back.

I cock my head to the side as I replay Law's promise in my head. This is actually good stuff. Maybe I should take notes? Law is definitely nobody's sidekick, so I should treat spending time with him as a learning opportunity. I wonder if Law would mind me filming him so I could study his mannerisms later? Okay, so Project Hero might be lagging, but I'm right on schedule with turning into a psycho. I should buy a bigger freezer for all those body parts I'll need to fit there.

All creepiness aside, I take note of Law's confident delivery. Maybe I can adjust it a bit and make it my own?

*You want to hire me as a tutor? Sure, I'll tutor the heck out of your team. They won't know what hit them when those A's start flying in.*

"Andy? You still with me?"

I blink, trying to get Law back into focus. "Sure. Absolutely. That was my listening face."

"Uh-huh."

*Note to self, learn to lie better.*

"So how about it? Personally, I think you're getting a hell of a deal. Think about it, you get paid, you get a stylist, and you get the man of your dreams, and all that for some light tutoring, two times a week."

I sigh. This is going to be embarrassing, but then again, it's not like my deep, dark secret is that deep and dark to begin with, so I might as well just explain it to Law.

"I have stage fright." That phrase sounds too tame, so I add, "I'm deathly afraid of public speaking."

Law cocks his head to the side. "It's seven people," he says slowly, looking confused, probably trying to remember the time he told me

I'd be tutoring eight thousand people on a stadium tour. It's the same reaction most people have.

Logically, I get it. Speaking is so basic that most people don't have any trouble with it. We all speak in front of people every day. I do, for that matter. It's the performing part that does me in. It doesn't bother me if I have to tell my roommates not to leave their dirty dishes in the sink. But whenever the attention of the room is on me, and I'm supposed to perform with everybody's eyes on me, my brain showers me with images of my fourteen-year-old self puking on stage of Woodbury Middle School, the whole school laughing at me, and the months that followed. I got to relive the humiliation because, with the invention of smartphones, everybody had a super easy way to show me clips of that event over and over again. I feel queasy just thinking about it.

"No, that's the thing. I can't speak in front of large crowds, sure, but you know the saying, three is a crowd? Yeah. That absolutely stands in my case. Speaking in front of people... I'll faint, or I'll puke, or I'll cry with great, heaving sobs, or there'll be some kind of combination of the three. Either way, it will be a horror show for me and for whatever poor souls have to witness the thing."

Law looks suspicious. "And you're not just saying it to get rid of me?" he asks.

I roll my eyes. "I'm capable of saying no."

"I'll take full responsibility for sounding like a dick, but have you tried lately?"

I flush and look away. "Kind of," I say. "Shaw offered me the position of his TA in spring semester. It did not go well." I panicked and ran out of the room when I had to introduce myself. I went full-on Forrest Gump for a moment there as I sprinted out of the building and ran home. Good times.

We sit in silence for a while. Except for the noises of the restaurant, but neither Law nor I say a word. Eventually, I gather my stuff, preparing to leave, because it doesn't seem like I'm needed here any longer. But as has become a tradition of sorts for us already, Law grabs my hand and stops me.

"Not so fast there. I'm trying to figure something out."

I dutifully resume my position next to him and fiddle with my water glass and the utensils as Law squints and frowns, deep in thought.

"I can ask around and help you find somebody," I offer.

"I've already done that. Most people in your department pointed me straight to you."

I frown and open my mouth to start protesting, because how is that possible when I've tutored none of them? Most people in my department barely know anything about me other than my major and my library seat.

"Don't even try and argue. I've got stories, dude. Michelle... something, I can't remember her last name, tells me you're the reason she understood electromagnetic field theory. Then there was a dude with a tattoo of an electrical circuit on his bicep who said you helped him ace thermodynamics. Liam... I want to say Wamboldt? It was something that I remember sounded vaguely like wombat," Law says thoughtfully. "Anyway, he gives you credit for helping him with"—Law's eyes go all squinty—"tensor fields in general relativity. Is that a thing?"

I nod mutely. I remember discussing those things with people, yeah. But I figured it was just us making friendly conversation. I distinctly remember the relief I felt in my freshman year when I got to talking with a girl from my Introductory Physics class after a study group because, for the first time in my life, I felt like, *Yes, that's the kind of small talk I can get behind.*

"Hear me out," Law says. "You can't deal with seven people because it's too much like your performing in front of a crowd, right?"

I nod. "That's the gist of it, yeah."

"What about one person?" he asks.

"What do you mean?"

"What about tutoring one person?" he asks.

I hesitate. Surely I could do one? Then again, who the hell knows? It's not like my anxiety is only about the size of the crowd. In fact, it's the smaller factor of the two. The main thing is still the performance part of the whole deal.

"Maybe," I hesitate. "With only two people present, it would probably be hard to make me feel like I'm on a stage," I joke.

Law nods, taking this whole thing completely seriously. "Probably," he agrees.

"But I can't give everybody individual lessons twice a week. I don't have enough time for that. That would be like a full-time job, not a temporary tutoring gig."

"No, I get it. The guys have summer jobs and we still train together a few times a week, so scheduling all those separate sessions would be a nightmare. That's not what I had in mind."

"So ," I hesitate because I'm not sure why I'm entertaining this whole thing. "Let's say I can do one person, how will you decide who gets the privilege of enjoying my shaky teaching skills?" I ask. "Because, let me be clear, you say you need me, but it'd be like... like... you're buying a pet in a bag."

I straighten myself, pleased with the analogy I came up with. "See, you think there's a dog in there. People say it's a cute one and knows lots of tricks, but you won't really know until you buy the bag and look inside and see that even though you might have been hoping for a golden retriever, you've ended up with a Chinese Crested and bulldog mix that can't do anything other than sleep and pee on the living room carpet. It's a dog, sure, but it's butt ugly and makes your neighbors wince when you walk the poor sucker around the block. Think about it, my alleged teaching prowess might very well be a myth, and you won't know until you've seen me in action."

"You'll be teaching me," Law says, unbothered about my rant, completely dismissing my awesome dog analogy.

His answer confuses me again, which leaves me to question Law's judgement in his tutoring pick, because let me tell you, I'm not coming off as particularly bright in this whole situation.

I squint my eyes at him. "Because you think it'd be fun to go over Freshman Physics again?"

He laughs. It's a nice sound. Deep and warm and friendly. It almost feels like Law enjoys talking to me. Like he's not laughing *at* me but *with* me.

It's been a long time since I was the outcast of my high school, not since Falcon moved to my hometown and took me under his wing, but every time I meet somebody new, there's still that moment of uncertainty. Is this person here to make me feel bad about myself? will there be taunts and ridicule? It takes a conscious effort to dispel these thoughts.

Even with Falcon, it took time to learn to trust him. For a long time, even after we'd become friends, I was suspicious about his motives and analyzed his laughs and teasing comments to death, trying to discover the hidden barbs beneath. Sometimes, late at night in my bed, I'd worried that the next day would be the day Falcon would reveal his true colors and turn out to be like everybody else at my high school. He hadn't. And after a while, I'd learned to trust him. Each new person in my life, though, usually presents the challenge of forcing away negative expectations. Coming to college has been a real test in that regard.

With Law, all those inclinations have disappeared. I don't look for hidden thorns in Law's words that could prickle me, make me bleed if I'm not careful enough and don't keep enough of a distance between us.

It's disconcerting.

Law looks all business now as he straightens himself. There's an excitement in his eyes because he's come up with a solution.

"You will tutor me. We'll go through each topic before the actual tutoring, and you'll tell me what to say to the guys. I'll take notes. We'll go through all the problems and solve them, and you'll tell me what to say to make the material comprehensible to people who might not be the next Richard Feynman."

There are ideas that are so good in the planning stages that later, when they fail spectacularly, you're left gobsmacked because you're so surprised something that good in theory could fail in real life.

This is not one of those times.

Law's plan is shaky at best on paper. There are so many ifs and buts that I can't even figure out which one to address first. I don't particularly want to be the one to rain on Law's parade since he looks so hopeful and excited. He's given the phrase *going the extra mile* a whole new meaning, which must mean that he feels like his position as assistant coach is on the line. I really don't relish disillusioning him.

My mouth seems to agree, since the next words that come out of it are, "That could work."

*Wait! What?*

"I could probably write you some sort of a list with bullet points to follow, and I can show you how to solve problems step by step."

*Abort! Abort!*

"It sounds doable."

*It sounds bonkers, and I have officially lost my mind.*

But Law smiles, and it's nice that he thinks of me as someone essential for his team's success, so I shut up and hope to god I won't turn out to be a mutt whose only talent is chasing its own tail.

# 6

# LAW

It's that time of the month again.

Lunch with my parents.

I've been dreading this thing for a week now, just like every month.

The thing about my parents is, they love me. In their own judgmental, controlling way. So we get together once every month and do our best to end the time we spend together on civil terms.

Today, I'm not as apprehensive as usual. Today, I've got something to look forward to. This afternoon, Andy is going to drop by and we'll have our first tutoring session, and I'm pretty excited about it. Fuck if I know why. There's something about Andy that is addictive. On the outside, he's so damn awkward, but he's also sarcastic and fun and just genuinely nice, and I can't even remember the last time I enjoyed just hanging out with somebody this much.

Maybe it's the fun factor Andy brings because, in my life, everything is about goals and fulfilling them. It's been like the goddamn Soviet Union in our house ever since I turned three. I had weekly goals and monthly goals and yearly goals. There were even five-year plans to follow, to give you the whole suppressive-experience package. The plans weren't theoretical. There were actual files and Excel tables involved, to track the progress, and family meetings where we discussed how well we were keeping up with our schedules. There might have even been awards for those who fulfilled their five-year plan in four years, not that I would know since I usually had trouble doing everything within the five-year schedule.

See, my parents are self-made, and they swear that they owe their success to rigorous adherence to schedules and religious following of the almighty plan.

It's too bad I threw a wrench in their plan for *me* by falling in love with hockey.

The thing with trying to force your kids into a mold is that at one point or another, most of us rebel, and when the parents are as pigheaded as the kid? Well, let's just say it goes to hell really fast. My parents and I barely spoke through my high-school years. They hated my dedication to hockey, and I hated their insistence that I should concentrate on school because I needed to follow in my father's footsteps. Somebody needs to take over the family business, but to keep the peace, none of us mentions it.

They wanted me to drop hockey and go to a respectable college and major in finance or business or law. I wanted to play hockey. After endless negotiations we compromised on Baril.

And then I got my diagnosis, which ended my hockey career before it had really even taken off. My parents were relieved as hell. And sure, they tried to hide it, but they both did a shitty job.

I still haven't mentioned to them that, even though I'll never play professional hockey, I still love the game and plan to make coaching my career. I'm planning to postpone that conversation for as long as I can.

Every month my parents fly to Vermont from New York. Dad has a pilot's license and a small Cessna that my parents bought when Dad turned fifty. It's the one hobby he allows himself to have and it's good for him. Makes him seem more human when he does something outside of staying in the office for fourteen hours a day, six days a week like a robot whose only energy source is paperwork.

The drive to Burlington from campus takes about forty minutes. I need every last one of those to condition myself for the two hours ahead. I park in front of the restaurant and take a fortifying breath before I get out.

I would love to have a better relationship with my parents, and it's improved a lot from when I was, say, seventeen. Still, there's this tension when we meet that shouldn't be there. We're all so afraid of a falling-out that we tiptoe around each other, scared of being honest and speaking our minds. It's exhausting, and I have a feeling we won't be able to keep it up much longer. Especially since I'm already done with my undergrad. I enrolled in an MBA program per my parents' requirements, but if all goes according to plan, that degree will just collect dust, and I'll be able to concentrate on the thing I love —hockey.

I enter the restaurant and the hostess smiles as she leads me to the table where my parents are already waiting for me. They both stand up as I approach.

"Darling." My mom reaches out her arms and squeezes my hands in hers as we both lean in and kiss each other's cheeks. I shake my dad's hand, and we take our seats. I haven't seen them in a month, but there'll be no hugs. My parents have never been overly touchy-feely. A pat on the back is as good as a bear hug by my father's standards.

We leaf through the menus and make small talk until the waiter brings us our meals. So far everything is going just like it always does. We cover my grades (I have a 4.2 GPA, but I could do better). My dad's job (he wooed himself a new, important client, but things could be going better). My mom's latest case (she won her client five million dollars, but she could have won more). It's the running theme in our family, no matter how well you're doing, you could always try harder, be better, achieve more.

That was also the reason sitting idly was seriously frowned upon when I was a kid. Every school holiday was packed with activities. Every moment of my day was planned. Before I discovered hockey, I felt like a hamster in a wheel, always going, going, going, but since I didn't particularly enjoy computer camp or Japanese for Beginners, I felt exhausted most of the time. It was an incredible relief when it turned out a hobby I enjoyed existed.

"I sent you an e-mail about a meeting I set up for you. Did you have a chance to familiarize yourself with it?" my dad asks, and just like that, the somewhat pleasant atmosphere is replaced by impending storm clouds.

I place my fork down on my plate and prepare myself. "Yes, I saw it."

"And?" He leans forward, a hopeful expression on his face. "It's a two-week internship, and it's an incredible opportunity for you to make a good impression on several key players in New York. An opportunity like that is a once-in-a-lifetime thing, son."

What I'm about to say next won't make me popular in my parents' household.

"It's in August," I say, hoping against hope that it'll ring a bell for either of them.

"Yes." Dad looks confused, since he obviously thinks nothing happens in August.

"What about camp?"

"The what?" Even more confusion, but something seems to register. "Oh, the hockey thing," he finally says.

Here's the main point of contention between me and my dad. Everything that I've worked toward, all those early mornings spent on ice, hours and hours in the gym, training, studying game tape—it's all reduced down to *that hockey thing*.

I sigh. They'll never understand, and they'll never support it. "Yeah, that hockey thing."

"Isn't that for kids?" Mom asks as she takes a sip of her water.

I close my eyes for a moment. "Yes."

They look at each other, and there are so many unspoken words flying between them that the air is thick with unvoiced thoughts.

"Does..." Mom starts. "Do you know if..." She throws Dad a helpless glance. Mom's always been the softer of the two. She's more empathetic and doesn't want to hurt anybody's feelings if there's another way. Don't get me wrong, she absolutely will if she feels it's warranted, but she prefers a somewhat gentler approach.

"What we want to say is, it's not exactly like you get paid to be there." Dad swoops in to save Mom. "It seems silly to throw away this great opportunity on a hockey camp for kids, where you volunteer."

"They are a great group of kids, and they're counting on me to be there." Which my parents would know if they had any interest in my life—the real one and not the one they wish I was living—but they don't, and I've long since given up on the hope that I'll get them to support me by making a wish on a falling star.

"But this internship would help you make several very important connections," Dad presses.

"I've committed myself to coaching those kids. I can't just fuck off into parts unknown because my dad found me an internship." My mom winces at the curse, but I don't even feel bad about it.

"Don't you have spares?" My mother, ladies and gentlemen.

"Sounds like a solid plan. I'll just give my spare coach a call," I say and try my hardest not to sound too sarcastic. I'm already toeing the line of being disrespectful, but in my defense, she started it.

My dad places his hands on the table and looks at me. "What is this really about? It's a great opportunity, why do we have to convince you to take it?" He studies me for a few unnerving seconds. "Please tell me you're still not entertaining this foolish notion of a career in hockey."

I'm not ready to have this fight, but there doesn't seem to be much choice. Where is an earthquake when you need one? Or a snowstorm that comes out of nowhere. I should have left my car doors unlocked. Maybe somebody would have stolen it, and I would have a reason to leave.

"It's my current plan for my future." I slip the p-word in there to make the dream seem more realistic. After all, plans are achievable, aren't they?

"I thought we agreed it's not a smart move," Mom says, and she seems to believe that all of us have, in fact, acknowledged that I should not pursue my dream.

"You and Dad agreed."

Mom looks stunned for a moment, as if that's something she really hadn't given a second thought to.

"It's a hobby," Dad says casually, brushing years of hard work aside like it's nothing. "It can't be anything more. Be realistic, Law." My temper is close to boiling point, so I stuff a large forkful of pasta in my mouth. My plan is to clean the plate as quickly as possible and get the hell out of here.

"It's not just a hobby," I mumble through a mouthful of food. Mom shakes her head, but she says nothing. It speaks to the gravitas of the situation that bad table manners seem to be the least of her worries.

"Son, you cannot still be entertaining the notion you'll make a comeback. The doctors were very clear that playing professionally was out."

I finish the pasta and take a long drink of water. "There are more ways than one to have a hockey career." I'm proud of how level my voice is.

What my parents don't get is that I know all the drawbacks they're dying to lay in front of me. I know the competition for the few available NHL coaching jobs is fierce. I know the statistics, and I know it won't be a walk in the park with extra time to smell the roses. I also know that, like with a lot of things, you have to start from the bottom and claw your way up. I know there is very little job security, and that a lot of the times, the pay is shit. It's fucking backbreaking, hard work, and like it or not, there's also the component of luck involved. I know all that.

The thing is, some people will make it to the top, and I want to be one of them no matter how narrow the odds. I'm not going to just step aside and be a forty-year-old financial analyst who's bitter about everything because he lacked the balls to try.

Parents should be proud when their child sets their mind to something and works their ass off to get it, but listening to my mom and dad, it almost feels like they're embarrassed.

It's like I'm the only son of a well-off family that has a shameful secret. Might as well face it: hockey is my drinking problem.

I can picture my mom's friends whispering, *Lawrence Anderson, yes.*

*Such a nice boy. Too bad about the...* And then they'd mimic hitting a puck. The image is almost enough to make me snicker.

"Don't gamble your future away on a long shot," Dad says.

"You took a risk when you started your own company," I argue. "Why can't I do the same?"

"The chances of me making a living in finance were much better than yours at hockey. Besides, you won't have that problem, seeing as you're going to inherit a successful company," Dad says.

It is my own fault that Dad still operates under the assumption that I'll be taking over, since I've never just come out and said that I won't be. Mom and Dad seem to think my grand plan right now is to dabble in hockey a bit, but once the metaphorical college gates fall shut behind me, I'll come to my senses and give the financial world a chance. Attempting to talk me out of coaching is just their way of trying to speed the process along. Why waste years on a silly game when I could graduate and start my cushy job as Dad's sidekick, right?

I don't even know why they're so insistent on me inheriting the company. It's not like Dad would retire as soon as I took over the reins. There's not a chance in hell that is happening. He'll stay on board until he dies, and even if he takes a tiny step away from the wheel, he'll still be around, micromanaging and checking my every move.

The two of us working together sounds like a nightmare, even if I had a deep passion for the finance world. I should just come clean.

*I don't want to take over the business, Dad.*

There. Is it really that hard? Why yes, yes it is. Otherwise I would have already said the fucking words out loud.

I should just force the words out. Rip the Band-Aid off and be done with it. It's family, though, and it's never easy when blood comes into play. Disappointing my parents is not something I want to do. I'd love to be interested in finance. It would make life easier for everybody. Unfortunately, when Mom and Dad combined their DNA, there must have been some sort of an error. How else do you explain that two people who are as unathletic as they come, managed to produce a son who lives and breathes hockey?

So we're at a stalemate.

*Say it. I don't want the company. Just man up and say it.*

I open my mouth… and Dad's phone rings. I slump back in my chair. Saved by the bell. It's cowardly as hell, but I'm fucking relieved I can postpone this conversation for at least another month.

*Cowardly Lion, thy name is Lawrence Anderson.*

"This is unacceptable," Dad barks into the phone, and it's the tone Mom and I are well acquainted with. Somebody has screwed up. I'd say I'm sorry for whoever it is, but Dad is actually very reasonable when it comes to work. Depending on the severity of the mistake and if it's a repeat offender, he'll either give them another chance or fire them. He's a fair boss, and even though people complain about the fact that he's strict and lacks a sense of humor, they respect him. I could never lead the company as well as he does, so really, should it come to that, selling is in everybody's best interest.

"I'll be there in a couple of hours," Dad says. He stands up and starts walking. It takes him a couple of steps before he remembers that a) he wasn't here alone, and b) he forgot to pay. Mom's already taken out her purse, and she tries to hold back a smile as our waiter hurries toward us. It always amazes me when she does that. How is that funny that your husband forgot about you because of a business call?

Dad is still distracted as he tries to wrestle his wallet out of his pocket and ends up handing his car keys to the waiter. Mom snatches them back as she gives the guy her credit card. It's a choreographed dance they've performed many times over the years. I leave a big tip to compensate for the mess that our sudden departure causes.

In front of the restaurant, Dad is pacing back and forth as Mom calmly takes the keys of their rental and navigates us all toward the vehicle.

"We'll see you next month?" she asks as she squeezes my hand in hers. I nod. They climb in the car and I think I'm in the clear, but just as Mom starts the car, Dad lowers his window.

"Read the e-mail," he says. "I expect you to contact Roy." He taps his fingers on the edge of the window. "Time to take your future seriously, son, and stop playing around."

With those parting words, the window rolls up and they take off. Tension has slammed into my body like Thor has put it there with his hammer. The parting shot about me playing around makes my insides vibrate with anger. I'm regretting now that I didn't say that I don't want the company. The petty wish to hurt Dad back has taken hold of my insides, so as if in a daze, I pull out my phone to call him and say my piece.

I weigh the phone in my hand before stuffing it back into my pocket. There's a good chance he wouldn't answer me, anyway. If there's a crisis in the office, he'll be busy handling it for the foreseeable future. There's also still some reasonable part of my brain that insists that it's not a conversation to have over the phone. Ugh! Just for once I'd like to turn the logical part of my brain off and act purely on instinct. Too damn bad today is not that day.

---

It takes a while to work my frustration off at the gym. I've been seething and muttering to myself so that everybody in the gym has given me a wide berth. I'm so preoccupied that, by the time I get out of the shower, I realize that I'm late. I'm supposed to meet Andy at my place at four, but it's already four-fifteen.

"Fuck," I snap as I quickly pull on a pair of sweats and a hoodie. I grab my bag, and I'm out of here.

*On my way,* I text Andy before I jump into my car.

I park in my space in front of the apartment I rent in Montpelier. The town is minuscule compared to New York, but I like it. The campus is only ten miles away. Most people prefer to live in the dorms, but I like privacy, so for the last two years, I've rented an apartment.

I used to rent a house with my teammates, but now that I'm not playing anymore, it doesn't feel like an appropriate setup. Living alone has taken some time to get used to, but it's fine. I'm not lonely, or anything. Plus, I have some serious neat-freak tendencies, and the mountains of beer bottles that littered the counters and living room corners in that house always drove me insane, so living on my own has its advantages.

I grab my bag and hurry inside, half certain that Andy has already left, which would be a huge waste of time for the both of us, since I'd have to track him down again and convince him to help all over again.

But he's not gone. He's sitting on the floor, leaning against the wall next to my front door, reading a book. His hair is in its usual disarray around his head, curls of it are falling in front of his face, and every once in a while, he brushes it away with his hand. He looks peaceful and nice and I have a sudden urge to sit next to him and just bask in Andy's presence, where there is no disapproval, expectation, or tension.

I must make some kind of noise because Andy's head shoots up, and he looks at me. He uses his middle finger to push his glasses back up on the bridge of his nose.

"So you do live here," he says. "I was starting to think you were pranking me when you gave me the address."

There's no anger in his tone. Most people would be pissed at me for being late, or they would already be out of here. Not Andy because, clearly, his mission in life is to be unpredictable. He just closes his book and looks at me expectantly.

"Sorry I'm late," I say. "I got caught up at the gym."

I don't know if it's imagination or wishful thinking, but Andy's eyes run over my body, and he seems to like what he sees. I force those thoughts aside. I already have too much on my plate with my parents' demands and hockey and school.

I like Andy. I like him a lot, but there's no way I can pursue anything with him. A hook-up would be nice, I admit, but Andy doesn't seem like the type, and I like him too much to complicate the tentative friendship we've got going on with sex.

And then there's the fact that Andy has a crush on Falcon Asola.

"No worries, I've been keeping myself entertained."

He waves a thick book in my direction. It has so many complicated words in the title that I can't even begin to guess what it's about. With his other hand, he points to the biggest bag of candy I've ever seen.

"Ooh." I sit down next to him, not caring that we're still in my hallway, and make a grab for the bag of candy. "I haven't had those in forever."

He scoffs, "Of course you haven't. You're an athlete. You guys hate things that make you feel good."

It's unexpectedly nice to hear Andy refer to me as an athlete. All my teammates and friends avoid the topic of my short hockey career like they're afraid I'm going to burst into tears.

Before I can stop myself, I run my eyes over Andy. "Not all good things," I say and damn if my voice doesn't sound suggestive. Andy looks startled, but before either of us can really think about what I said, I stand up. "Let's get inside."

I reach out my arm. Andy looks at it for a second before he grabs it, and I haul him to his feet. I ignore the tingles that run over my skin as Andy's palm touches mine. I let go of him as soon as he's on his feet and turn to unlock the door.

We step inside. I put my bag in the hallway closet and motion Andy to the living room.

"It's a nice place," he says as he looks around for a moment.

There aren't many options for rentals in Montpelier, but I got lucky. It's a small one-bedroom apartment, but it's plenty of space for me. It's a bit on the older side, but that just means it has character. I especially love the exposed red-brick wall in the living room and the fact that the bedroom is separated from the living room with a book shelf instead of a solid wall. It makes the place seem bigger and airier.

"Do you want something to eat?" I ask as Andy sits down on my dark-blue couch and starts taking things out of his backpack.

He lifts his massive bag of candy and shakes it in my direction. "I'm good. Gotta finish these bad boys before I head home."

I take a seat next to him on the couch. "Why can't you eat them at home?"

He sighs and looks at the candy forlornly. "Falcon," he says as if that one word explains everything. "He thinks it's his mission to save my arteries from trans fats."

"Ah," I say. "How's that going, by the way? Ready to confess your feelings yet?"

He throws me an annoyed glance. "But of course. I brought up the topic of my undying love yesterday during a house meeting. We voted on it, and then we fucked all night like two crazed rabbits."

I'm going to ignore the uncomfortable feeling that squeezes my insides at the mention of Andy fucking somebody else.

"No, I haven't told him," Andy continues. "I still need to look the part before I go and throw myself at him. And with that in mind, let's get to work."

While we've been talking, Andy has laid out the contents of his bag. Holy shit, the guy has been busy. There are three textbooks, a spiral notebook, and a bunch of notecards. Everything is color coded and organized to death. He's also brought some weird instruments with him that I've never seen before.

I've always considered myself a well-organized person, but compared to Andy I'm a slob who writes his notes on rolls of toilet paper that I store in a box, mixed with regular toilet paper.

In thirty minutes flat, I learn two things: first, Andy is a phenomenal teacher, and second, to be even halfway on his level during the actual tutoring session, I'm going to have to record everything Andy says and learn it by heart.

Andy looks all easygoing and laidback, but when it comes to teaching, he's pretty strict. "Gotta know the basics," he says as he hands me a paper with units of measurement on it.

We go over length, weight, time... and on and on it goes until my head swims. It's made worse by the fact that, instead of the good old foot-pound-inch, there's meter-kilogram-second. Then Andy makes me convert between different measurement systems. From there, we jump to scientific notation, because physicists love numbers that need a whole page to fit all the zeroes.

After a while, Andy seems to be happy with what we've covered so far. Since the guys are coming over tomorrow night, I feel fairly confident that I'll be able to duplicate this lesson. I've got to hand it to Andy. He made an otherwise boring lesson just fly by. It's only been about thirty minutes, and we're already done. Andy has taught me the material, and he's also checked and deemed my efforts of conversion satisfactory, and has had me parrot all of it back to him to see if I can be trusted with bestowing that knowledge onto our rookies. I'm impressed with his efficiency.

"And now, onto the first lesson," Andy announces as he opens his laptop.

I do a double take. "Wait, that wasn't the lesson?"

He stares at me like I'm nuts. "That was an introduction. I thought about skipping it, but I figured it would be better to go over it just in case. Shaw starts his class with the concept of speed, so that's where we're headed."

I go and grab two bottles of water. This is going to be a long evening.

And it is, but to be honest, I don't really think about the time because Andy, wonder of wonders, makes that topic interesting, too. He has video clips and real-life examples, and he gets so into the lesson he veers off topic more than once, explaining things like escape velocity. He almost knocks over my lamp as he gestures wildly while explaining why it's necessary when traveling to Mars. From there he moves to challenges of inhabiting Mars and before either of us realizes it, it's dark outside, and we've been at it for three hours.

We finish the chapter and I'm relatively confident that I can deliver at least the most important points of this lesson to the guys by using the examples Andy has given, but I guess the only way to be sure is to wait and see tomorrow. My goal is to be at least fifty percent better than Shaw, so we'll see how it goes.

"Shit! Is that the time?" Andy asks as he stares at the clock on his laptop screen. "Why did you let me go on and on like that?" he asks as he throws himself back onto the couch.

I shrug. "It was interesting."

He rolls his eyes at me. "I've already agreed to tutor you. You don't need to butter me up anymore."

I straighten myself and look him in the eye. "I'm not saying it to stroke your ego. You're a very good teacher. Have you ever considered working as one?"

He toys with the cord of his laptop as he considers my words. "I've thought about it," he eventually says as he gets up and starts packing his things. He doesn't say anything else, though.

"And?" I prompt.

"You only think I'm a decent teacher because I feel comfortable enough with you not to puke on you."

Andy feels comfortable with me? For whatever reason, that feels like a lottery win. My insides go all warm as I let the thought settle. I would have persevered with the tutoring thing even if it turned out Andy hated me and every moment he was forced to spend with me because I need him, but the fact that he actually likes me is like an ice cream cone on a warm summer day. Without thinking, I grab Andy's arms and force him to look at me.

"You're an excellent teacher, Andy Carter."

He flushes slightly and shakes his head, but there's a small smile on his face as he pulls away and continues putting his things away.

"Hey, you want some dinner?" I ask before I can consider whether or not it's a good idea. I just know that I don't want Andy to leave yet. I'm having too much fun hanging out with him to call it a night, even though I have an early practice tomorrow at the camp and on a normal day, I would never do something like this.

Andy looks surprised at the offer.

"I'm a decent cook," I add.

Andy looks torn as his eyes flitter between my kitchen and the front door. He scratches his head. "I kind of told Falcon I'd be home for dinner. It's this farewell thing since he's going away for the summer. I'm going to regret it later when I'm trying to force down tofu or Brussels sprouts or something equally as horrifying, but raincheck?"

Why the hell am I disappointed? There's no reason to be bothered by the fact that the guy I've known for a grand total of two weeks has other plans.

*Plans with a guy he has a crush on,* I remind myself, and instantly I tell myself to shut up. Good for Andy. He can flirt and make Asola notice him. I'm kind of surprised Asola hasn't figured out yet that Andy has a crush on him. It's not like Andy is especially subtle about it, but maybe it's easier to detect it from an outsider's perspective.

"Sure," I say. "I'll just eat that chicken alfredo myself then."

Andy glowers at me. "You evil bastard."

I grin as I watch him pull his sneakers on. "It's my grandma's recipe with extra cheese."

Andy shakes his head. "Keep talking. But just remember, people have gone to hell for less, and God is always listening."

It's fun to tease him. Andy picks up his bag, and that brings me back to reality. He's here to help me with tutoring, so I should do my part, too.

"Before I forget, I found you a stylist."

Andy takes a step back and gapes at me. "Already?"

"Well, yeah, it's Jordan's sister. Jordan's our goalie. And don't worry, she's a pro. Has a client list and everything."

"Oh," Andy says faintly. He looks a bit green.

"You sure you want to go through with it?" I ask with a frown.

Andy blinks a couple of times and starts nodding. "Absolutely. Yup. It'll be great. Super great."

"Uh-huh." It doesn't look like his heart is fully in it, but I guess the thought of change can be scary, and it'll take some time to get used to it.

"I was also thinking you should come to the gym with me," I continue.

The look on Andy's face is priceless. Already freaked by the stylist news, his eyes go wide and he closes and opens his mouth a few times. "The gym?" he repeats like it's a foreign word, and he's testing it out to get the pronunciation right.

"We can go in the morning. I usually run on the treadmill before work. You should come with," I propose.

He laughs. "Phew, for a moment there, I thought you were being serious. Good one."

"I think it makes perfect sense. First of all, exercise is good for you."

He gasps. "You take that back."

"And secondly, think about it, Asola is really into sport, so if you start running and going to the gym, you'll have something else in common. Is there really anything more romantic than working out together?"

"I can think of lots of things," Andy mutters.

"Well, you wanted my help with Asola, and that's my first lesson. Find a common interest. You can start going to the gym together, or even on a morning run. You'll have all this time together, just the two of you…"

Andy doesn't look convinced, but eventually, his shoulders drop and he lets out a resigned sigh. "Fine. I guess we can try."

I rub my hands together excitedly. "It'll be great," I announce. "We'll start tomorrow. I'll pick you up at six."

"Six!" he yelps. "My alarm clock didn't come with the six a.m. option."

"It'll be great," I assure him once more.

Andy opens the front door wordlessly. He steps out and takes another disgusted look at me. "I rue the day I met you," he announces.

I laugh as I watch him sulkily trudge down the stairs.

My mood is great for the rest of the evening.

7

## ANDY

Five forty-five in the morning is a ridiculous time to get up. The sun is rising, true, but the apartment is still dim, for Christ's sake. That must be a clear sign from God that He does not approve of doing anything other than sleeping at this hour of the day, and who am I to contradict the big guy? Clearly, people aren't meant to be up this early. The sun looks like it's trying to convince itself that rising is a necessary feat. As it is, only murderers, lunatics, and prostitutes are out at this time of day, and since I'm none of those, I feel like I should have stayed in bed to avoid false advertising.

I'm slumped over the kitchen table, trying to gather enough willpower to make myself a cup of coffee when my phone rings. I grab at it blindly and slide my thumb over the screen. "I hate you," I mumble into the phone.

Law laughs too damn brightly to be human. "Rise and shine," he says in a singsong voice. "I'll be there in five."

"I hope you get some kind of embarrassing disease," I yell into the phone before he can hang up. The bastard only laughs at that.

Precisely five minutes later, I drag my sorry ass downstairs, where Law's car idles by the curb. I climb in, buckle the seatbelt, and we're off. Law takes one look at me and wordlessly hands me a thermos. I take a sip and groan as the glorious taste of coffee hits. "Fine, I take back the embarrassing disease wish," I say.

"Well, I, for one, am relieved," he deadpans.

The drive to the gym takes us only five minutes. The campus is silent in the early morning. It's that quiet time of the day when diligent students aren't out to go to class yet, but even the most avid parties have called it quits for the night. The only good thing about the six a.m. wake-up call is the fact that all my roommates were still dead to the world because of last night's goodbye party, so I was spared the conversation where I would have had to explain why I'm up at six and ready to go exercise. Falcon would have probably hired an exorcist had he witnessed me this morning. By the time I'm back, he'll already be gone. For the whole summer. For whatever reason, I'm not as bummed as I usually am about it.

Law and I get out of the car and make our way into the gym. "Is this the right time to mention that running, and exercise in general, is against my religion?" I ask as we drop our things in the lockers.

"And what religion is that?"

"I worship on the altar of Mars Inc. and Hershey Co."

He laughs at that. "Relax. We're just going to do some light running."

"Oh, okay. See, I should have told you before, in my religion it's only acceptable to run when somebody's chasing you."

Law's looks me up and down. "I mean, I guess I could run behind you if that's what you need."

"Cool. Thanks. Could you also emulate an angry carnivore, like a tiger or a bear or a T-Rex? It helps if I feel like my life is in danger."

"Man, I've gotta go practice my roaring," he says, and to his credit, he manages to sound like he doesn't think I'm completely ridiculous.

"Now come on, we've only got an hour before I have to go to practice," he says as I gape at him.

"Why are you here if you've got practice later?" I ask.

"Warming up." Law's lips twitch as I stare at him in horror.

"I'll never understand athletes," I mumble to myself.

He puts his hand on the small of my back and starts pushing me out of the locker room. I ignore the tingles that run through me at Law's touch.

"I work as a coach at hockey camp. The kids have practice, not me. I mean, I skate a little, but it's mostly just yelling at them to tell them what they're doing wrong."

I stop and Law bumps into me. He's big and warm and standing so close to him feels good. Too good. I step away. "Is that why I'm here? You want to practice your yelling on me? I'll probably give you lots of reasons to get frustrated, just a fair warning."

"I'll use all my best curse words," he assures me with a twinkle in his eyes.

"Lead the way," I tell Law with a resigned sigh, and not a minute later, I find myself face to face with a row of treadmills.

"Ah," I say, doing my best to emulate the dude from History Channel. "Ancient torture devices. In the Middle Ages people who were accused of being witches were made to run on those archaic machines until they collapsed of exhaustion and admitted that they were, in fact, in cahoots with the devil and were practicing witchcraft."

Law barks out another laugh. He throws his arm over my shoulder and leads me to one of the deathtraps. "Let's see if you've got the power, then."

He walks me through his plan for me, which is basically a lot of walking, intercepted by short bouts of jogging every couple of minutes. It doesn't sound exactly pleasant, but since I expected him to make me run at full speed for three hours straight, it's better than I thought.

As far as workouts go, this one's okay. Not once do I feel like I'm about to die. Law runs beside me, predictably with a much tougher regime that includes sprinting uphill. I glance at him from the corner of my eye every once in a while. I can't help it. He's... hot. There's no other word for it. His powerful muscles flex as he speeds up, legs measuring the miles steadily. It's impossible not to appreciate the sight.

After my thirty minutes are up, I step off the treadmill and sit down on the floor. I know I hated the idea of a workout in the beginning, but

I feel good. Those pesky endorphins really know what they're doing. I empty Law's water bottle just to mess with him, because I'm a good friend like that. Finally, after twenty more minutes, Law slows to a walk and after another five minutes, steps down from the treadmill.

"So?" he asks with a knowing smirk. He doesn't even sound tired, damn it. I sound more winded when I have to walk up the stairs to my apartment. Maybe Law was onto something with this gym thing?

"It was not totally unenjoyable," I allow as he beams like he's a new father and I've just complimented his newborn.

"Great. Same time tomorrow?" he asks. He heads toward the locker room as I scramble to my feet and almost lose my balance in my haste to get to Law. "Wait a minute," I call after him. "What do you mean tomorrow? I thought it was like a once-in-a-lifetime type of deal?"

"Exercise is good for you," he repeats like a mantra. "But fine, you can have Sundays off. That still leaves us with six mornings of fun each week."

I gape at him in disbelief. "Don't you have other friends to torture?"

A shadow crosses his eyes, but it's so quick that it might also only be a trick of light. "That just means I like you best," he quips, and I'm taken aback by how good that makes me feel, joking or otherwise.

We reach our lockers and Law undresses. No hesitation, no insecurities. Just pulls off his shirt and drops his shorts. I realize belatedly that I'm staring at Law's ass, so I quickly turn my back because he's about to lose the boxer briefs, and if I'm not mistaken, things are about to get embarrassing for me.

"Six times a week is crazy," I say to distract myself. My face is firmly turned away from Law, but I can hear the rustling of fabric, so I'm determined to drown that sound out with my voice.

Law is quiet for a moment before he sighs and says, "Fine, five times a week."

"Two," I counter.

"Four, but we'll go for a hike one of those days."

"Two days and a hike. That's my final offer."

"Three days and a short hike," Law says.

"Fine," I grumble. "You get three mornings, a hike, and my eternal hatred."

"Deal," Law says. I'm afraid he'll want to shake on it, so I quickly busy myself with rummaging through the locker to seem busy. No way will I be able to shake hands with a very naked Law—who by the way, doesn't seem at all bothered by the fact that he has no clothes on —without giving him a hint of how his nakedness is affecting me. Because yes, I'm sporting a major boner.

"For the record, I would have been fine with four days," I say, just to get the last word and distract myself.

Law laughs as he walks past me, and I can totally see his bare ass. His magnificent, fantastic bare ass that flexes as he walks and is all sorts of muscled and firm. He turns his head and glances at me over his shoulder. I quickly lift my eyes, but I'm sure he's noticed me look-ing. He has a satisfied smirk on his face as he says, "I would have been happy with two."

Awesome.

That same afternoon, I get a call from my new stylist, Tricia. She sounds like the epitome of no-nonsense. In five minutes, she's proposed for us to meet this evening in a coffee shop near campus. She has that whole take-charge attitude down pat, which is good because on my own, I'd probably procrastinate the hell out of this makeover and get to it by the time Falcon has proposed to somebody who looks like a GQ cover model.

The thought propels me to say yes, which is how I find myself in The Jumping Bean at six o'clock in the evening, sitting opposite a thirty-something blonde with a pixie cut, who has been silently studying me for the last ten minutes. If this was a blind date, I'd be sweating bullets, trying to figure out why she's staring at me like that.

But since it's not a date and she has literally shushed me and told me to let her work, I'm almost stoic about the process.

*This is what you wanted,* I remind myself every time the staring becomes unnerving, and strangely enough, it helps.

"What are you looking to accomplish?" she asks as she keeps looking at me.

"Well, I guess I want to look more presentable," I say. I knew this was coming, so I've been practicing my answer, and I sound relatively sure of myself, which is always a plus. I've opted out of telling this stranger about Falcon. I don't need another lecture about how I should be who I am and stay true to myself, so I roll out the more socially acceptable reason. "I'm graduating next year, so I'll need to ditch the sweats and look like a grown-up." She says nothing at that. "Maybe do something with the hair?" I say, and once again, I sound hesitant, instead of confident.

"You do have a lot of hair," she finally says.

"Yes?" Where is she going with this, and will I like it?

"What products do you use?"

"Umm… shampoo?"

"Conditioner?" she asks.

"No?"

"I figured. Here's the plan. Drop the shampoo and use only conditioner for now. You look like somebody electrocuted Einstein, so you've got to get some moisture into that mess." She waves at my hair. "I've made you an appointment with my hairstylist for Saturday. She'll tell you what products to use. She's going to chop off a couple of inches of your hair, but it'll still be on the longer side, since Law tells me that under no circumstance am I allowed to shave your head."

I gape at her. Law doesn't want her to cut my hair? I don't know how to feel about it. On the one hand I want to be all, *Roar, I'm my own person,* and shave my head out of spite, but on the other hand—and that's the dominant part—I get a warm feeling in my belly. He likes my hair! What does it mean?

Meanwhile, Tricia has continued talking, so I quickly concentrate back on her and make a face to show that I've been listening the whole time. "The stylist's also going to show you how to style your hair step by step, because right now, it's a mess."

There's obviously not going to be any sugarcoating, but oddly enough, it relaxes me. I almost feel like a canvas, and that's fine with me. I need an artist to paint a nice picture on me, because all evidence points to the fact that, if left to my own devices, the result will look like a preschooler's finger-painting.

"I also need to see your wardrobe."

"Why?"

"To separate the wheat from the chaff. I've got to see what I'm working with here. Usually, when I'm working with a new client, we make two piles: keep and toss. That way we can figure out what additional items to buy."

I wince at the thought of buying clothes because I hate shopping, and I can already imagine the price tag I'll be looking at, shopping with somebody as stylish as Tricia. No way did her clothes come from Amazon with the offer of *buy two, get the third T-shirt for free.*

Tricia notices my reaction, so she smiles for the first time since we said our hellos and pats my hand. "Don't worry. Most people don't realize that you don't need to buy a whole new wardrobe. We need some key elements, and I'll show you how to mix and match them. Also, you're in luck. I love shopping, and I adore thrift stores, so stop looking so worried. It'll be great."

She sounds very optimistic about the whole endeavor, and I'm reluctant to bring her down to Earth with my pessimistic outlook, so I just take a deep breath and give her a hesitant smile. "Sounds good. Let's do this."

"That's the attitude. Come on. We'll do the wardrobe now, so we'll have a general idea of what we're up against."

She gets up, drops some money on the table, and we're out of there. I'm tentatively hopeful, which turns out to be a mistake, because an hour later, Tricia has declared most of my clothes useless.

"How do you not have a single suit?" she asks as she picks up a green dress shirt. "And the only dress shirt you have looks like a Granny Smith apple vomited it out." She continues looking through the tiny keep pile, still picking out things to toss from there. "You don't have khakis, but you have overalls. How is that logical human behavior? Help me out here, Andy." I don't have an answer for her. "You have one pair of jeans. One! Are you even American? Jeans are our uniform. I have nine pairs, and I hate jeans."

"Sorry?" I offer.

"This is worse than I thought," she mutters.

In the end, most of the things Tricia picks out are the ones my sisters have forced me to buy. If nothing else comes from this venture, at least they'll know their taste has earned a seal of approval from an actual stylist. I should have Tricia write them a certificate since I won't be able to afford actual birthday presents once I've used all my money on new, acceptable clothes.

*It's what you wanted*, I remind myself. And I do. I really do, but the prospect of change is still scary. It'll probably get easier after I've taken the first steps, though. I hope.

I must look pretty defeated because Tricia pats me awkwardly on the back. Two quick, consecutive taps. No one could accuse her of not being efficient. "There, there. Now cheer up," she says. It's not exactly a warm, motherly hug, but I guess even a drop of water is something when you're parched. "The hard part's done, so now the fun begins. You and I have a date in the near future. Spoiler alert, we'll go shopping."

I give her a weak smile. Somehow I don't think she and I have the same definition of fun, but I've come this far, so I'm not giving up now. New Andy, here I come.

# 8

## LAW

It's been two weeks since Andy started teaching me how to tutor the team. We've arranged all our sessions so that Andy comes to my place the evening before the actual tutoring, so I'll remember all the information when I step in front of the guys and try my best to duplicate Andy's lesson from the night before.

The first tutoring session was... okayish. Everybody seemed to get what I was saying. Andy had put together a little quiz of his own for them to take at the end of the tutoring session, and they all passed, so I counted it as a success.

Since then, though, things have gone progressively worse. I mean, Andy does his part, and he's going way overboard with all the extras he adds, like the quizzes and notecards. But the thing is, even if I parrot everything Andy tells me beforehand to the guys the next evening, I don't know the answers to all the questions they have for me, and boy, do they have questions.

With the previous tutors the guys just sat there, looking bored and uninterested. They gave mumbled answers and there were never questions, except that one time Jared wanted to know what time it was because he had a date.

It turns out Andy's lessons are so good that people actually understand what he's talking about. Instead of reciting the material from the book, Andy ties every single topic to real life, which makes the otherwise difficult concepts easier to grasp.

The problem is, I'm still an unskilled teacher, so I say the wrong things and I doubt myself, and it shows. And that leads to the team having even more questions, and when I stumble my way through them—because Andy has anticipated a lot of those beforehand and made notes on what to say—it's time for the dreaded follow-up questions, and that usually means I'm in deep shit because fuck if I know if the final total momentum when two objects collide equals the initial total momentum.

Some of my old teammates all have gotten into the habit of sitting through tutoring because they know I'm getting in way over my head, so they pitch in and try to play teacher with me. Or maybe they're just in it for the laughs. I feel like I'm an incompetent dad who's trying to fumble his way through his kids' seventh grade math assignments.

Tonight has been especially brutal. The lesson is about vectors, and even though Andy explained it to me yesterday, I could tell that today was going to be difficult because my knowledge of vectors is more than shaky. I understand it on an abstract level but passing my knowledge on to somebody else is a big, fat no. I learnt Andy's lecture by heart and delivered it, but that didn't stop the barrage of questions. And dear mother of dragons did they have questions.

At the end of the night, I'm feeling like the dumbest motherfucker on planet Earth because, as is becoming our new habit, I've done subpar work with the tutoring.

Mark, our center, flops face first on the couch as the front door shuts, and mumbles something into the pillow. Jordan just stares straight ahead like he's reliving a nightmare he can't wake up from. I can't blame him; he's an excellent goalie, but kind of hopeless when it comes to physics.

The three of us used to share a house my junior year, and we were good friends, but ever since I accepted the position of assistant coach, there's been this tension between the three of us. My new position doesn't really allow me to go out and drink with the team any longer, and there's an awkwardness between us that didn't used to be there. Still, at least there's a bit of camaraderie left between us. My other teammates have taken the stance that, since I'm now part of the coaching staff, we can't be friends any longer. I guess it was to be expected, but it still bums me out from time to time.

"Is it me, or are we getting dumber every day?" Mark lifts his head from the pillow and frowns.

"I'm not gonna lie to you, man," Jordan says. "You've always been like this."

Mark flips him off. "At least I have my looks going for me."

"Way to be an optimist. And you're right, there has always been a certain demographic who prefers to go for the dumb, pretty ones, so you'll be fine."

We sit quietly for a while until Mark sighs. "What the hell is the point of this?" He looks at me. "No offense, man, but you're not equipped to deal with this shit. None of us are. I mean, fuck, I barely passed Freshman Physics myself, and that was pre-Shaw."

Jordan bites his lower lip and grunts in affirmation.

"Besides, it's not like it's even our fucking problem," Mark continues and yawns. "It's not like *we're* failing. I say, let them figure it out themselves. They fail, they fail. Case closed."

"Well," I point out. "They fail, and more than half of them can't play because their GPAs will be too low."

It's not the first time we've had this conversation. Mark's a good guy, but he had a rough childhood, living in the foster care system. He had some shitty temporary placements in less-than-ideal foster families, so there's a firm every-man-for-himself attitude planted in him he still struggles to shake most of the time. He's getting better, though. When he joined the team, he used to hog the puck like he was the only person capable of scoring a goal.

"Maybe it'll be the kick in the ass they need to get their shit together." Mark shrugs.

"Maybe. Or, and bear with me here, maybe we're a team, and we have each other's backs."

Mark just rolls his eyes at that. "You have the worst hero complex."

I bristle at that. It's not the first time I've heard that about myself, and I fucking hate it. I'm a decent person who likes to pitch in when I can. What's so wrong with that? It's not like I actively try to find people in trouble and force them to accept my help. "It's not a hero complex. I just give a shit. What's your solution when we don't have enough decent players on the roster because half of them are stuck behind a failing grade in physics?"

"All I'm saying is maybe we should stop coddling them, and they'll man up and pass the class," Mark replies.

I groan in frustration. "We tried that already."

"All I remember is you pulling some strings and schmoozing your way into the dean's office where you convinced him to force Shaw to let them retake the class this summer, which is probably why he got so pissed off in the first place. He'll probably fail all the hockey players on purpose from now on."

"Over seventy percent of the class failed," I say calmly. "I just pointed it out to the dean. He merely agreed that it might not be solely the students' faults. I didn't ask him to demand Shaw repeat the class. That was his prerogative."

"You meddled," Mark states flatly.

"Fuck you," I snap. "I did what was necessary, and I got results. And can I just point out that nobody asked you to be here. If you don't want to help, you're free to go."

"Mom, Dad, stop fighting," Jordan's bored voice drawls from the other side of the room. He turns toward me. "Law, you fucking meddled. Own it." Next, he faces Mark. "And you can stop whining. Wrong or right, if Law wasn't prepared to go through fire and water for this team, we'd be fucked and you know it."

We both glare at Jordan, but he's right and we both know it.

"Yeah, all right," Mark finally sighs. "Sorry, man. It's just fucking frustrating. Are you sure this Andy guy wouldn't be willing to come teach himself? We could probably pay him more, right?"

If only it was that simple. Andy has refused to take my money, saying that I'm already helping him with Falcon, so it would be unfair for me to pay him.

"It's not the money," I say. "He has a legitimate phobia. You should have seen his face when I told him he needed to tutor seven people. He went pale so fast I thought somebody had removed all the blood from his body."

"Still sounds like a made-up excuse," Mark grumbles.

I push his shoulder. "Way to be an insensitive ass. Besides, it's not like we can force him to tutor the guys. If he says he can't do it, he can't do it and that's that."

"What if..." Jordan purses his lips and frowns like he's trying to catch a fleeting thought. He stays silent for so long that Mark gets impatient.

"What if what?" he snaps. "Dude, just spit it out."

Jordan glares at Mark. "It's just a thought, but what if Andy comes to the tutoring sessions? Not to teach, but to sit in the back row and listen, and then he can, like, write down the answers to all the questions and we'll read them out loud or something."

I rub my forehead. It's an idea. Maybe not a great one, and fuck knows if Andy would even be willing to do it, but let's face it, we're all in too deep in this ridiculous plan, so we might as well see it to the end.

I sigh. "I guess I'll talk to him."

* * *

As expected, Andy isn't thrilled with the idea, but he agrees to try it after I've sent him about thirty different text messages. I tried asking him on the phone, but he hung up on me, so I've been shooting him text after text, trying to make my case.

I'm practically begging by the time he replies, *Fine. I'll do it. Now stop harassing me.*

He might be a wee bit frustrated with me. Doesn't matter. As unethical as it might be, the ends justify the means, so even though I feel conflicted about forcing Andy further and further away from his comfort zone, I'll do it because I'm a selfish asshole.

On Monday we have our next session. I haven't seen Andy since

Friday morning when we went to gym. When a knock sounds on my door, I'm already expecting it and hurry through the apartment much more quickly than could be considered cool.

I throw open the door and freeze.

The guy standing in front of me is... well, it's clearly Andy, but he doesn't look like the Andy I know. It takes me a second to put my finger on it.

His hair.

Somebody has tamed it.

When before, it flew all over his head in crazy waves and strands, now there are neat curls. It's still longish, but the wild lion's mane that used to be Andy's hair is now restrained.

He looks good. Definitely. His gray eyes stand out even more now that you can actually see them. So yeah, he looks good. Absolutely. I have no idea why I feel a pang of longing for Andy's old hair. It's dumb.

Something else registers right at that moment and I do a double take. His eyes.

"Where are your glasses?" I blurt out.

"Contacts. Not sure about those yet. It took me two hours to get them in. I'm not sure it's worth the trouble."

I just stare.

Andy, for his part, looks uncomfortable. He's fidgety and sort of nervous as he plays with the strap of his bag. Almost like he's waiting for my opinion.

"You look different," I say because I have to say *something*. I can't just keep standing here, staring at him. The initial shock has passed, but I find it hard to shake this change off and act like a normal person.

"Yeah," Andy says and clears his throat. He licks his lips, straightens himself, and looks me in the eye. "It was time for my annual haircut," he jokes and I laugh, but it sounds forced. Andy's shoulders deflate again, and he looks away. "Can I come in?" he asks, and I hurry to get out of his way.

He takes off his shoes and jacket and goes to the living room, holding his backpack in front of him like a shield.

I go after him, and we take a seat on the couch. Andy gets his books and notes out in complete silence. Why is it so awkward? And then it hits me. I've hurt his feelings. As easygoing and low maintenance as Andy seems, he wanted this makeover because he didn't feel comfortable in his own skin. Didn't feel like he was good enough for people to notice him. And instead of giving him a compliment, I've stared at him like he's grown an extra head. I officially suck. But I can do better.

"I like your hair," I say. "You look good."

He clears his throat once more and throws me a quick glance over his shoulder. "Yeah. I met up with Tricia the other day, and she sent me to this hair stylist. Umm, she wanted to do a pompadour. I had no fucking clue what it was, and I couldn't exactly do an internet search in front of her, so I opted out of that one. She was disappointed, but I looked it up after, and no way would I have been able to style it so that I wouldn't have looked like I had an unfortunate incident with a lawn mower. So yeah, good thing I didn't say yes to that. Anyway, this is what she came up with." He fiddles with the ends of his hair. "It's less hair than before, but I don't look unrecognizable, so I figure it's a win."

He's rambling, but it's kind of cute. I've never seen Andy so flustered before.

"You look hot," I say and immediately start overthinking it. Is that something you'd say to a friend? Would I say it to Mark or Jordan or any of my other teammates? And that's a no. Mark would laugh his ass off if I were to give him an estimation of how sexy I think he looks. Maybe I shouldn't have said it? Andy and I are friends, and friends do not flirt with each other.

But Andy visibly relaxes and smiles at me. The real, wide, toothy Andy-grin that I've come to like, and I think, fuck it, he's hot, why shouldn't I let him know? Andy could use a boost of confidence, and what kind of friend would I be if I wasn't the one to give it when opportunity presents itself?

"Thanks. I like it too. For a second there, I thought that I couldn't go through with this makeover thing, but I like the result. Gives me hope for when Tricia and I get to the clothes-buying part."

"When is that happening?"

He shrugged. "Don't know yet. I've got to come up with a budget first, but probably soon. She already cleaned out my closet, so from now on, if you see me wearing only two shirts and one pair of pants, it's because I literally don't have other clothes. Apparently my closet is a disaster zone."

"She threw away your T-shirts?" I ask, startled. "I like your shirts. They're hilarious."

Andy flushes and shrugs. "She left me some, but they're not exactly screaming successful grown-up, so most of them had to go. It'll be fine. I can live with shirts that don't have slogans on them."

I paste a smile on my face. Andy doesn't look like he's missing the clothes too much, so I guess he's fine, and there's no reason for me to be upset on his behalf.

"As long as you're happy," I say because I'm being a supportive friend and that's what I'm supposed to do.

"Eh." He shrugs one shoulder and shoots me a half-smile. "I can always go back to the way I was if I don't like the result."

I nod. "Sure. Hair grows back and all that."

"Exactly." He nods.

And I nod.

We're like a pair of ventriloquist dolls with our heads bobbing up and down.

"Should we get started?" Andy asks.

"Oh yeah. But before we do, I just wanted to confirm that you'll be at the tutoring session tomorrow?"

Andy looks resigned. "Yeah, I'll be there."

Guilt gnaws at me. I'm being a shitty friend, and I feel like crap doing it to Andy, but we need him, and it's not like I'm forcing him to talk or anything. He can just sit and listen, and maybe later he'll have some thoughts on how to make this process less painful. Yeah. It's a reasonable enough request. I mean, it would be different if I made him teach the class or something, but he's just there to observe. Or that's the way I'm spinning it in my mind.

"Okay. Good," I say.

"Yeah," he replies. The awkwardness is back, and it lasts 'til Andy leaves two hours later.

I might have screwed up on that one.

———

Andy is late.

"He's not going to show," Mark says, ever the optimist.

I check my phone. No messages.

"He'll be here," I repeat stubbornly, like I've done countless times over the last twenty minutes.

Mark just shakes his head and throws himself onto the couch sulkily. I have a whole new appreciation for parents of teenagers.

"Hey coach." Kevin, one of the rookies, hovers in the doorway that leads to the dining room, which we've set up for tutoring. "Can we maybe start? I've got this thing later."

He disappears as I get up and drag myself to the dining room to entertain everybody with my take on Newton's three laws. With each lesson, I feel my confidence take so many hits that the thing is already beaten black and blue. I need this lesson to go well or it'll be very difficult to continue telling everybody, myself included, that this secondhand tutoring is a good plan.

I'm in the middle of an explanation when I lift my gaze and see Andy slip in the room.

"Sorry," he mouths as he rests his back against the wall and settles in to listen. It's nerve-wracking, to give a tutoring session in physics when an actual physics major is present. It doesn't matter that I'm reciting what Andy has told me word for word.

I explain force, inertia, and mass before I recite the three laws of motion. I think I'm doing pretty well, but when we whip out the section where the formulas come out to play, it all goes to shit. As much as I try, I'm out of ideas for how to explain this topic in a way that won't have people staring at me blankly. I parrot whatever Andy has written out for me, but it's obvious that I'm about as knowledgeable in Newton's laws as a squid.

The guys are looking defeated. My shoulders drop. I've failed. In fact, I've screwed the team over because Mark is right. If I hadn't meddled and gone to the dean, the man wouldn't have forced Shaw to repeat the course and he wouldn't hold a grudge against the students.

Logically, I know that I should have just let it play out without sticking my nose into it, but I love hockey. Have always loved it and will always love it, and coaching is the only way I get to be part of the game.

The doctor's diagnosis of hypertrophic cardiomyopathy came as a complete shock, and coming to terms with the fact that I had to hang my skates up at the grand old age of twenty-two, when I really thought I was heading for the NHL, has been the hardest thing I've ever done. Somehow, I kept going, even though back then my only prospect for the future was working for my dad.

But then Coach Williams approached me and offered me the position of assistant coach, and suddenly, my life didn't look so bleak anymore. I threw myself into work, and it turns out, I'm not half bad at this whole coaching thing. At first, I was afraid it'd feel like a consolation prize. That I would end up resenting the guys who still had a shot at the NHL, but I've been at it for two years now, and with each week, I like it more and more.

Which is why it's so important for the team to do well. I have to fix this physics situation or the team is screwed, and I can't help but feel like my chances will be screwed along with the team. And I already know how bleak life was, thinking that I'd have to spend the rest of my life working for my dad, so failure is not an option. I'm doing my MBA to please my parents. I'm not going to give up on my own dream because of physics.

I look at Andy, prepared to see an expression of pity because of how badly I'm fucking this lesson up, but I'm in for a surprise. Andy stares straight ahead, pale and sort of looking like he would rather make a run for it than stay here a moment longer. He doesn't leave, though. Instead, he slowly straightens himself, and even though he looks ready to bolt, he clears his throat and starts speaking.

"Okay, imagine you're on the ice. There's a goal and there's a puck. Since you're a hockey player, you want to give the audience what they're looking for and score. So you hit the puck, and it slides over the ice. But wait! There's a player from the opposing team, and he sticks his stick where it shouldn't be and touches the puck. The puck changes its motion, and you don't score. So essentially, what Newton says is that the only way to get something to change its motion is to use force. If nothing stops the puck, it'll keep moving in a straight line. Forever."

All the guys have turned around to face Andy. The look on his face is pure terror, but instead of running away, he looks at me, bites his lower lip, and slowly and hesitantly makes his way to the front of the room. He's still pale and looks like he'd rather have lunch with a fire-breathing dragon than be here, but he soldiers on.

"Can you maybe all look at your notes and pretend I'm not here?" he asks. As if recognizing that Andy might be their saving grace, everybody snaps their eyes firmly to their notes. Andy lets out a deep breath. In a quick bout of inspiration, I push a chair toward Andy and grab one for myself and sit down in front of him.

"Tune them out," I say. "We're in my apartment, and this chair is just a very uncomfortable couch. So… repeat what you told me yesterday. I'm a shitty student, so I can't remember."

Andy takes a deep breath. He still looks a bit green, but he keeps his gaze on me and starts speaking again. "So now you say, *but Andy, there's no such thing as a perpetual motion machine*, and you'd be right. There isn't, but…"

And he's off. It only takes a minute for Andy to get going. He keeps his gaze firmly locked on mine, and slowly relaxes enough so the lesson really starts to feel like it's just one of our sessions. The ones we hold in my living room. Eventually, Andy looks away from me, sending furtive glances toward his audience, and he stands up to write a formula on the whiteboard.

Andy goes through all the three laws using everyday examples. He inserts formulas into his lecture almost seamlessly and even cracks a few jokes. Granted, they're physics jokes, so absolutely nobody gets them, but the guys seem to realize that Andy is their best shot to pass Shaw's class, so they chuckle politely and keep their what-the-fuck faces for when Andy turns his back to them.

Andy explains all the problems so effortlessly that I'm having a hard time remembering why I couldn't talk about Newton with the same ease. The guys look more engaged than I've ever seen them.

At the end of the session the guys clap Andy on the back. "Dude, why didn't you bring this guy from the start?" Jared asks me as he passes me on his way out. "No offense, but you kind of suck at tutoring."

"Thanks," I say as Mark snickers somewhere behind me, but he sounds happy. "You better get him to agree to keep on tutoring. I don't care what it takes. Money, your car, a fucking blowjob, just get him to agree to continue," he mutters before he stalks out after the others.

Andy has taken a seat. He looks dazed, but he's not as pale anymore, and there's a small smile on his lips.

He looks up as I approach and his smile widens. "Is it pathetic that I totally got an adrenaline rush from this?" he asks. He shakes out his hands. "Is that how BASE jumpers feel? Because if so, sign me up."

"Good, I'm kind of hoping you'll want to repeat that, say twice a week, same place, same time?" I jump in to ask, and I'm not joking. Not even a little bit. I feel guilty for pressuring him, but not enough to let it go. I mean, if Andy refuses to come back here, there's nothing I can do about it, but fuck do I hope that's not the case. I think the guys would riot if they have to endure my pathetic attempts at teaching.

"I'm pretty sure this is what being high feels like," Andy mutters to himself. "Fuck it. I'm sure I'll regret it later, but I'll do it."

Relief. That's all I feel. I'm pretty sure I can now safely say that I've done all I can for my team.

# 9

# ANDY

Adrenaline highs are short. Who knew, right?

I do.

Now.

I'm in the bathroom, hyperventilating. I've got tutoring in an hour, but I can't seem to force myself to move. What was I thinking agreeing to this shit?

Better yet, why didn't I just remain quiet while Law was trying to fumble his way through Newton's Laws? But no, I just had to feel sorry for the guy, and have my moment of bravery where I stormed in and saved the day. That was probably my one and only heroic deed I'll do in my lifetime, so why the hell did I choose to waste it on a measly tutoring session instead of, say, running into a burning building to save a puppy? It's anybody's guess.

A knock on the door brings me back to reality and reminds me that I've been occupying the bathroom for the last forty minutes. I remember that I have roommates who might need to use it for something other than staring at themselves in the mirror, cursing and swearing, while simultaneously breathing into a paper bag.

"I'll be right out," I call weakly as I splash another handful of cold water on my face. I open the door and find a scowling Falcon. He's back in town for a teammate's birthday party, but it's the first time I've seen him since he arrived because last night I was hanging out with Law again, and this morning we went to gym, then I had work, and now I'm supposed to prepare for tutoring.

"Shit," I yelp as he grabs my elbow and pulls me into my room, slamming the door behind us.

"Sit," he orders, and I immediately drop into the chair by my desk. Judging by the speed with which I follow his order, I would have made an excellent soldier.

"What?" I ask defensively as Falcon glares at me from across the room.

"Are you doing drugs?" he asks.

I laugh, but Falcon doesn't crack a smile. "Wait... are you serious?" I ask. His answer is in his humorless expression.

"I'm not... Why would you... What the hell, man?" I sputter.

He drags his hand through his hair and shakes his head. "What else am I supposed to think? I've been gone for two weeks, and you barely pick up your phone. You don't answer any of my texts. Rory and Paul tell me they haven't seen you in ages. And now you're talking to yourself in the bathroom, all pale and shaky."

"And your first thought was, *Jeez, Andy must be on drugs?*" It's such a weird accusation that I'm finding it hard to decide if I should be offended or laughing my ass off.

It's true that I've been busier than usual. With tutoring and work and perfecting my application to MIT, I've hardly had time for my afternoon naps. In fact, lately I've been skipping them more often than not.

He looks embarrassed, which is good because: drugs? Seriously? What the fuck?

"It might have been a gut reaction, but look at it from my perspective. I leave again on Sunday, Andy. I don't have time for an intervention," he says.

"Oh. Well, that makes it all right," I say, my voice dripping with sarcasm.

He stares at me for a long time and with each passing second, he frowns more and more and starts squinting his eyes. "What the hell happened to your hair?" he finally asks.

My hand flies to my head and I pat at my hair self-consciously. "I got a haircut," I say defensively.

*Don't ask if he likes it. Don't ask if he likes it.*

"Do you like it?"

*Damn it, Andy!*

He glares at my hair like it has somehow offended him, which is crazy. If anything, my previous messy excuse for hair should have been considered a public eyesore. I did everybody's retinas a favor by finally fixing that mess.

"Well, I like it." I raise my chin higher.

He must detect something in my voice because he raises both of his palms. "It's very neat," he says, but he keeps glaring at me like he doesn't appreciate the change.

"What a glowing review," I mutter to myself.

"What do you want me to say?" He lifts his hands in exasperation.

"I got the haircut two days ago," I say. "I sent you a picture."

Jesus Christ, we're having a married couple's fight, and we're not even close to being one. What the hell is wrong with me?

He must realize the same thing. Falcon sits on my bed and looks at me. "I'm sorry," he says. "For the drug things and for the"—he gestures toward my head—"hair thing."

I sit down next to him. "I'm sorry too," I say. "I'm just nervous, I guess. Gah!" I groan. "It's embarrassing. I'm trying to tutor some people, and I'm freaking the fuck out because it's a group and, well, you know me and public speaking don't exactly mesh."

"You're tutoring?" Falcon asks with raised brows. "When did that happen?"

"It's the thing I've been doing when you thought I was at my super-secret drug meetings with my new drug buddies."

He smacks the back of my head as I duck and snicker. "We've been injecting umm… ecstasy? Can you inject ecstasy?"

Falcon shakes his head. "You'd make a shitty drug addict."

"Aren't friends supposed to be supportive?"

"Not about this."

I sigh dramatically. "Fine. Be that way."

We sit in silence for a few moments. Falcon is the first to speak. "I miss hanging out with you. In the past, we called and texted a lot more, but now it's like I don't hear from you at all."

My heart lurches in my chest. The fact that Falcon misses me is a good sign. It must be. Somehow I've inadvertently implemented the principle *absence makes the heart grow fonder*. I try to bask in that knowledge for a moment. It's funny, I imagined it would feel better. Sort of like a victory. Instead, I don't feel much of anything. I just seem to register what Falcon has said, but I'm lacking the appropriate emotional response.

Falcon nudges me with his shoulder. "What about you?" He looks adorable, all uncertain and slightly bashful. "Have you missed me at all?"

"Sure I have," I blurt because I have. I totally have. I just haven't realized it before now because I've been so busy with school and work and tutoring. That's all.

"A lot," I say emphatically, because my first response doesn't feel too sincere. I'm trying to fix it, but now I fear I might have gone overboard and sounded too eager, which would be weird, so I hit Falcon's forearm with my fist and say, "Who wouldn't miss that ugly mug of yours, eh bro?" The Canadian accent might be overkill.

He stares at me for a moment, but thankfully doesn't bring up the drugs again, which let's be honest, wouldn't be unwarranted after that little display.

"So then we should try harder," Falcon says, and God bless him, he still seems to mean it.

"Absolutely." I refuse to say anything else in fear I'll make this whole conversation even weirder.

"Shake on it?"

I nod as we do just that. "I'll come home next weekend, and we'll hang out. Just the two of us. It'll be like the old days."

"Sounds good," Falcon says before he gets up to leave. Just as he's about to exit my room, he turns around and says, "I really do like the new hair. It suits you."

The comment distracts me enough that I get to the tutoring session without succumbing to another freak-out, which I count as a win.

Of course then, I trip on one of the hockey player's ginormous feet while I shakily make my way to the front of the room and land on my face, which concludes with a nosebleed and Law clucking over me like a mother hen. It's simultaneously irritating and cute how freaked out a person can get about a bloody nose.

"I thought hockey players beat each other up regularly," I grumble. I'm sitting on the lid of the toilet, and Law is pressing an icepack against my nose. "Shouldn't you be telling me to man up and tutor through the pain?"

"I would, but we still need you, so I figured I should be nice to you lest you decide it's too dangerous and never come back."

"Self-serving wound tending," I joke, but Law frowns and his expression turns sour.

"You know I was just kidding about that, right?" he asks, looking as if he's worried I might not have realized.

"Relax, even though all the evidence points to the contrary," I say as I gesture toward my swollen nose, "I believe a tiny smidgeon of you cares about my physical wellbeing."

He nods, even though he doesn't look totally convinced, and he keeps standing close to me, pressing the ice against my nose and trying to wipe the blood off with his other hand. It's a miracle he hasn't tied his arms into actual knots.

"Holy crap." I laugh. "Quit hovering. It's just a bloody nose."

It takes five more minutes for Law to declare me all right. I wash my face in the sink as Law calls out the door, "Logan, can you cancel tonight's tutoring session?"

"Hey! I can keep going," I protest, but he ignores me, and secretly, I'm relieved.

Logan peeks his head inside as he passes by the bathroom. "They're already gone," he says. "Ran out the door like it was the beginning of summer vacation."

Law looks annoyed as I snicker. "It still counts as a nice gesture, even though there's no one to witness it," I assure him.

He rolls his eyes. "I wasn't doing it for them. I was doing it for you."

My insides go all warm at that. I don't know what to call this feeling inside me, but I guess *cherished* is the word that comes closest. It feels too big for our friendship. Logically, I know that, but the feeling remains.

"Come on," Law says. "We'll go to my place and relax for the night."

I squint my eyes at him. "That doesn't sound like you. Have you been body swapped?"

"Yes," he says. "Enjoy it while you can. Tomorrow, the selfish version will reappear."

It sounds like a joke, but his tone is flat as if he finds it hard to convince himself that the statement is meant as one, which is weird. The guy has given his all to help his team pass this class. He found them multiple tutors. He negotiated a deal with me. I saw his tutoring session on Newton's laws. It was clear as day that Law had learned by heart what I taught him. The whole thing is far from being selfish.

I don't have time to tell him, though, because he's already halfway out the door by the time I catch up to him.

It only takes about five minutes to get to Law's apartment. I settle in on the couch and he prepares a bowl of popcorn for us and places it in my lap.

I grab the remote and turn on the TV while Law is in the kitchen, grabbing us something to drink.

"What do you want to watch?" I ask him as I scroll through the list of channels.

He shrugs. "Don't care. You choose," he calls over his shoulder.

"Have you seen *Nuclear* yet?" I ask because there are a lot of options, and I'm shit at choosing. I've already seen the first episode and would like to see the rest, so I figure we might as well go with that. Falcon was supposed to watch it with me but thought it was boring, and I haven't found a moment to watch it by myself yet.

Law plops down next to me and puts his feet on the low coffee table he has in front of the couch. "Nope. I've heard of it, though." He throws a handful of popcorn into his mouth. "Put it on."

"You sure? It's kind of depressing."

"Are you trying to talk me out of it?" he asks with a laugh.

"Not exactly. I really liked the first episode, so I'd like to see the rest, but I don't know if it's your thing."

"You don't know if nuclear disasters are my thing?" he asks with a smirk.

I press play on the remote. "And your time to pick something yourself just ran out. Enjoy the death and misery."

I've seen the first episode already, but we'll start from the beginning. It takes no time for me to completely get lost in the episode. It's a tragic story, and the series is appropriately dark and grim, but it's so fucking captivating that before I realize it, we've already finished the second episode.

"Wow," Law mutters as he stares at the rolling titles. "Can you imagine volunteering to go search for survivors from a system of shelters underneath the city after a nuclear bomb has been dropped on it? That bomb wiped the place clear. How are they supposed to find the shelters? In the middle of the night. With the threat of another bomb dropping whenever that dickhead of a general decides to give the order." His head is resting against the back of the couch, but he turns it toward me as he speaks.

"They designed the system, so they knew where the shelters were supposed to be," I say.

"Yeah, but you just saw it. It was pitch black down there. I can barely orientate when I have to go to the bathroom at night, and the streetlight shines right in the living-room window," he says.

I chuckle.

"No but seriously, they volunteered," he says. "Volunteered to walk through a radioactive town. I mean, man, talk about being stupidly brave."

I shrug. "I guess some things are just worth dying for."

"Hmm," he mumbles his agreement. We're quiet for a little while before Law speaks again. "If it happened in real life, do you think there'd be volunteers? Or are we all so self-absorbed that we'd just shake our heads and say, 'Nah, let somebody else do it.' I mean, dying for the greater good is fine in theory, and it's easy to picture yourself being the hero from the safety of your own couch, but would any of us really have the guts?"

I stare at the ceiling as I ponder what Law just said. "I think when push comes to shove there would be volunteers for sure. Even if you only have the wimpiest losers out there to do the job, one of them will come through."

Law smiles at that. "You're way more optimistic than I am."

"I'm a realist." I straighten myself and turn toward Law, "Think about it, though. If you don't do it, everybody who's ever mattered to you will die. Your parents, your siblings, husbands, wives, boyfriends, girlfriends. Maybe people wouldn't be willing to die for themselves, but a lot of us would do it for our loved ones."

"You don't think an average person figures somebody else should take care of that problem?"

"I guess there will always be extraordinary people," I say.

"I really wish I was one of them."

"You don't think you are?"

"I'd like to think I'd do the right thing, but who the hell really knows?"

"I don't think any of us know before we're faced with an impossible situation," I agree.

He grins. "It really sucks that I might never know if I'm a decent person or not."

I think about that one for a bit. "Do you have to be a hero to be a decent person?" I counter. It's getting personal, what with all of my revelations about the sidekicky nature of my life. I'm as unheroic as they come, but even then, I'd like to think I can be very much unexceptional and still be a good person.

"I guess not," he says. "But I think there's this inherent need within people, where each of us wants to be the hero."

It mirrors my own thoughts from the day I began this whole Project Hero makeover thing, that led me to this moment.

My mouth seems to open as if it has a will of its own. "I'm the sidekick."

I've heard of alien hand syndrome, but right about now it seems I have a good case for alien mouth syndrome.

Law raises his brows in question. Dear God, I want to keep my mouth shut, but the words are out there, and there's no stopping me now.

"You know. There's the cool hero that everybody wants to be like, and then there's that other guy. That's me. The sidekick."

Law frowns and sits up straighter. "What makes you say that?"

"Extensive research and thorough analysis of my character."

Law chuckles. "Of course. Care to elaborate?"

"I'm the person that makes the hero look better with my mediocrity," I say like it's the most obvious thing in the world.

"Since when are you mediocre at anything?" Law looks genuinely confused.

"Dude," I drag out and gesture at myself.

Law squints his eyes at me like that explanation wasn't enough. "Yes?"

I sigh. "I'm just... I'm not enough, okay? I've never been cool enough or tall enough or handsome enough. I'm unremarkable. And I'm not saying it because I feel sorry for myself or something. I'm making an observation."

"How do you figure that?" Law asks. "That you're unremarkable. Not good enough."

I gesticulate with my hands for a while, the words stuck somewhere in my windpipe. "Just... I don't have the qualities to be the hero. People usually have something. You know, the thing that makes them stand out of the crowd. You know what my thing is?" I don't let Law answer. That question is more rhetorical in nature anyway. "I don't have one. You know what they wrote about me in my yearbook? Most likely to be seen with Falcon Asola. That was my most memorable quality."

A frown creases Law's expression as he keeps staring at me. It goes on for the longest time before he scratches his head and says, "I can't believe I get to say this, but I don't think your logic applies."

That makes me do a double take. "What do you mean? I have years' worth of data. You can't just dismiss my research like that."

"No. What you have is comparisons. Unfavorable ones, it seems, which means you, my friend, have done something extremely unscientific and cherry-picked your data."

I gasp. "Are you questioning my methods?"

Law snorts and rolls his eyes. "All I'm saying is that if you go by that logic, everybody's a sidekick."

"How do you figure that?" I echo Law's question from before.

"You can always find a person who's better than you at something." I want to argue, but Law stops me before I can get the words out. "It works the other way too, you know? When you're good at something, you can always find somebody whose talents lie elsewhere."

I can't help but chuckle at that. "Very diplomatic."

Law tips an imaginary hat before he continues. "All I'm saying is, don't compare yourself to others. And I know it's borderline impossible these days when everybody shoves their supposed accomplishments down your throat via social media. It's hard to keep a cool head, but most of what you see from everybody else is a façade, isn't it? We all try to look better than we really are. Human nature, I guess. Don't let them get to you."

"It's easier said than done," I mutter.

"Unfortunately," Law agrees.

"The... the makeover thing?" I ask. Shit, this is going to be embarrassing, but I can't seem to stop myself. The alien mouth syndrome strikes again. "I call it Project Hero in my mind. You know, turn the sidekick into a hero."

I refuse to look at Law. I should have just kept my mouth shut.

We're both quiet for a moment before Law starts speaking again. "I don't know if my opinion counts, but I love spending time with you. My solo gym sessions are super boring now that I know what it feels like when you're running next to me and cracking me up with your jokes. Or right now"—he gestures toward the TV—"just hanging out has been more fun than I've had in forever. You're smart and dedicated and nice. Not to mention you're also doing me this huge favor that might very well be the key to getting my career on track. You're a good person, Andy Carter, and as far as I'm concerned, that makes you a hero in my book."

My mind goes blank. This might just be the best thing anybody has ever told me. And Law does it so casually. Like it's obvious. Like that's how he really sees me. And it's not as if he just threw around some generic words to appease me. We haven't known each other for that long, but it's startling to realize how much Law's opinion of me matters.

Suddenly, I feel lighter than I have in months. And it's not because Law said the h-word, even though that was nice to hear. It's the fact that somebody as awesome and great as Law Anderson sees me—the real me—and likes that person. Somehow it feels more momentous than the fact that my family seems to like me well enough. Then again, they're stuck with me. Law's opinion feels more... impartial.

This conversation has given me a lot to think about.

I look at the clock on my phone. It's already twelve thirty at night. "Wow, it's getting late," I mutter.

Law's eyes twinkle as he says, "Want to watch another one?"

I should really go home. It's late, and we both have an early morning tomorrow, but my apartment is empty because the guys are out at their birthday party, so no one will care if I'm there or not. I'm not used to being alone.

With six kids, my family's house was always noisy and if you wanted privacy, you had to bribe somebody by doing their chores for a week to get them to leave the bedroom. Half the time that didn't even work because you bribe one brother, but your other five siblings don't give a shit that you promised to rake leaves for Ian to get him to leave your shared bedroom. When I got to college, I shared a dorm with Falcon, and later an apartment. I'm not sure I even know how to be alone. Still, staying here with Law feels like a bad idea.

"What the hell," I say, completely disregarding my own good sense. "Turn it on."

Law laughs. "Oh good. I've gotta tell you, I'm kind of relieved I don't have to lie to you later about not having seen the third episode when I watch it without you after you've left."

I gasp. "You would have watched it without me? That's, like, treason or something."

"Hey!" he protests. "Blame the creators of the series. I need to know if the suicidal dudes find any survivors."

I pretend to wipe a tear from the corner of my eye. "I thought our friendship was more important to you."

He lifts his hand and lowers it step by step like he's mimicking the steps of a ladder. "It goes TV, you and then everything else," he says.

"Wow. I'm before hockey? I'm impressed."

"Oh." He pretends to frown. "I forgot about that. Okay, correction. Hockey, TV, you, everything else." His grin is so wide and carefree that I forget myself and stare at it for a moment.

I gasp in mock outrage. "The suicidal dudes get stuck in a shelter when another bomb drops," I say and enjoy my revenge as he sputters.

"Spoilers!" His eyes go comically round. "I can't believe you'd do that. I've got to reconsider the order of importance. You might have just lowered your position to the bottom. Right below pineapple and blue cheese." Then he squints his eyes at me. "Wait. How do you even know that? Have you seen the next episode?"

I raise my palms as I laugh. "No. I promise you, I haven't. I've only seen the trailer, and they make it pretty obvious that's what's going to happen next."

He stares at me. "Fine, but how can I be sure you won't spill any other major plot points?"

"I solemnly vow on... hockey," I say, "that I will not watch *Nuclear* without you. I'll even quit watching sneak peeks."

He snorts. "Does it even count if you don't like hockey?"

"Yeah, because you like it, and since I like you well enough, I wouldn't dream of disrespecting your favorite thing with a broken vow."

He reaches out his arm. "Shake on it."

We do it. And then we turn on the next episode.

# 10

# LAW

I wake up slowly, blinking at the ceiling as my mind catches up to the fact that I somehow seem to have fallen asleep on the couch last night.

It takes me another moment to realize that I'm not alone. I'm not sure how, but I'm lying on my back, my head on the middle section of the couch and my feet hanging over the edge. Next to my head, there's Andy's head. He's in a similar position to mine, eyes somewhere near the region of my mouth, cheek next to my cheek. His body is stretched out on the other side of the couch, and his feet are hanging over the armrest.

We're so close that our cheeks are almost touching. His mouth is right next to my eyes, and I can feel the soft puffs of air against my skin. He's still deeply asleep, breathing softly. His hair is back to its usual messy curls and waves. A strand of it sticks to his cheek, and another one falls over his left eye.

Before I can think better of it, I run my finger over it. It's soft to the touch as I follow the wave the hair creates with my finger. I repeat the movement. It feels like I'm hypnotized as I keep caressing Andy's hair.

As if on cue, Andy's eyes flutter open. He doesn't seem at all surprised to find me practically in his face, with my hand in his hair. He just blinks, and the sleepy confusion leaves his gaze quickly as he yawns. His eyes move over to the window where the first rays of sun are starting to peek in.

"We fell asleep," he says. His voice is gravelly with sleep and the morning wood I'm sporting takes it as its cue to perk up even more.

"Yeah," I say, my own voice sounding just as raspy.

Andy yawns once more but doesn't make a move to sit up. "What time is it?"

I reach out my hand and pat at the surface of the coffee table to locate my phone. "Seven," I say.

"I've got work in an hour," Andy says lazily but still doesn't move.

I've never woken up with anybody in my life. My only serious boyfriend was in high school, and there were no sleepovers back then. My parents would have rather given up all their worldly possessions and joined a nudist colony than let me invite my boyfriend over for a night of sex and cuddling.

In college, it's only been hook-ups, and I've never felt comfortable with a stranger sleeping next to me in my bed, so once both parties have gotten off, we amicably part ways.

Now, lying next to Andy, though, I must admit there's something to this whole waking up to somebody in the morning thing. It's endearing to see another person early in the morning when the matter-of-factness that encompasses people's everyday lives hasn't settled in yet. It's like I get to peek at something sacred. Something most people don't get to see.

The Andy I usually see is efficient to the max. He comes to my apartment, and he gets things done, which I appreciate and respect because I admire dedication. Hell, dedication is my middle name.

This Andy, on the other hand, is seemingly in no hurry to get up. The attitude and clever comebacks are all in hiding right now. Instead, he's softer, his sharp corners duller in the early morning light. The way he stretches himself reminds me of a cat, lazing around in the sunlight.

"Anything interesting planned for the morning?" he asks me and turns his head toward me.

We're practically nose to nose now, and it makes thinking a real chore. Andy's gray eyes look like they're made of silver. I've never noticed how long his lashes are or that he has a small beauty mark just above his right eyebrow.

"Law?" he asks, and only then do I remember that he asked me a question.

"I have a coaches' meeting at eight," I reply. My voice sounds too loud in the quiet room, so I lower it. "We should probably get up."

Andy nods but that's the full extent of effort he puts into moving his body, so I push myself to my feet and reach out my hand. "Come on, you can have dibs on the shower, and I'll make us some coffee."

He grumbles something under his breath as he takes my hand and lets me pull him to his feet. His clothes are rumbled and locks of his hair fall over his eyes.

I busy myself with grabbing a carton of eggs from the fridge. I'll whip up some breakfast while Andy takes his shower.

Andy disappears into my bathroom, and the ten minutes that follow are a real test for my brain as I recite the names of all the states and follow that up with naming European countries in alphabetical order. I get stuck after Slovakia, which is a problem. Not because I'm especially fond of countries starting with an S and am now upset that I can't remember some of them. No. It's more about not having anything to distract me from the sounds of Andy showering, and the accompanying mental images of wet, naked flesh my brain helpfully sends my way with no regard for the fact that my body gets a lot of ideas very quickly.

The water turns off, but my body still refuses to cooperate. I'm wondering if I should sneak into my bedroom and jerk off real quick. By this point it'll only take a couple of tugs, so I probably wouldn't even get caught.

"Spain. Switzerland," I mutter desperately. "Transylvania. Fucking Tatooine."

I glare at my cock, which absolutely refuses to deflate. Time to bring out the big guns. Grandparents. Having sex. Wrinkly flesh. Gray hair.

That does it, so when Andy emerges from the bathroom, I look decent enough, or at least I'm not greeting him with a sight of my dick so hard that it looks like it could hammer nails into a wall.

"All yours." Andy comes to stand behind me and peeks over my shoulder at the eggs I'm scrambling on the stove. I'm clutching the spatula so tightly that my knuckles have turned white.

He smells like me. Well, my shower gel, but that's also what I smell like, so by default, Andy smells like me, and it's unbelievably hot. The citrusy aroma mixes with Andy's skin and creates a whole new scent that reminds me of me but also smells distinctly like Andy. I will never be able to shower without getting painfully hard again. It's getting ridiculous. By this point, I would be surprised if the sight of lemons at the grocery store would leave me unaffected.

"Ooh, breakfast," Andy says like he has no clue what his proximity does to me, and to be fair, I'm pretty fucking certain that he really has no idea how he affects me.

*He's in love with another guy*, I remind myself.

*Get a grip, Anderson.*

I drop the spatula into the pan and flee the kitchen. "Can you stir it?" I call over my shoulder, and I practically run into the bathroom.

"Sure thing, boss." Andy's reply makes my feet move even faster, so I sprint through the apartment and slam the bathroom door shut behind me. I pull off my pants and shuck off the T-shirt. The water is too hot, but I don't give a fuck as I pull the shower curtain shut.

My hand grips my cock, and I almost cry out in relief. It's quick and it's rough. A couple of tugs with my wet palm, and I punch my hips forward, coming all over the white, tiled wall of the shower with a grunt.

It takes me a whole five minutes of leaning my arm against the wall and panting, hot water raining down my back, before I get my bearings.

I turn off the water and stare at myself in the mirror, even though it's so foggy with condensation that I can only make out a faint outline of myself.

As I stand there, one thing becomes very clear.

I want Andy Carter.

I groan at the realization.

I'm fucked.

# 11

## ANDY

I am in a real-life reenactment of expectations versus reality.

There are people all around me, slamming down shots like they're dying of thirst in a desert and vodka is the only source of liquid they could find.

This is not what I had in mind when I drove home for the weekend to hang out with Falcon. I was thinking something more in the line of there being just the two of us, maybe playing some video games like we used to when we were in high school. To be fair, we'd started out that way, but then Falcon had suggested shooting some pool, and we just happened to pick a bar where a bunch of people from our high school class were having their TGIF moment. At least that's how I'm choosing to interpret it.

In reality, our choice of the bar hasn't been that accidental. The way some of those guys high-fived and bro hugged Falcon and shouted greetings like, "Asola, man. About time. Fucking finally!" has been a pretty big clue to how we ended up here.

I feel bad about it, but I'm not exactly enjoying myself. It's not that Falcon's friends are dicks to me. Falcon wouldn't let that shit fly.

It's just that these are the people who laughed at me in sixth grade when I fell on my lunch tray and ended up wearing my food for the rest of the day. These are the people who always picked me last in gym class, the people who only started talking to me when Falcon came into the picture. And I use the word *talking* lightly, since I don't think any of us is really making that much of an effort to find common ground. We're a bunch of polite semi-strangers. It's not like with Law, where yes, I don't watch hockey, and he isn't exactly passionate about physics, but when we're hanging out, we seamlessly find tons of things to talk about.

And now I kind of miss Law. No. Definitely not miss. That would be ridiculous. I just wish he was here. It's not like I'm pining for him. But Law and I have a lot of fun, and with him here, I wouldn't feel so out of place. Right. That's the version I'm sticking to.

With people from high school there is a forced air. I talk. They talk. But it's so much fucking work. I'm always freaking exhausted after a night like this one, even though hanging out in a bar should be a relaxing thing. I mean, people do that shit because it's fun, for crying out loud, but all I feel right now is left out. Also, slightly bored. Man, I'm not coming off as a good friend.

I glance around the crowded place, and if I felt shitty before, the feeling multiplies as a twinky blond approaches Falcon at the bar. I reluctantly admire the guy because he doesn't exactly look confident. He smiles shyly and there's seemingly not a whole lot of super obvious flirting going on, but Falcon smiles back, and it's clear that the twink has at least made his interest known to Falcon, even if it doesn't pan out for him. Not a minute later, Falcon is back at our booth, carrying the beers he'd promised to get.

"Strike out?" Davis, who used to play basketball with Falcon, yells over the noise of the bar to Falcon. He's a giant even by basketballers' standards.

"As if." Falcon snorts and starts handing out bottles. "I'm just not interested."

Falcon has never had a big, official coming-out-of-the-closet moment, but he's never hidden the fact that he's gay. As far as I know, nobody has given him shit about it.

Jerome stretches his neck to the side as he searches out the twink

Falcon has apparently given the brush-off to. "Why not? He looked into you."

Falcon rolls his eyes. "Yeah, but I wasn't into him."

"Plan to continue that romance with your right hand?" someone yells as Falcon flips the whole table off. "Nope. I'm left-handed," he says seriously. As far as jokes go, this one's pretty bad, but everybody's so drunk that they roar with laughter anyway.

"He's still checking you out," Jerome says helpfully. "Just saying."

We all turn toward to look where Jerome is pointing with his head.

"How very subtle," I say, even though I'm also staring. And yes, thank you for asking, my high horse is very nice and comfortable.

"Just drop it," Falcon says. "I won't sleep with him."

"But you still haven't told us why," somebody calls.

"Holy shit, just look at him. And I mean, really look at him," Falcon groans. "It should be obvious." He drains his beer while all of us stare at the poor blond who's still oblivious to the fact that ten people are ogling him from across the bar.

"Oh," Jerome says after a minute. "Yeah, okay." He turns back to his own drink.

"Legit." Davis nods. One by one they all seem to get what the mysterious flaw is.

Me? I just keep staring like a creep.

The guy is with two other people. They're huddled in a booth, nursing their drinks. They seem a bit uncomfortable. Like they'd prefer to be anywhere else, or more accurately, like they're afraid somebody will come and ask them to leave. I have no idea why. It's a bar, unless you're drunk off your ass or flashing somebody, you're free to stay.

Unless... He looks very young. Maybe he's underage? Is that it? Did I get it? I look at Falcon, but shockingly, because he's not a mind reader, he hasn't heard my silent questions.

"See?" Falcon says and everybody nods. I follow suit because I'm almost confident I got it right, and if everybody else understood, I don't want to be the lone dumb one who doesn't get it. Man, here I thought I was better than that, and wouldn't allow herd mentality to affect me.

"Yup." Davis makes the p-sound pop as he nods sagely. "Virgin alert."

I'm in the middle of finishing my beer, so the next thing I know, I'm coughing, trying to get the beer out of my windpipe.

Falcon claps me on the back. "You all right there, Andy?"

"Absolutely," I gasp. "Wrong hole."

"That's what he said," somebody mutters and everybody roars with laughter.

"Virgin alert?" I finally ask when I regain the ability to breathe.

Falcon looks uncomfortable as hell as he looks at me. Almost as if he wishes he hadn't said anything, and slept with the guy just so he wouldn't have to have this conversation. "He didn't seem to be that... experienced," Falcon reluctantly explains.

"I'm not blaming you for not being interested, in that case," Travis says. He's one of the people who's always been cool to me. Or, at least, he hasn't actively sought me out to pick on me, so I'm not as hesitant as I would be with others to ask, "Why would you exclude anybody from a potential pool of datable people just because they lack, and I quote, *experience?*"

Travis raises his brows at my, admittedly, hostile tone. "I'm interested from the scientific angle. Human behavior is fascinating," I say with as much dignity as I can, and I hope like hell that my own inexperience doesn't ring through, loud and clear. I don't care about what everybody else thinks of me, but I'd like to keep my dignity when it comes to Falcon.

Travis rubs his jaw as he considers my question. "I guess it's a personal preference," he finally says. "It's like this. Remember, in fourth grade, Mrs. Pearson made us all play block flute for a semester? And we all sucked? But we practiced for a few months, and then when we had that concert for the parents we could all play *Twinkle, Twinkle Little Star* passably well."

I cock my head to the side at that little speech. "Did you just compare sex to playing block flute?"

Travis shrugs. "Good sex takes practice, is all I'm saying."

"Exactly," Davis says. "Like, it's hot in porn, but then she"—he looks at Falcon—"well, in your case, *he*, goes down on you, and there's all this fumbling and uncertainty, and indecision about what goes where and how, and it's just not that good in the end."

Falcon still looks like he'd rather change the subject, but he nods. "I'd rather do and not teach," he agrees.

There are a lot of murmurs of agreement. I feel like I must have gotten all my knowledge of sex from porn, because I honestly hadn't thought of virginity as a roadblock. It's just a thing. That is there. It's more of a social construct than anything else, to be honest. I've never considered it that important.

I'm not totally inexperienced. I've kissed a couple of people. Molly Burk in the ninth grade because I had a hypothesis about my sexuality, and I needed to confirm it. I was successful, I might add, because while Molly was as sweet and nice as they come, kissing her did absolutely nothing for me.

Not like with Gavin, sophomore year of high school. I felt all sorts of things then, the most life-changing part of which was the wood I sprang while we were at it.

Then there was Steve at my graduation party. He was the older brother of one of my classmates, and I was a bit drunk, which surrounds the whole experience with a bit of haze in my mind, but there were hands involved, and both of us got off.

There have been a few other guys during college, all of them unremarkable, so my scientific conclusion is that I'm about thirty percent a virgin. Probably. I've done some things, but I've never gone all the way because of the whole in-love-with-my-best-friend thing. It might sound stupid, but sex feels too intimate to do it with a complete stranger, at least for the first time.

There have been times when I've figured I should just get it over with and do it, but I guess I'm not wired that way, which is why right now, I'm cursing Past Andy. He's the reason I'm in this predicament in the first place, with yet another obstacle in my way. Should have just done it with Steve, and I'd be golden right now. It wouldn't even have to have been anal. One measly BJ, and I would already be in a decidedly better position in my quest to make Falcon realize I'm the one for him.

Great. Maybe I should see if the twink Falcon rejected is desperate enough to fumble through sex with me so I could gain some valuable insight?

What a great night this has turned out to be.

## 12

## LAW

Andy is distracted. It's been his constant state the whole week. I've got no clue what has occupied his mind so thoroughly that, for our last three gym sessions, he hasn't bitched and moaned at all. He just runs like a robot, brow furrowed, like he's trying to simultaneously cure cancer, stop world hunger, and eliminate all forms of violence from planet Earth.

After Thursday's tutoring session, a couple of guys actually approached me to ask if Andy was alright. It hadn't been a bad lesson, per se, just way more subdued than usual.

It's a Saturday, and I've picked him up for our hike. Andy stares out the window without saying a word, which is new. Usually he keeps up a random commentary on things he sees, things he thinks, and things he wants to ask. Today, however, he says nothing, just stares, frowns, turns away. Occasionally he opens his mouth as if to say something, but then seems to change his mind and turns away again.

It's weird as fuck. Andy isn't really the type to contemplate silently. He thinks out loud. He comments. He jokes. I don't think he even realizes how much he speaks and how funny his self-deprecating humor is.

An hour of driving and we reach the Thundering Falls trail. I've been before. It's not really a backbreaking hike, more like a stroll through the forest, but it's beautiful, and when I asked Andy if he'd ever been here, he just raised his brow at me as if to say, "Hike? Me? Seriously? No. Duh."

The thing about Andy is he doesn't like to try new things, which is why he protests going to the gym (which he secretly likes now) and teaching (which he excels at). He just needs a little push to get going, so I've decided to nudge him a bit from time to time because, let's face it, the guy needs to loosen up a bit to show everybody what a great person he really is. The world should give me a pat on the back for exposing everyone to the awesomeness that is Andy Carter.

Andy mutters something as he gets out of the car.

"Pardon?"

"I'm praying to the patron saint of hikers to make my inevitable death as painless as possible," he says as he bends down to lace his boot, giving me a magnificent view of his ass. It takes a certain kind of talent to look hot in hiking gear, but Andy definitely pulls it off.

I distract myself with getting my backpack out of the trunk. "It's a trail suitable for kids."

He stops. "You're serious?"

"As a heart attack, and coincidentally, people who have suffered one find this hike a breeze."

Andy's lips twitch as he tries to glare at me. He throws a twig at my head but misses.

"I'm not sure if I should be offended or amused that you think I have the endurance of a heart-attack patient."

"I also said kids," I protest. "Kids are notorious for having lots of energy. Shit, a three-year-old can be crazy active. Who knows, maybe this trail is so hard that only somebody with the energy levels of a toddler can complete it successfully?"

"I guess we're about to find out," Andy says as he picks up his own backpack and starts walking.

We're here early for a Saturday, so there aren't very many people around. The trail gets more foot traffic after people have consumed their pancakes and enjoyed their coffees. There aren't many of us who'd be out and about at seven on a Saturday. We've had to postpone our weekly hike twice already because Andy went home last weekend, and the weekend before that, I'd volunteered to take the camp kids swimming. But today we finally managed. The weather is perfect, except for maybe the early morning chill, but I figure once we get moving, it'll be all right.

I like Vermont. It's crazy different from New York, but in a good way. I like the nature and the fact that there aren't people everywhere. I like the fact that people are friendly but reserved and not overly invested in everybody else's lives.

I like the seasons. Even mud season is fine with me, since I haven't had the misfortune of getting my car stuck in the mud yet. I love the snow and winter weather just as much as the summer. Summer in the city gets old really quickly. The heat is oppressive when you're surrounded by concrete and glass. Here, though, summer means a soft breeze cooling my skin and the sun caressing my cheeks. Mild summer nights and swimming in lakes. It's kind of perfect, to be honest.

I imagine I look like an idiot as I half walk, half skip down the raised wooden walkaway. There's a goofy smile on my face that I can't seem to get rid of, and in all honesty, I'm not trying that hard. I freaking love nature and being outside.

"You look way too perky for this hour of the morning," Andy remarks as he walks next to me. For all his complaining about physical activity, the guy isn't that out of shape. In the three weeks we've been going to the gym together, he's graduated from his five-minute runs, intercepted with bouts of walking, to a solid five miles. He still complains and makes snarky comments left and right, but ninety-five percent of the time, those are just because Andy's being Andy. Plus, I enjoy the sarcastic remarks a lot, so the mornings Andy is at home and not working out with me are straight-out boring.

"What can I say, I like mornings," I say.

"Did you, by any chance, happen to be that nightmare child who insisted on getting up at five every day?" he asks with a smirk.

"You know it, but my parents didn't mind. They thought it was great. Start the day early, get a lot done."

"That's literally the worst family motto I've ever heard." Andy shudders in disgust.

"I take it you like to sleep in?"

He nods. "It's genetic. We're night owls, all of us. My mom did her best to get us on a semi-normal schedule while we were in school, but I function better after ten o'clock in the morning."

"You have a big family?" I ask.

"Depends what you call big. There's my mom and dad and I have two sisters and three brothers." He grins as I gape at him.

"That's a lot of kids," I finally manage. I'm an only child, and I've always wanted a brother or a sister, but my parents said one was enough. Six is a lot, though.

"Tell me about it. It would be halfway understandable if my parents had had five sons or five daughters in a row and just kept trying for a boy or a girl, but those lunatics just seem to like kids," he says with a smirk.

"Even after experiencing the toddler years and teenagers slamming doors and being unreasonable and smug as fuck?" I ask. Not that I know a lot about the hardships of having a toddler from firsthand experience, but I can imagine raising a child is a shitload of work.

"Yup, go figure. Apparently my older sisters used to throw temper tantrums like somebody paid them to see who can make more noise, them or a jet engine."

"And yet, your parents decided to keep reproducing," I say with a laugh. It's clear Andy loves his family a lot, but the trademark self-deprecating humor is still firmly in place.

"To be fair, after Cecilia and Emily, it was my turn to make an appearance, and I was a delight. Still am. No wonder they had two more after me. Too bad Ryan and Landon were so much trouble that Mom and Dad opted out of having more kids."

"Six kids wasn't enough for you? Was the house too quiet?"

"Hardly a quiet moment from morning 'til late at night," Andy says cheerfully.

"Are you close with your family?" I inquire. I've already admitted to myself that I'm more than a little intrigued by everything about Andy, so I file every new morsel of information away to add to the overall picture of Andy in my mind.

"To an unhealthy degree. I told my mom about my first kiss the next morning it happened."

I let out a startled laugh. "Why?"

He shrugs. "I didn't have a lot of friends, and awkwardly smashing my lips against Molly Burk's seemed like a great accomplishment at the time, so I had this incessant need to brag to somebody. My dad and Ian were on a fishing trip, and Mom was the first person I saw that morning. Of course, that story earned me a lecture about respect toward women and not a hearty congratulations like I was expecting, but you live and you learn, I guess. She still hasn't heard about my first kiss with a boy. I'm saving that baby for a special occasion."

Andy smiles at me. A lock of hair falls over his eye, and I have to stuff my hands into my pocket so I wouldn't do something stupid, like push it away from his face.

"Do you miss them?" His family sounds very close and just plain lovely. I can't imagine having so many people in your corner. Like your very own tribe. My relationship with my mom and dad is mostly just strained. Love from my family has always seemed conditional, and I don't think it could ever be this effortless as Andy makes it seem.

"I visit often enough, so I can't say I pine for them," he jokes. "I miss spending time with them from time to time. We have these board game nights that get crazy competitive. Used to have them every couple of weeks, but now it's cut down to Christmas and Thanksgiving and such."

"Is that why you chose a school close to home?"

Andy scrunches up his nose, which I've learned is a sign that a topic makes him uncomfortable. He hesitates before speaking. "College is expensive, and with six kids, it just wouldn't make sense to add the extra expense of living out of state. It would have been even better if I could have lived at home, but a two-hour commute would be a bitch."

I don't know what to say to that. Money's never really been a problem. My parents instilled a strong work ethic in me, and they've always stressed the age-old *money doesn't grow on trees* wisdom, but paying for college or hockey or camps has never been an issue. Andy's confession makes me feel bad for complaining about my parents so much because, for all their faults, they've given me everything I've asked for.

"What about you?" Andy asks. "Big family?"

"Nah. It's just me and my parents."

"Are you close?"

It's my turn to shrug. "We love each other in our own way, but they don't like hockey. They want me to take over my dad's finance consulting firm. He's very successful. Lots of important clients."

"You sound like the idea thrills you about as much as eating dog food for the rest of your life would." Andy is so blunt in his assessment. No pussyfooting around the topic for him, but it's liberating to talk about it straightforwardly, unlike how I talk about it with my parents.

"The prospect of an office job bores me to tears," I confess. I think about what I just said and can't help but smile. "Wow. I've never said it out loud. Feels kind of nice."

"I imagine it's a point of contention between you and your parents?"

"We've been arguing over it since I was about fifteen. We had a compromise. Sort of. I played hockey in college, but I majored in finance, so we had a truce of sorts. But now I'm the assistant coach, so it's starting to sink in that I might not be heading in the direction they've planned for me."

Andy purses his lips as he keeps giving me speculative glances.

"What?" I ask.

"I have a question, but I don't want to bring up bad memories."

"Ask, and I'll tell you if I don't want to talk about it," I say, even though I already know what he wants to ask.

"Why did you stop playing?"

*Bingo.*

I wait for the bang of sadness that usually follows when somebody brings up my doomed hockey career, but it's not there anymore, which makes me pretty damn happy. Maybe it's a sign that I'm on the right path?

"I have a heart condition," I say in answer to Andy's question. "Hypertrophic cardiomyopathy."

To my surprise, he doesn't look confused by the name of my diagnosis. "Thickening of the heart muscle," we say in unison, and I laugh, which is something I've never done before when my heart problem has come up.

"That must have sucked," Andy concludes succinctly.

"Kind of," I agree. "I've been dreaming of the NHL since I was ten, and then that dream died in a matter of seconds. It took some time to get used to it."

"But then they offered you the assistant coach's position?"

"Yeah. It came out of the blue, but Coach Williams said he thought it'd be something that'd suit me, and he was right. I love it."

Andy beams at that like he's truly happy for me, and it feels fantastic. Nobody has supported me like this before. My former teammates seem to think being an assistant coach is a shitty substitute for an NHL career, and my parents hate that I still live and breathe hockey.

As if reading my mind Andy asks, "But your parents still don't approve?"

"They don't consider it a real career, I suppose. I still haven't told them I'm not going to take over Dad's business. They keep making those statements, like, *after you're done with school, you're going to be so happy when you have a job and don't have to scramble to make a living like a lot of your peers will.* I need to just man up and tell them, but they'll be so disappointed, and I don't relish being the fuck-up of the family."

"Must be rough."

"You have no idea."

"None whatsoever. My parents are super supportive of everything

I do," he says, and as per usual, the unexpected thing that comes out of Andy's mouth makes me laugh out loud.

"I can't believe you just said that. Rubbing your great family in my face like that."

"What can I say? I'm a shitty friend."

I bump my shoulder into his as I shake my head. "No, you really aren't."

His smile is barely there, but I can hear it, clear as day, in his voice as he says, "Well, I hope you'll be singing the same tune when I sell that information to your parents for the big bucks."

"I trust you," I say. I mean to say it as a joke, but as the words leave my mouth, I realize that it's the God's honest truth. I do trust Andy. Trust him enough to speak freely in front of him. Trust him not to laugh or belittle me for my decidedly first world problems. Trust him to keep the things we talk about between us.

Andy's cheeks flush as he looks down at his feet. "Thanks pal," he says and bumps my shoulder with his fist. "I trust you too."

He stops so suddenly that I walk another couple of steps before I even realize Andy is no longer next to me. I turn around, only to see him standing in the middle of the trail. His eyes are fixated on the horizon, but there's that vacant look in them that tells me he's not really seeing anything around him. "I trust you too," he repeats as if talking to himself. He cocks his head to the side, and for the longest time, he stares at me with a strange, intense look in his eyes.

"Well... good," I say as I trudge back to him. A picture of my face could be in the encyclopedia entry for *perplexed*.

"No. You don't get it," Andy says, his gaze burning with intensity. "*I trust you.*" He looks like he's just solved a problem worthy of the Nobel Prize.

The perplexed thing still stands.

"That's nice. Are we going to keep going or...?" I take a step away, ready to get moving again, when Andy grabs my hand and pulls me to a stop.

His eyes are glittering in the sunshine. "Have sex with me," he blurts.

I take an involuntary step back out of sheer surprise, but somehow, in my state of shock, I trip on a protruding rock. My arms flail and the next thing I know, I'm about to land on my back. I try to stay upright, but fail, and instead of falling on my ass like a normal person, I stumble forward.

Andy has stepped toward me to help, but that only means that in a flail of limbs and bodies, we crash together, and I take him down with me. Andy falls on his back with an oomph, and I land on top of him.

"Oh shit," Andy says.

That sounds about right.

## 13

# ANDY

*Oh shit* is right.

Law lies on top of me. I feel dizzy and lightheaded, but not in a good way. More like I just had my breath knocked out of me by a two-hundred-pound hockey player.

"Ouch," I mutter as I slowly lift my hand and try to rub the back of my head. There's a nice lump already forming from smacking it against the walkaway.

Law lifts his head and looks at me.

He's so close.

I can see the green of his eyes. I never noticed how long his lashes are. I could probably count all of them if I wanted to. His nostrils flare as he breaths in, and I can feel the short puffs of air move over my cheek as he exhales.

Law's gaze is on me. I don't think anybody has ever watched me with such intensity. His tongue slips out as he licks his lips, and I groan. The lightheaded feeling is quickly transforming into something much better.

I can feel my body reacting to Law's proximity. He's heavy and wide and covering me like a big, warm blanket. I definitely like that. My dick swells in my pants, which is both good and bad. Good, because I'm trying to get him to sleep with me. Bad, because I don't know how Law feels about that. If I'm being honest with myself, it seems like him losing his balance and almost faceplanting on the ground might not be a sign that he's on board with that plan.

"You're heavy," I say. I'd love to stay just like this, me on my back and him on top of me, but I really think we should talk before I start rubbing my cock against him. I mean, it's basic courtesy.

"Shit! Let me help you." Law scrambles to his feet and grabs my hand to pull me up, but I wave him off. "I'm really sorry." He looks all frantic and alarmed. It's kind of adorable, which is a weird thing to think about somebody as big as Law, but there it is. Maybe I have a concussion, and that's why I'm having these crazy thoughts?

I push myself to a sitting position, lean my back against one of the poles that is on the side of the walkaway, and tilt my head back to look at Law. "Spending time with you is becoming a hazardous hobby. First a nosebleed and now this." I try to lighten the mood with a joke, but Law looks like an honors student who'd just gotten caught smoking weed and is now terrified about it going on his permanent record.

"Do you feel okay? Maybe we should go to the ER. I'll call 911." I grab his hand before he can go searching for his phone. He willingly lowers himself to the ground next to me.

"I'm fine. Just got my breath knocked out of me for a moment."

"You sure?"

"That's a resounding yes."

"Okay then." He still sounds like he's about to start looking for his phone again at the slightest hint of something being out of the ordinary.

"I'm fine," I assure him once more, but it's hard not to be amused by his concern.

He nods and finally seems to relax. Neither of us makes a move to get up even though we're sitting on the ground, but my ass is already numb, and Law doesn't seem to be in a hurry to move either, so I settle in.

We're both quiet, and it's nice. Everything around us is moving.

Leaves are rustling in the gentle wind. Birds are taking flight from the trees and singing. I can hear the faint sound of water falling down in a rush. It would be downright idyllic if it weren't for the massive elephant of a proposition sitting between us.

I should address it, but my you-should-sleep-with-me speech and the following collision have taken the wind out of my sails. Maybe we'll just ignore what I said and pretend nothing happened.

Yeah.

That sounds like a good plan.

"Should we get moving?" I ask just as Law blurts out, "You want to have sex with me?"

Okay. Clearly we're going to talk about it.

"Any chance we can pretend I didn't say anything?" I try to take the coward's way out.

"Umm, that would be a no."

"Awesome," I mutter.

"What..." Law opens and closes his mouth. "How..." He shakes his head, but to his credit, he keeps going. "Why would you... just... what?" he finally asks.

"You're gonna have to elaborate on that," I say. "What was I thinking? What did I mean by it? What is sex?" He just gapes at me in reply. "Come on, Law, help me out here."

He sighs and rubs his palms over his face. The bandana he's wearing on his head tilts to the side, exposing one of his ears, so without thinking, I reach out my hands and straighten it. He sucks in a breath as my fingers touch his cheeks. I'd like to think it's because of the skin-on-skin contact, but it might just be that my fingers are all dirty from scrambling around on the ground, and Law is sensitive to dirt.

"We should definitely get up," I say as I push myself to my feet. Law looks at me for a second and follows my lead.

"Do you want to go back to the car?" he asks, but I shake my head. "Let's just keep going." I have a feeling the conversation we're about to have will be much easier if I don't have to look at Law and, instead, can stare at my feet. I'll have the excuse of making sure that I don't step on any squirrels.

We follow the trail, and we get to the base of the falls in no time. It's beautiful. Way better than what I expected when Law proposed this hike. I bet it looks even better during spring when there's more water. I guess we'll just have to come back. I stumble at the thought. I'm making future plans for us now? What the hell?

Law leans against the railing and pulls off his bandana. Warmth and sunshine chase away the chill of the morning, so I follow suit and take off the baseball cap Law gave me before we started our hike. It had been in the back seat of his car. I take out a bottle of water and drink, offering it to Law who takes it wordlessly and empties it.

For a while, we both just stand, elbows on the railing, and watch the falls.

"So," Law finally says. "You want to have sex with me."

His tone is neutral. There's no hint about how he feels about that prospect. Curious? Amused? Disgusted? There's nothing there, so I go for a simple, "Yes."

Another moment of silence stretches between us, but I'm not in a hurry to fill it. I'll let Law take the lead on this one.

"Okay," he says. "I've got to say, I was certain I'd gotten the hang of how your mind works, but clearly that's not the case. So, any hints about what put that idea into that fascinating brain of yours?"

I'm speechless. He finds my brain fascinating? He's not being sarcastic? That's unexpected. It's much more common for me to evoke things like mild exasperation and aggravation in people.

Law is still waiting for my response, so I choose my words carefully. "It's been brought to my attention recently that people enjoy... intimate encounters more if both parties have a certain level of experience to bring to the table." I think I come off as mature and rational.

*Yeah because that's what's hot, Andy.*

Law says nothing, and after a couple of minutes, which are probably more like seconds, the need to fill the silence becomes unbearable.

"Not that I'm planning to do it on a table," I add quickly. "A bed is fine. Or I suppose a table is also fine if that's your thing."

I think about what I've just said. Great. It's a small step from mature and rational to prudish. No wonder people aren't lining up to sleep with me. And my mouth just keeps going, seemingly independent from my brain.

"Umm... up against the wall would work too, and maybe on the floor. And, I mean, shower sex has never seemed like a good idea because of the slippery factor, but I'm prepared to be convinced otherwise," I ramble. "I'll try anything once," I add just to give Law the impression I'm adventurous. In reality, I have no idea what kind of lover I'd be, but that's why I need his help, damn it.

Law just stares at me, unblinking. This is going *so* well.

"I saw a clip once where two guys were going at it on the roof, but that's where I draw the line," I continue, because dear, almighty God, the silence is killing me. "I know what I just said about trying anything once, but it's implied that common sense must be applied. I want to have sex, not die gruesomely. My mom would not be happy to receive my naked, dead body from the coroner, so if that's something you—"

That's all I get out before Law hauls me against him and crashes his lips to mine.

"Oomph," I say elegantly because I'm cool like that, but I forget about it instantly since I'm kissing Law. Law!

Okay, so technically he's kissing me, because I'm just standing still, not moving a muscle. I think I'm in shock.

Law pulls away slightly after a moment. Our noses are almost touching, he's that close. "Andy?" he whispers, and that one word, my name sounding like a question on his lips, is all it takes to jolt me out of my shock. My fingers go to his hair and I pull his face back, so our lips meet again.

I don't remember my last kiss. It was that unremarkable. Some dude at a party. Both of us drunk. Just a totally ordinary encounter between two strangers who accidentally bumped into each other. I do remember that he was about my equal on the nerdiness scale, so I guess he didn't have any better options. We both probably took a long look at the other and thought, *Eh, he'll do*. The kiss was about as unmemorable as the guy I shared it with had been.

This right here, though? I think I could fall on my head and wake up from a coma two years later with amnesia so bad that I couldn't remember who I was, but this kiss would surely stay with me.

Law's lips are warm against mine. He wraps himself around me, and I feel every inch of him. His nose bumps against mine, and he smiles against my mouth. I smile back, but we don't move even an inch away from each other.

Law's lips are super soft. He licks over my lower lip, prompting me to open, so I do. Of course I do, and then our tongues tangle and lick and caress each other, and it's hot and awesome and just the best feeling ever.

What the hell? Why has kissing never felt like this before? Is it just me? Does Law feel it too? I have so many questions, but nothing in this world will make me disentangle myself from Law, especially for something as ordinary as speaking.

Law's hands move behind my back. One of them lands on my ass, and he pulls me even closer. His fingers squeeze my ass, and I shiver because that feels fantastic, and I want more.

My cock is rock hard in my pants, trapped and squeezed against Law.

If kissing Law feels this amazing, I can't wait to see what sex with him feels like. I've given a finger to the devil, and I can't wait for him to grab my hand and drag me to his lair.

My hands move all over Law's body. Why is he wearing so many clothes? It's like fifty-five degrees outside. I'm sure he could go shirt-less. And maybe he could also ditch the pants. We haven't seen a single person on this trail so far, so he should feel free to flaunt that fit body of his for my viewing pleasure.

But before I can unzip anything, Law pulls away. We're both breathing harshly. Panting, really. Law's hair is messy, his bandana is on the ground, in front of his feet. His eyes are huge, glittering with arousal. His lips are swollen, and I can't wait to taste them again.

"Why'd you stop?" I blurt out the only question that circles my mind.

"I have no fucking clue," he mutters as if to himself. He lifts his gaze to mine. "You need some time to think," he declares as he picks his bandana up and stuffs it in his pocket.

"About...?" I ask. "The benefits of taking this inside? Because you're hot and you make me hot, but if we keep this up, we'll give the other hikers an eyeful," I say.

"About sex." Law's voice is patient. He sounds like he's explaining the basic principles of gravity to a five-year-old who wants to use an umbrella to fly from the roof of the barn.

I take a step closer. "After that kiss it shouldn't be a problem. I'll be thinking about sex for the foreseeable future."

He laughs. "Flattering, but that's not what I meant." He looks down. "We're friends," he says.

"Yeah," I say, confused. "That's the best part."

And it is. It's the only reason I feel so comfortable with this situation.

"Sex might complicate things." He thinks for a moment. "Scratch that, sex will definitely complicate things."

Now Law's the one being all mature and reasonable, and if I scoffed at those qualities being sexy before, from now on, I'll be singing a different tune. This serious, look-at-every-angle, rational part of Law is really doing it for me.

Ever since I went out with Falcon and his friends, my mind has been preoccupied with my very limited number of sexual encounters. I've been analyzing the situation from every angle, and the only logical conclusion I've reached is that I need to gain more experience.

The problem is that the most common way to do that—finding a hook-up—does not appeal to me at all. Casual sex has never been my thing. I mean, it would be so much easier if it were, since I wouldn't be in this pickle at all right now if I could just go to a club and sleep with somebody. I've tried it a couple of times over the years, but I've failed miserably every time I found somebody who seemed willing to entertain the idea of sleeping with me at all. Strangers don't turn me on. It's that simple.

So unless I want to hire myself a hooker and go all *Pretty Woman* on him, which doesn't really seem like the best idea because of the whole illegal aspect, I'm all out of ideas.

Only about half an hour ago, when Law mentioned trusting me, did I have the lightbulb moment. I'm starting to think I exaggerated when I said that I have good problem-solving skills. All the evidence points to the contrary, since it's becoming clear that, if a person is uncomfortable sleeping with a complete stranger, the only other option they have left is sleeping with a friend. The hell if I know why it took me a week of serious thinking to figure that one out. So I immediately moved on to deal with the next part of the problem— finding a friend to sleep with. I don't have a lot of those, so my options are limited. Let's see: there's Falcon—sleeping with *him* to gain some experience in order to be more appealing to *him* seems like circular reasoning—and then there's Law. That's it. That's the full extent of my friend pool.

"It will only complicate things if we let it," I say. We're both adults. We can be reasonable about it. Plus, there'll be no complicated feelings involved. Law is a friend, a very good one, but that's it. I don't have feelings for him. I like him. A lot. I like how he goes the extra mile for his friends and his team. I like the way his nose crinkles when he laughs out loud. I like how, when he concentrates, he sticks his pen behind his ear and then forgets about it. I like how he yells at the TV when he deems somebody's actions too stupid to endure in silence. I realize I could go on and on. I have an endless supply of Law facts stored away in my mind. I like that he's smart and fun and loyal. Spending time with Law is the most fun I've ever had. Well, not the most, I remind myself. I have fun with Falcon too. He's my best friend, so it's great when we hang out.

*Only you haven't done that in forever,* my brain helpfully reminds me.

*Nah-uh, we went to a bar just last week,* I counter.

*It wasn't just the two of you, and you haven't missed him that much, have you?* My brain snarks back. I frown at the thought but dismiss it immediately. I've been busy. That's all.

I almost start laughing because I'm arguing with myself. How very normal and not at all creepy and weird.

"Can't it be one of those things where it won't be awkward if we don't let it be awkward?" I ask, and I'm only half joking.

There's a conflicted look in Law's eyes. "What if… what if feelings get involved?" He looks at me with such intensity. There's a hidden question beneath what he actually said.

He means me. He means, what if *I* develop feelings for *him?* And I've got to hand it to him, it's a fair question. The guy has seen me moon over Falcon, and according to him, my feelings were clear as day. Considering what he knows about my history with Falcon, can he really be blamed for thinking there might be a chance I'll get a crush on him as well? No wonder he's so hesitant, he just doesn't want to deal with my pesky crush, so I force myself to laugh.

"No way is that happening. My… thing for Falcon is rock solid. It's an impenetrable stone wall of feelings," I say. I try to insert the word love in there somewhere, but my mouth refuses to cooperate and the word just won't come out. It's fine, though. I'm sure it's implied. "Lots and lots of feelings," I add to hammer the point home.

Law looks down, and for a moment, I swear there's a look of disappointment on his face, but I dismiss the thought. I must have imagined it. Besides, what's he got to be disappointed about here? It's not like Law's harboring his own secret crush on me. That's an idea so ridiculous that the fact that Donald Duck wears a towel around his waist when in everyday life he doesn't wear any pants seems sane and logical compared to what I just came up with.

"We have nothing in common," I say because Law is suddenly acting all weird, and I can only imagine it's because he's still not convinced of my ability to keep myself from developing feelings. "I'm this science geek and you're, well, you're you." I gesture toward him with my hand, trying to encompass everything that is Law in this one movement. A fun, popular, great person, who is kind and good and all-around awesome.

I've never really concentrated on how different we are, but it hits me now, full force. I've thought about it before, but it's been in passing. How did we get to this moment?

It would be easy to explain Law's continued interest in spending time with me with the fact that he just tolerates me because of the whole tutoring thing. Only it's been weeks since I agreed to help, and we've both kept our ends of the deal. So I'm thinking it's not because he feels like he should kiss my ass just to make sure I don't suddenly bail. I guess he could be a psychopath who's playing me, but scientifically speaking, the odds are low. I'm talking, like, one ten-billionth of a meter tiny.

Still, it's weird, because I'm so very much the opposite of Law. He's like the sun, bright and warm, and I'm like one of those brown dwarves, too small to be called a star and so insignificant most people don't even know they exist.

I force myself to laugh. "I mean, what would we even talk about, right?"

For some reason, Law's smile seems just as forced. "Right," he says.

Maybe I shouldn't have brought his attention to the fact that he's wasting his time hanging out with me? Maybe this is the moment where he realizes he could be doing something else with much cooler people?

My gut has an uncomfortable, hollow feeling in it.

Way to go, Andy.

## 14

## LAW

It shouldn't sting, but it does. Andy is right. He's the smart one, and I'm the jock who'd never be able to keep up with him if he went in depth about his classes or his job or his thoughts on some famous theory or physicist during a conversation. My knowledge about Andy's chosen field is embarrassingly poor.

It's stupid to be hurt because Andy pointed out the simple fact that dating me would be impossible simply because we would have nothing to talk about. We don't seem to have that problem now, but it'd probably arise at one point. How could he take me with him to work functions if I can't keep up with the conversation?

He's right. It's better we remain friends. Not to mention the fact that I'm not even in the market for a boyfriend, so this whole thought sequence is pointless.

The thing is, I want Andy. Have for a while now. There's something about him that pulls me in and refuses to let go, so the offer to have some no-strings sex is extremely hard to resist. Especially because I'm not so sure I should.

It's just like Andy said, we're both adults. It shouldn't be hard to leave emotions out of the equation. Sure, I like Andy. A lot. But I'm not in love with him, so it's not that big of a deal if, in addition to being friends, we throw sex into the mix.

"Just to be clear," I say, "by saying you need to gain experience, you mean what, exactly?"

He looks away and his cheeks turn a dark shade of pink. "You're going to make me spell it out, aren't you?" he mumbles.

"It's one of those things where there shouldn't be any miscommunication, so it's easier for both of us to be as honest and straightforward as humanly possible."

He huffs out a breath through his mouth, which makes his hair fly around his head. "Fine. My experience with sex is limited," he says and looks at me with a frown as if waiting for me to make a joke.

"Okay." I keep my voice as neutral as possible.

"I've kissed a few people, and there was a hand job thrown in there somewhere, but otherwise I'm a blank slate, and to be honest, it's been a while since I've… done something that doesn't involve my own hand," he soldiers on, chin up, looking almost defiant. And good for him. It's nobody's business to judge what the other person does with their body, so he damn well shouldn't be ashamed. Although, this all raises the question of…

"Why are you suddenly so interested in changing that, then?" I ask.

"People don't want to sleep with somebody this inexperienced," he says. "They want somebody who knows what they're doing, and I don't. The way I see it, you'll be doing a public service. Based on the distinct lack of naked people in my life, I might not even recognize somebody else's cock. Think about it, if you let me go into the world with the knowledge I have right now, I might go in for a blowjob and start to lick somebody's elbow or something."

"That sounds like a problem a few sex ed classes might solve. Or biology," I joke weakly. I go hot all over at the casual mention of blowjobs and cocks. My own cock is trying to make itself known in a very obvious way, but I'm a good friend, so I ignore it.

"Believe me, I'm familiar with the theoretical part. In fact, I watched a documentary just the other day." He thinks about it for a moment. "Or should porn be considered a mockumentary?" he asks with a thoughtful frown.

I slam my hands into my pockets to try and conceal my very obvious erection because the thought of Andy watching porn is a mental image that makes me want to forget everything, and just attack Andy right here and now. Fuck the tourists, they can walk around us. Or stand and watch. I don't give a shit.

Unlike Andy, per his own words, I'm good at the practical part. There have been many compliments given over the years, five-star ratings and glowing reviews all around, if you will, so we would complement each other nicely. But that line of thinking must stop immediately.

*Do it! Do it!* My insides chant, not giving a shit about being a decent friend, and my dick is begging me to grab this opportunity and run with it.

Andy takes a step toward me, and fuck me, he glances down and smirks, a knowing look in his eyes as his gaze collides with mine. This whole conversation has been about teaching Andy about sex, but to be honest, he doesn't exactly behave like a blushing virgin. The part where he asked me to sleep with him might have been a bit awkward on his end, but for everything else, he's been sure of himself and straightforward. Hell, it's almost as if he's seducing me.

Case in point:

"You could teach me," Andy says. It would seem almost innocent, but there's a calculating look in his eyes, and he's one step short of sliding his fingers over my chest and biting his lip. Here's a man who knows what he wants and is going for it. It reminds me of the way I pursue my own goals. There's an almost cunning look in his eyes, and it's really hot. I have no idea what's wrong with me that I think that, but God help me, I do. He's playing me like a world-class violinist does a Stradivarius, and I don't mind one bit.

"It could be hot," he says. I don't know who he's kidding because there's no *could* about it. It will definitely be hot.

I'll be forever proud of my self-control as I take a step back and force myself to say, "You need to take a few days and think about it. To make sure this is what you want."

He huffs out an impatient breath. "I've already thought about it. It's not like I came up with the idea on the spot. It's been on my mind for a while already."

"Really," I say skeptically. "You've been thinking about sleeping with me. Had a list of pros and cons, did you?"

"The *you* part might have been a stroke of genius that happened today," he admits. "But come on, those are legitimately the best things ever. Think about it, there are a number of cases where a solution comes to you suddenly. It even has a name. The Eureka Effect. And in the spirit of how we met, I'll even give you some examples. Think of it as a private tutoring session: Newton and gravity, Hubble and nebulae, Paul Dirac and antimatter, Fleming and penicillin, Percy Spencer and the microwave. I can go on and on about how people accidentally stumbled on ideas that turned out to be genius."

"I bet Fleming took an evening to think it through instead of handing out antibiotics to people all willy-nilly," I say reasonably.

He looks at me for a long moment. "I change my mind. The responsible streak you're displaying is most definitely not hot."

"I feel the same," I mutter, which makes Andy snort out a laugh, but he immediately glares at me. "Don't try and be all cute about it."

"I'm not. But you do need to think about it some more."

"God, you're stubborn," Andy says.

"Like a mule. It's one of my better qualities, actually."

"I heartily disagree."

"Let's just get back to the car. I'll take you home, and you can do an actual pros and cons list."

"Yeah, because that's how I solve all the great dilemmas in my life." The sarcasm is thick, but I ignore it. I want Andy to think this thing through before we move on with the plan. Hell, I'll probably make a list of my own.

Later that night, I'm lying in bed. It's early still, and I can't sleep for shit. All I can think about is Andy's proposition, and how much of an idiot I must have been to self-sabotage myself like that. Who says no to casual sex when it's offered to you? Me. That's who.

"Motherfucking moron," I mutter to myself as I pound my fist into my pillow to make it more comfortable.

I'm in the middle of tossing and turning when my phone dings on the bedside table. I swipe over the screen.

*I made that pros and cons list you wanted.*

I grin despite myself as the messages start pouring in.

*Sex counts as exercise (5 calories per minute. We could do it instead of the gym sessions if you're worried having sex with me will be hard to fit into your schedule)*

*Sex improves sleep (you could be asleep right now if you'd taken me up on my offer before)*

*Sex boosts your immune system (you'll thank me when you won't have to skip games because of a common cold)*

*Sex lowers heart attack risk (I mean, you're young, but being proactive about your health is never a bad thing)*

I can't help but laugh at the list. I especially like the casual way he doesn't shy away from joking about my heart condition. It makes me feel normal. Andy isn't done yet, I get about ten more messages, each one getting more ridiculous than the last, before I give up and text back.

*What about the cons?*

The reply is quick and swift.

*Sex relieves stress. Let's do it, and you won't have to worry about the cons anymore.*

*You're like a dog with a bone,* I type back.

*Is your subconscious taking over, letting us know you want to bone me? I'm all for it, just saying.*

I laugh out loud, because how can I not? The last dregs of resistance are disappearing, dismantled by Andy with his cheeky humor and quick wit. All those reasons I've been resisting him seem less important than they did earlier. They're replaced by a burst of can-do attitude.

We *can* have sex and remain friends.

I *can* keep myself from developing feelings for Andy.

This *won't* end up being a total disaster.

So, before I can hesitate, I type three words and send them off, heart thrumming wildly like I've just scored a winning goal.

*Let's do it.*

## 15

### ANDY

I pace on the street in front of Law's apartment building.

Last night, when I was sending the texts, it was easy to hide my nervousness behind humor. After all, no one but me knew how much time it took me to compose the messages (three hours of research and writing different versions of them in my laptop when I should have been studying).

It felt like I'd won the lottery when Law's *Let's do it* appeared on my phone screen. The problem is, there's been twenty-four hours between that message and this moment, which means there's been ample time for my brain to come up with a cons list that keeps replaying in my head.

I'm probably not that good in bed. How many of us are experts at something on our first try? It took me eight months to learn to drive, and I still can't drive a stick, even though my dad tried to teach me. Well, he tried to teach me for an hour or so, but it didn't really look like his heart was in it.

My siblings think it's a conspiracy theory, but the thing is, Dad's car has manual transmission, and none of my siblings know how to drive it, even though supposedly we've all received lessons from Dad. Call me cynical, but I think I'm onto something here. But I digress; the point is, even with an automatic, it took me an embarrassingly long time to pass my driving exam. What if I'm as bad at sex as I am at driving?

What if I make weird noises?

What if I *do* develop feelings for Law? Other than the friendship feelings I'm already feeling, I mean.

I almost jump out of my skin when my phone vibrates in my pocket. I pull it out and groan as I look at the display.

Law.

Great.

And here I thought this couldn't get any more embarrassing.

I clear my throat before I pick up, doing my best to sound confident and relaxed.

"Yellow!" I say cheerfully and close my eyes as what I just said registers in my brain.

There's a long silence in the phone before Law's amused voice says, *"Should I just pretend I didn't hear that?"*

I let out my breath in a whoosh. "It's probably better for everybody involved."

*"So... whatcha doin'?"* he asks. He's still laughing at me, but I decide to ignore it. Challenging him would only make it worse in my current state of mind. I'm not decent with comebacks even at the best of times. Throw in nerves about having sex with Law for the first time, and the result will not be pretty.

"Oh, you know, I'm out on a stroll. Little evening exercise. It's supposed to be good for body and mind."

*"I see I've turned you into a fitness fanatic."*

"Oh shit, you think? In that case I should probably stop going to the gym with you. Otherwise I'll do something drastic, like join a team or something."

*"The horror,"* he deadpans.

"It might as well be a sign of the apocalypse."

Silence falls between us.

*"Are you gonna come up?"* Law asks, and now his tone is decidedly more serious.

I whirl around. "You can see me?" I ask like the moron that I am.

*"I have windows, you know?"* he says, and the smile is back in his voice.

My eyes scan over the front of the building and there on the third floor, leaning on the windowsill, is Law. He looks effortlessly hot, like always. His eyes are intent, focused on me and only me.

"I'm really selling that whole I'm-smart-let-me-tutor-you angle, huh?"

*"I thought I was the one that convinced you to help us out,"* he remarks.

"Ah, that was just my clever ploy to get you to have sex with me."

He chuckles, his voice warm and soothing in my ear. *"Come up, Andy,"* he says and hangs up.

I take a deep breath and go inside.

Usually, I dislike stairs. People have gone through a lot of trouble to come up with the concept of an elevator, so I'm a firm believer that we should honor their work and let ourselves be whisked through the air in metal boxes, where the only physical activity involved is lifting our fingers and pressing a button.

Today, though, I'm perfectly happy to slog myself up the stairs. The more time-consuming the activity, the better. Too bad Law's apartment is only on the third floor.

I feel like I'm about to enter a dentist's office, not like I'm about to have sex, which as I understand, is a favorite pastime for a lot of people.

Law's door is already open when I reach his floor. I go in and shut it behind me, get rid of my jacket, slide off my shoes, and follow Law's voice into the kitchen. He's making dinner and singing. I've never heard his voice before. It's nice. Deep and, unlike me, he can keep a tune.

I take a seat at the small table. I've been a bundle of nerves ever since last night when I finally got Law to agree to the whole sex plan, which has resulted in some fairly ludicrous thoughts forming in my brain:

I'll trip over my feet and fall face first into Law's lap, injuring his dick—among other things—after which we'll be forced to spend an awkward night in the ER, and then Law will never want to see me again, because penis injuries are no joke.

I'll make weird noises while in bed with him. It's totally a possibility, since I've never gotten past second base, or whatever the gay equivalent of an awkward hand job is, so I don't know if I have a tendency to do that.

Maybe I *will* actually lick Law's elbow without realizing it's not his dick.

The possibilities are endless.

I take a deep breath and concentrate on the sound of Law's voice. It calms me down quite well. Not all the way, but I stop trying to call the whole night off out of fear that I'll embarrass myself. Law has that effect on me.

"Can you set the table?" he asks over his shoulder as he pours sauce into a big pot. I get the plates, cutlery, and a couple of glasses from the cabinet above the sink. I've been here so many times already that I know where all the necessary items are.

After I've set everything up, I go to peer over Law's shoulder. I inhale deeply and groan as the delicious scent hits my nostrils with full force.

The spoon Law uses to stir the pasta stops for a second. He continues after a moment, and I can see the corner of his mouth curl up in a small smile. "I hope I can coax a repeat of that sound out of you later tonight," he says casually, like he doesn't have any idea what kind of effect his words have on me.

I feel like I'm about to hyperventilate because all the oxygen seems to have been sucked out of the room.

"That…" I croak. "That would be most pleasant." No one could ever accuse me of being suave.

"Indeed," he says and the twitching of lips is now a full-blown smile. I'm still standing behind Law, unable to move. I'm so close that I can smell his body wash on his skin. The citrusy smell is addictive. The shorter hair at the back of Law's neck is standing up as my breath whooshes over it. Without thinking, I lean forward and run my nose through it. It's exactly as soft as it looks. I repeat the motion again and again. I'm like a cat, rubbing against his owner.

Law leans forward on the counter. He drops his head, exposing more of his neck, as his breathing becomes louder and harsher. It's the only sound in the quiet apartment.

I'm not sure if it's the right thing to do, but I stop myself from overthinking everything and just go for it. My lips land on the soft skin and I move up and down, leaving small kisses. The tingling in my lips, Law's scent, and the soft noises that drop from his lips make for a heady combination. I could stay right here all night. This small patch of skin is fascinating enough to explore for hours.

But Law lets out a loud curse as he drops the spoon he's been clutching in his hand. He whirls around in my arms, and in less than a second, he has turned us so that now I'm the one pressed against the counter.

"I thought I was supposed to be the teacher tonight," he growls before he covers my mouth with his.

The kiss goes from zero to sixty faster than a rocket ship. As soon as our lips touch, it's clear that neither of us has time for slow explorations. Our lips smash together, and I slam my palms down on the counter so as not to lose my balance. Law presses against me with every inch of his body. You'd need a chisel to pry us apart.

The outside world disappears. It's just him and me and that hot-as-fuck kiss that makes a desire sizzle inside me.

Kissing should definitely be Law's major. And minor. And his future career. He should just walk around and kiss all day long because he's that good. But not other people. Just me.

The unexpected flash of jealousy at the thought of Law kissing somebody else causes me to lose my balance for a second. I move my hand upward to steady myself, but somehow end up pressing my palm against the hot burner on the stove.

"Shit!" I yell as the burning sensation registers.

"What?" Law looks dazed as he pulls away from me. His face is only about two inches from mine, but even that distance is too much. I erase it by slamming my mouth back on his.

"Your hand," he mutters against my lips.

"Don't care." It doesn't feel like a serious, third-degree burn. Maybe like a superficial second-degree one at most, so I ignore the throbbing in my palm and concentrate on the kiss. Unfortunately, Law cannot be swayed so easily. He pulls away and grabs my hand to examine it.

"It's fine," I protest as I try to kiss him again, but he dodges me.

"It's just a little red," he mumbles more to himself than to me. "Cold water," he decides and pulls me to the sink where he blasts a spray of icy water on the damaged skin.

"Any long-lasting effects, Doctor Anderson?" I ask.

"You'll thank me when you don't die of infection. Now be a good boy, and maybe I'll kiss it better after I'm done with the first aid." He waggles his brows.

My body immediately goes hot all over, and it has nothing to do with the burning sensation in my palm.

He holds my hand under water for a few more seconds before dabbing it dry with a clean towel. He examines my palm under the kitchen light and is seemingly satisfied with whatever he sees there.

"What—" I ask, but my words get stuck somewhere in my throat as Law slowly lifts my hand and presses his lips to the center of my palm.

"Holy fuck," I whisper as he stays true to his word and kisses it better. Literally. And he doesn't stop with my palm. His lips track the inside of my wrist and follow the path of the lines in my palm. Heart line. Or lung line. Or brain line, something like that. I can't remember my mom's name at this point, so body parts and everything related to them seem like the obscurest of matters.

His eyes stay focused on me the whole time, which makes the experience even more intimate. He sucks my fingers into his mouth, one at a time, and I nearly come in my pants.

My cock is pressed against the zipper of my jeans, and I already regret wearing them. I wouldn't care if they were the most popular pants in the history of the universe, right now they're uncomfortable as hell. I should have stayed true to my trusty sweats. Damn Tricia.

Law pulls away from my fingers with a pop and a last soft kiss to the pad of my thumb. "Bedroom," he orders.

"Dinner?" I reply stupidly. I don't know why I say it. I don't care about dinner. I'll skip dinner for the rest of my life if it means Law will keep doing what he's doing.

"Later," he all but growls.

"Good," I say. It seems we're only able to come up with one word at a time, and I wholeheartedly approve. Who needs to waste time with full sentences?

Then we're kissing again and stumbling across the apartment toward his bed. Luckily, it's a small place, so in no time, we reach the bedroom. We land on the bed together with no finesse whatsoever. My elbow presses into Law's gut and his teeth clatter against mine, but who cares? I like the realness of the moment.

Law maneuvers me onto my back and kneels above me. He's breathing harshly, in perfect rhythm with my own panting breaths.

I wiggle out of my T-shirt and throw it over the edge of the bed. Law pulls his own shirt off. Seeing all those cut muscles and the six-pack—something I'll never have because I'm too lazy and only tolerate the gym and love junk food—makes me self-conscious about my body in a flash.

I cross my hands over my chest and Law blinks as if trying to clear the haze from his mind. "What just happened?" he asks.

"What?" I repeat, even though what I mean is, *Let's turn off the lights and do it in the dark.*

"You," he accuses. "You turned cold."

I want to wave him off and say *it's nothing*, but it's Law. We're friends, first and foremost. There isn't, and never has been, any room for games between us, so I just blurt it out. "I got self-conscious." He looks at me like he truly doesn't understand what might have possessed me to feel that way. I wave my hand toward his upper body. "You're very hot."

"And?" He cocks his head to the side, still confused but looking a bit more amused.

"I've got a Snickers body," I say. "Not in the sense that I look like a Snickers bar. Just that I eat too many Snickers and it shows."

He blinks a couple of times and then he lowers his head. I figure he's checking if what I've said is true, and I'm instantly regretful. If his brain was in some kind of misty state of lust that prevented him from seeing how not in-shape I am, I should have sucked it up and not said a word. Maybe he'll now look at me and be all, *You do look like a noodle. What was I thinking? I better go and find me a hotter hook-up. Sayonara, bitch.*

Law's shoulders shake. It takes me a moment to realize that the bastard is laughing.

"I don't know about you, but sex feels real good right about now," I say loudly. "Tell me, as an expert, is the feeling of intense humiliation part of the package?"

He lifts his head and smiles at me. "Sorry. I'm not laughing at you. I swear. It's just... *Snickers body*. You should have your own podcast or something. I'd listen to every episode. I swear."

"I'll call it *The Dad Bod Pod with Andy*. Don't forget to click subscribe." I roll my eyes.

Law's eyes track over my body again. Slowly, so I can feel his eyes on every inch of me. He's not laughing anymore, but I squirm because it feels like a horrible version of Judgement Day. *You, Andy Carter, are... not worthy of having sex.*

Law's gaze is still fixated on me, but before I can do anything, like hide under the sheets or put a bag over his head, he kisses me on my solar plexus. His lips linger, and all the arousal that had started to wane while I was worrying about my lack of abdominal muscles, comes back with a vengeance.

Law keeps kissing me all over my upper body. My chest, my stomach, my flanks, my hip bones. He doesn't leave a single inch unkissed.

"Do you know what I see when I look at you?" he asks in between kisses.

I shake my head, unable to form words as he flicks his tongue over my nipple and scrapes it with his teeth. My hips punch up.

"I see somebody I'm very attracted to. Somebody I want to touch.

Somebody I want to kiss. Somebody I want to see with my hands all over him."

He slides both of his palms over my chest and stomach. "We wouldn't be here if I didn't find you hot as fuck," he says.

I take a deep breath and let the insecurity go. This is Law. The guy has never lied to me and has always spoken his mind. If he says he's attracted to me, he means it.

"I don't care about six-packs. If you want one, I'll help you train. But otherwise, you don't need it to be the hottest person I've ever been with." Law keeps talking and kissing, and I keep squirming and fighting the need to come right here and now.

It's a feat that is doubled in difficulty as Law pops open the button of my jeans and drags the zipper down. My dick jumps up like it's a prisoner being freed from its shackles.

He straightens himself as he grabs the waistband of my jeans with both hands. "Lift," he orders, and I immediately push my hips up. He drags my pants down along with my underwear. He's being very efficient, and I wholeheartedly approve. My cock slaps against my abdomen. Precum forms a line between the head of my still bobbing dick and the skin of my stomach. Law stares at it, mesmerized, and before my mind can compute what he's doing, he swipes the precum up with his thumb, lifts it to his mouth, and licks it clean.

I grab the base of my dick with shaky fingers and squeeze so hard that I half expect my eyeballs to pop out like I'm some sort of a cartoon character.

*Do not come, Andy,* I lecture myself. *I forbid you. This is your Super Bowl. Or whatever the hell the sex equivalent of the Super Bowl is. Do not blow it.*

That last thought does not help at all, since blowing is exactly what my body wants to do.

Law seems to decide he might as well make my task more challenging. He takes hold of my cock, right above my own fist, and I watch as he lowers his head and licks over the slit of my dick as if in slow motion.

I howl. There's literally no other word for the sound that comes out of my mouth. Law chuckles against the sensitive flesh, making goosebumps rise all over my skin. He then proceeds to take the crown of my dick into his mouth and suck on it.

I dig my nails into the mattress and force myself not to thrust so far into his mouth that I sink down his throat. It takes inhuman willpower, something I never thought I had, to keep my thrusts shallow. I mean, I don't want to choke the guy. Seems a bit rude when he's giving me so much pleasure. If I'd known a mouth on my cock would feel that good, I would have trained to become a contortionist and done it myself. My own mouth might not be in the same league as Law's but based on how I'm feeling right now, even a poor substitute would do the trick.

By now, Law's head is bobbing up and down my shaft, and all I can do is repeat, "Oh shit! Fuck! Oh shit!" on a loop. It's so good that my toes curl, and I just want to stay here forever, lying on Law's bed with my cock in his mouth.

Law pries my fingers loose from the base of my dick and starts jacking me in his fist as he continues sucking me.

"Too good! Too much!" I babble, but there's no stopping Law, and to be fair, I'm not really trying.

It's over embarrassingly quickly. Law's hand moves up and down once, twice. He lifts his head and looks me deep in the eyes while he presses his thumb to the slit and rubs at it, before sliding his palm down again, and that's all it takes for me to go off like a Fourth of July fireworks display.

Ropes of cum shoot from my dick. The orgasm is like an explosion. There's no easing into it. It's just suddenly there, and it leaves me shaken and wrung out, panting on Law's bed like I've just ran a marathon. Even my ears are ringing, so there might very well have been a real explosion, and I just didn't notice in my blissed-out state.

My limbs feel like jelly, and my heart slams against the inside of my chest like it's got a hammer and is trying to chip its way out of there and make a run for it. It's the perfect plan. No way would I be able to chase after it in my current state. I'd die a happy man, though, so there's that.

Law's palm moves over my cock once more before he throws himself on his back next to me. He pushes his sweats down with one swift move and grabs his cock. His hand moves so quickly that I can only blink as I watch, mesmerized as he jerks himself off. It only takes a couple of tugs, and then he's coming with a loud groan. Cum spills out, covering his stomach and chest. It gathers between the dips and valleys of his abdominal muscles, forming little ponds there. My spent dick jerks as if giving its nod of approval. Law sprawls out on the bed, panting.

We stay quiet for the longest time, and even though I'm lying here, naked, my dick limp and my body covered with remnants of my orgasm and sweat, it's not awkward or embarrassing.

Eventually, Law turns his head toward me. His eyes are sleepy and there's a lazy grin on his face. "So?" His voice is scratchy and, since it might have something to do with the fact that my cock was in his mouth, it's unbelievably hot.

"We might have to retest the hypothesis." I sound like I've been drugged, and I can feel the dopey smile on my face.

"What was the hypothesis again?" He turns to his side and throws his arm over my chest and presses his face into my neck. Law Anderson likes to cuddle. Who would have thought?

"Sex with Lawrence Anderson is good," I say.

He smiles against my neck. "Just good?"

"Fantastic," I amend.

"That's right," he says with a rumbly, happy voice and falls asleep almost immediately.

I'm not the least bit sleepy, though. My body is buzzing with the aftershocks of my orgasm, and I feel more alive than ever before. How did I not know sex could be that good? I'm definitely up for another round. I mean, I could go right now, but it'd probably be rude to wake Law up to demand him to fuck me. I should reciprocate anyway. Work a little on my oral skills. I look down at Law's body, and even in near darkness, it's magnificent. I definitely want to touch and kiss and lick, and I can hardly wait for the morning to arrive, so I could do just that.

But morning is still hours away, and since I'm an overthinker at the best of times, doubts start creeping in. What's the etiquette here, anyway? Should I go? Should I stay? If I stay, should I sleep here? On the couch? Sit at the kitchen table the whole night and pretend I'm an early riser in the morning?

Would Law even want me to stay? Maybe he hopes I'll go away before the morning?

I turn my head to look at Law. His lips are slightly parted as he breaths softly. His eyelids flutter as he falls deeper into sleep, but he just keeps holding me, and slowly, I start to relax. Law and I are friends. If he wanted me gone, he would have said so.

It feels good to be held, so I burrow even closer, and before I know it, I'm asleep too.

## 16

## LAW

I don't know what to expect when I wake up in the morning, so I keep my eyes closed to avoid reality for as long as possible.

I manage a mere minute before my alarm clock starts screaming its head off. Andy flings himself to a sitting position at the obnoxious sound. He looks rumpled and adorable, pillow creases covering one cheek and his hair a mess.

"Where's the fire?" he asks, blinking rapidly to get rid of the haze of sleep.

It takes him a couple of moments to figure out the shrieking is coming from my alarm clock. He stares at the thing with utter confusion for another moment before he flings himself back on the bed. "Drown it. Throw it out of the window. I don't care what happens to it, just for the love of God, destroy that satanic noise maker," he mumbles as he presses the pillow over his ears.

I quickly turn off the alarm because Andy looks like he's ready to burn the thing himself.

I lie back down next to Andy. I should probably get out of bed, but a lazy Sunday morning feels too good to pass up.

"Why does your alarm clock make such ungodly sounds? I mean, mine isn't like an angel choir either, but at least it doesn't make all the babies' ears bleed in fifty-mile radius," Andy mumbles.

He snuggles in closer to me, still sleepy, and I find it hard to think because, man does it feel good. "Otherwise I'll be too tempted to stay in bed," I say, explaining the logic behind my obnoxious alarm clock.

"You're weird," Andy concludes. He throws his arm over my chest and falls asleep again. I don't move, even though I was planning to go to the gym. It's not like me at all. I used to be the guy that snuck in a workout on Christmas morning. Training was my life, and even though my dreams of going pro have been dashed, I still train religiously, if not as intensely as before. Yet here I am, in bed on a perfectly good Sunday morning and I'm not even sorry, because having Andy cuddled up against me feels so good. After a while, I doze off too.

I wake up some time later. The sun is shining through the open curtains, and I'm alone in bed. There's noise coming from the kitchen nook, though, so after pulling on a pair of sweats, I head that way.

Andy's back is to me. He's also wearing a pair of my sweats, but he's so much slimmer than I am that they have fallen low on his hips. The dimples on his lower back are on full display and if he were to bend over even a little bit, I would probably have a great view of his bare ass.

He's stirring something in a bowl, stopping every once in a while to throw in extra flour. I pad over and stop directly behind him.

"Pancakes?" I ask. Andy jumps and drops the spoon into the batter. He scowls at me over his shoulder. "Sorry," I say, but I'm really not.

"I figured we'd need some sustenance since last night we kind of got distracted before we could eat," Andy says and flushes, and it's all kinds of cute. He fishes the spoon out of the batter and pushes past me. In a minute, the kitchen is filled with the smell of pancakes, and my stomach growls.

Andy points to the table with the spatula. "Sit. Let me take care of you."

I blink, suddenly overcome with emotion because I don't think anybody has ever said something like that to me. The weird thing is how much I like it. My parents have raised me to be independent. They have never coddled me. Whatever the opposite of helicopter parents is, they're it, and I haven't minded. But as Andy slides a plate of pancakes in front of me and squeezes my shoulder as he passes me to get the utensils, it feels nice.

We eat our pancakes in silence and then we do the dishes. I wash and Andy dries, and I have to give myself a stern talking-to while we're at it because, as much as I like this whole domestic morning routine we've got going on, it's not real. Andy and I are not a real couple. We have an arrangement and no matter how good it feels to play house with him, it's not something I should let distract me.

After we're done cleaning up, we both lean against the kitchen counter. I'm not sure what to do next. I don't want Andy to leave, but if he stayed it would only feed this weird delusion I have, where it feels like Andy and I are something more than a hook-up. I don't know why it's so hard to keep my thoughts in check.

I clear my throat, determined to tell Andy that it's been nice, but I have to go to the gym now. Before I can do that, he turns toward me and kisses me. Every rational thought flees my head like it's being chased out by a wildfire. What's left is only raging desire and a need so deep that I can hardly take it. I've never felt this attracted to a guy before. There's something about Andy that just does it for me, and I'm beginning to think I might not be as well equipped to handle this situation as I thought I would be.

"Can I try something?" Andy asks.

All I can do is nod mutely. I have no idea what Andy has planned, but with a single kiss, he's turned me on enough that I'd probably agree with anything.

I don't know what exactly I expect, but it's definitely not Andy lowering himself to his knees in front of me. He looks up through the mess of his hair and, without breaking eye contact, pulls my sweats down, freeing my dick. I'm rock hard embarrassingly quickly, and when Andy places a soft, innocent kiss on the tip of my cock, my whole body stiffens. I give myself a stern lecture and recite some capitals again because I'm not going to blow in under a minute like a freaking thirteen-year-old who sees a pair of boobs at his first boy-girl pool party.

Andy licks his lips, seemingly unsure how to continue. I can almost hear the clicks and whirls as his brain tries to take the scientific route and compute the best way to approach a blowjob.

I cup his jaw with my hand and make him look at me. "Just… follow your gut. Do what feels right. Don't overthink it."

Andy licks his lips and nods, a determined expression on his face. "Tell me if I do something wrong."

I let out a strained laugh. "Not possible."

He cocks his head to the side. He looks intrigued at once. And thoughtful. This does not bode well.

"You sure about that?" Andy asks, lips inches away from my dick. The puff of warm breath makes all hairs stand up on my body, and I grip the edge of the counter so that I won't push myself into Andy's mouth. "What if I bite?" he continues, studying my cock with the concentration of a scientist looking at a never-before-seen species.

I close my eyes and let my head fall back as I groan and try not to let my frustration show, because my dick is rock hard and in front of Andy's face. I can feel his breath on it, and he wants to discuss the effect of biting my dick, which I'm sure even the most inexperienced of people know not to do. "Yeah, maybe don't do that."

"What if I suck too hard, and you end up getting a hickey? On your penis," he clarifies unnecessarily.

I rub my forehead. "I'm not sure if that's even possible."

"Technically, there are blood vessels and capillaries in a penis, so it should be possible," Andy says thoughtfully.

"Okay," I say with a choked voice. "Just to clarify, you were about to give me a blowjob, but you got sidetracked by dick hickeys?"

Andy blinks and looks down at my, by now only half-hard cock. "Oops," he says, but just as quickly, a determined look appears on his face. "We can fix this."

"I don't think I'm in the mood any—" I start, but Andy wraps his fingers around my shaft and sucks the tip into his mouth, and I take back everything I was about to say because he's absolutely right. He can—and does—fix it in an instant.

Andy's tongue slides over my hard flesh as he licks me. He pumps the hand that holds the base in synchronized rhythm with his tongue, and my hips snap forward. "Shit! Sorry," I mumble, but Andy seems only more determined by whatever he sees on my face and hears in my voice. He pulls off me with an audible pop, and even that simple sound is turning me on like nobody's business. "Don't think," he orders. "I can handle myself, just let go."

I nod because I know Andy is capable of anything he sets his mind to, so why not blowjobs, right? If he says he can handle it, he can handle it, and he'll stop me if it's too much. I start pushing into his mouth as he sucks me.

Andy might never have given a blowjob before, but he's a damn quick learner. He observes my reactions, taking in every moan and sound, adjusting his pace and the tightness of his grip according to whatever he sees on my face and hears in my voice. I'm mindless with pleasure and need in no time at all, pumping into his mouth with abandon.

"Andy," I choke out. *So close. I'm so close.*

Andy locks his gaze with mine, and I feel his other hand between my thighs as he cups my balls and rolls them between his fingers.

"Andy," I repeat. It's a warning and praise in one because his name seems to be the only thing in my mind. Andy looks nervous for a second, but then the same determination that was there at the beginning takes over once again. He doesn't pull off. He sucks harder, and I let go. I throw my head back and my spine arches as I come into his mouth. My dick spurts so much cum that some of it runs down from the corner of Andy's mouth. It's the hottest thing I've seen in my life.

It takes forever for my body to relax, and when it does, I slide down onto the floor. My ass hits the cold tile, but I don't care. I'm in orgasm heaven, and it's fucking spectacular.

Andy kneels in front of me, a hint of uncertainty in his eyes. "Was that okay?" he asks.

"Jesus." I swallow hard before I pull him to me so that he can straddle my thighs. I take his face between my palms and kiss him hard. "That was incredible," I say, and Andy smiles brightly like the sun, as my insides go all gooey and happy.

Later, we lie on the couch and talk about nothing in particular.

I'm not in the market for a boyfriend. Relationships take time and effort and all my energy goes into hockey right now. I may not become an NHL superstar, but I damn well intend to leave my mark as a coach. To do that, I can't afford any distractions.

But when Andy looks at me with hesitation as he starts to leave sometime around noon and asks, "So... I'll see you around?" with that hopeful expression on his face, my heart beats faster and excitement bubbles in my stomach like a fizzy drink.

I pull Andy to me and plant a firm kiss on his lips. "Tonight," I say and the smile he sends my way is blinding.

## 17

# ANDY

Before I know it, it's the beginning of July. Where has the time gone? The summer classes end at the beginning of August, so I effectively have about four weeks to help Law's hockey players pass Shaw's class.

The tutoring is going better. I haven't fallen on my face again. Nor have there been any episodes of fainting or puking. I'm far from okay with standing in front of the makeshift classroom, and the thought of my tutoring sessions usually makes my throat dry and my palms sweaty, but it's getting better. The process is slow, but there *is* some progress.

It doesn't hurt that every time I get nervous, Law is there to distract me. And while I'm still struggling with my tutoring role, Law is a natural when it comes to our very own, private tutoring sessions. We're taking things slow at Law's insistence. I guess he doesn't want there to be any regrets, which is probably smart. If it was up to me, we'd probably already have gone the whole way, but Law has a different approach. We're learning each other's bodies and preferences slowly, in the most enjoyable way imaginable, and I'm not complaining one bit. The things Law can do with his hands and his mouth should probably be illegal. Hell, who am I kidding? They probably *are* illegal in some parts of the world.

I've always been a good student, but under Law's skillful hands, I excel. I love teasing him and tasting him. I love the way his breath hitches when I lick over an especially sensitive spot. I love finding erogenous zones on Law's body. I love to watch him lose control and know that I was the one who helped him get to that point, where the only thing he can feel is mindless pleasure.

Today, however, even the images of our nights together can't quell my nerves. To mark the halfway point of the summer courses, Shaw gave the guys a test, and they're getting the results back today. So I'm sitting in the library, but instead of working, I stare at the clock on the wall, counting down the minutes. Even though I've only been tutoring them for about a month, I still feel like they're my students. So if they fail, it'll also be my failure, which would really be a nail in the coffin of the teaching career I've tentatively started to consider again. I mean, I haven't puked on anybody, so it must be a sign from God that He approves and is nudging me in that direction.

Well, I should say I haven't puked *yet*, because when my phone rings a minute later, and I see Law's name on the screen, I definitely feel queasy.

"So?" I croak into the phone instead of a greeting.

"You in the library?" Law asks.

I nod for several long seconds before I realize that Law can't see me. "Yeah," I manage to say.

"I'll be there in five." And then he hangs up.

I stare at my phone because, what kind of a depraved monster leaves another person hanging like that?

Law's saving grace is that it only takes him three minutes to get to my desk. Then again, it's three minutes too long, which means I've let anxiety overtake my brain, and am now certain that they've all failed.

Law takes a seat next to me and raises his brows at whatever he sees on my face. "Dude, why do you look like you're about to pass out?"

"I'm fine," I mutter, even though evidently, I don't look the part.

"You sure about that?" he asks.

I swallow hard. I'm not ready to hear how badly I've failed. Maybe if I can postpone it just a little bit it will be easier? I fan myself with my hand. "Is it hot in here? I feel hot. Let me just get myself a bottle of water. I'll be back in a minute."

Before I can stand up, Law has placed a bottle in front of me. "You're in luck. I just filled it up."

There goes my plan of climbing out the window and hitchhiking to Canada.

I take my time drinking, but I can't guzzle the whole thing, so all too soon, I'm forced to face the music. I cross my fingers and send up a quick, silent prayer. "Okay, lay it on me."

"They passed. Every single one of them." The words rush out, accompanied by the biggest smile I've ever seen on Law's face. "There were even two A's," he adds, looking dazed.

I'm one to talk. I'm not in better shape. I'm having a hard time even hearing Law through the roar of blood in my ears. "Really?" I need to confirm that he said what I think he said, because I can't seem to believe it.

"It was a total triumph. Well, Kevin triumphed with a D, but that was better than everybody expected, so we'll call it a win for now. And it's all thanks to you."

I let out the breath that I've been holding for what feels like hours. I'm ridiculously relieved by the news. I don't think I had as much to do with those grades as Law seems to think I did, but at least I didn't make things worse.

"Congrats," I say. My smile could probably rival the Cheshire Cat's.

Law slumps in his chair. It looks like he's relaxed for the first time in weeks. "I don't know how to thank you," he says.

"We still have four weeks to go, so you're not allowed to express any gratitude yet."

Law laughs, happy and carefree, at least for today, and I smile. I'm not going to rain on his parade with any more of my realism. Let him feel good about how things are going.

He stretches out his legs and places his hands behind his head. "And now I'm going to sit here and watch you work. It's the best way to relax, and after the summer I've had so far, I feel like I deserve it at least a tiny bit."

I laugh and push my laptop away. "Sounds festive."

"Sounds lame, huh?" Law grins, but then he straightens himself. "You know what we should do? Go out."

I don't know what's wrong with my mouth, or my brain for that matter, but the first thing that comes out is, "On a date?"

Law looks confused for a second, and why wouldn't he, when the tutor he's hired is twisting his words to score a date? But then Law says, "Exactly."

My mouth falls open. Surely Law has better options for celebrating? I imagine the team is having a wild party tonight to let off some steam, so why would Law want to spend the evening with me?

"It would be like practice," Law adds. "If I'm going to help you with Asola, I need to see you in action."

*Oh. So not really a date, then.*

"In action," I repeat. This does not sound good.

"Yeah. We'll go on a pretend date. We'll do the whole thing." He ticks off items on his fingers. "Dress to impress. I'll pick you up, or you can pick me up, whichever works for you. We'll go to a nice restaurant. Talk. Flirt."

I swallow hard. "Flirt?" I ask with a faint voice.

"You're going to have to be on top of your game for Asola, so we need to practice."

"I don't know how to flirt."

"Hence the pretend date." Law stands up and stretches. "It's a plan. I'll pick you up in two hours."

"But…"

"What?" Law asks.

I have nothing to use as a good argument against doing this, other than the fact that I'm afraid I'll make a fool out of myself, and I don't think Law would consider that an acceptable reason to cancel the date.

"Nothing," I mumble.

There's no way I'm going to do well on this date.

Law is buzzing the intercom precisely two hours later, and I drop the bottle of styling oil that I've been staring at for the last ten minutes, trying to remember what the hair stylist told me about using it. I buzz him in and curse as I'm forced to crawl under a bench by the door, where the bottle has rolled.

There's a knock on the door, and I slam my head against the underside of the bench. "Shit!" I crawl out from underneath it and open the door.

And then I stare.

Because, man, Law cleans up nice.

It's not like he's been a slob so far. He always looks good, but now that he's dressed in a nice pair of dark gray slacks and a purple button-down, it becomes painfully clear just how devastatingly handsome Law Anderson is.

He quirks his brow at me and his lips twitch. "Hi. Can I come in?"

"Uh. Sure. Of course. Step right into my humble abode," I say and step aside, gesturing toward the inside of the apartment with a flourish. There might be something resembling a curtsey there as I watch him pass me. I can't be sure since I immediately block that embarrassing part of the evening from my memory for good. Law gives me the side-eye, and he makes a valiant effort to restrain himself, even though he can't help letting out a stifled laugh.

The start of this date is super promising.

I follow Law to the living room, but as I pass the mirror on my way there, I glance at myself, and I almost choke at the sight. The front of my dark blue shirt is covered in dust. It looks like I've been practicing my tie-dye techniques only in boring blues and grays. I guess it sums up my personality quite well.

Nevertheless, I hold my head high as I face Law. "I'm gonna go change real quick. Wouldn't want to show up on our date in my lounge wear." And then I let out a shrill laugh.

"Sure." He manages to keep an almost straight face, bless him.

I start for my bedroom, but when I pass Law, he stops me with his hand on my elbow.

"What—" I don't get to finish my question because Law kisses me softly. It's a short kiss, almost chaste, and Law pulls away way too soon for my liking. He presses his lips to my cheek in another quick kiss, and his low voice rumbles through me as he says just one word.

"Relax."

And I do.

I take a deep breath and force my shoulders to drop. My nerves, which were wound tight like guitar strings, loosen a bit and the tight knot in my stomach eases. I nod as he smiles at me.

I head to my bedroom and leave Law to wander around the apartment. I shuck off the dusty shirt as I open the door to my closet. Thanks to Tricia's shopping trip I have a small selection of new clothes that a stylist has pre-approved. Since I told her my makeover was something I needed to better my chances of getting a job after I graduate, my new wardrobe is heavy on button-downs and slacks. I just grab a new shirt in a slightly different shade of blue.

"So this is your room." I whirl around at Law's voice. He's standing in the doorway, shoulder leaning against the frame, and he lets his eyes scan over me slowly and unashamedly. "It's nice."

"Thanks." My voice is husky as I return the favor. I can't help it. I enjoy looking at Law. I like that he's strong and tall, but somehow also possesses a kind of unexpected grace as he moves around. He commands attention. I don't think it's possible to look at anybody else when he's in the room.

"Sorry," he says with a small smile. "I couldn't let the opportunity of seeing you half naked pass me by."

I blush. It's one of those chest-goes-red-like-a-tomato type blushes, which is most likely highly unattractive, so I quickly pull on my shirt. I drag my hand through my hair to get it out of my eyes. Curls flop around my face, and there's a good chance that I look like I've just stuffed a pair of scissors into an electrical outlet, but it'll have to do.

"Ready," I announce as I grab my jacket. Law is still staring at me with an unreadable expression on his face. "Shall we?" I prompt, not sure what's with the intense look.

"Absolutely." Law smiles, and we head out.

Even though Montpelier isn't exactly a booming metropolis, it has a wide selection of restaurants, most of which I haven't visited because of my less-than-excellent monetary situation. But I have some savings left even after Tricia's shopping trip, so for once, I'm going to let loose, and not worry about my finances.

Law has made us a reservation. The restaurant is small and cozy with lots of nooks and corners that make the dining experience feel more private. It's a very nice place, which immediately makes me feel self-conscious, but then Law places his hand on my back as we follow the hostess through the restaurant to our table. My loud, nervous, I-don't-know-how-to-behave-in-a-place-like-this heartbeat pounds even harder, and for a whole new reason. The fuck-I-hope-this-night-ends-in-Law's-bed reason.

We take our seats and that is when things turn awkward as hell, because I'm very much aware that Law is going through all this trouble for me, and I feel like I should repay him by being the best date ever. So I'm trying to think of something interesting to say to get the conversation rolling, but nothing good comes to mind. I read a fascinating article about the Crimean-Congo hemorrhagic fever the other day, but I feel like *depressing* isn't the mood I should go for here. I could flirt, but I'm not good at that, so I'm not banking on that option.

Law is sitting there, a small smile on his face, and he doesn't seem that bothered by the silence that has gone on for a long time by now.

"So," I eventually say. "Here we are."

Law's lips twitch. "Yes."

"Umm... how exactly is this supposed to work?"

"Well, we've safely arrived at the restaurant, so I'd say we're on the traditional route so far."

"Ha. Very funny. I meant, what's next? Should I just... say something sexy? How do these things usually go?"

Law chuckles softly and looks me in the eye. The low lighting of the restaurant makes his emerald eyes dark and intense. "Just relax, Andy. You're supposed to have fun on a date, not hyperventilate and worry."

"Really?" I say drily. "Because in my, admittedly, limited experience, dating is supposed to make you sweat like a pig and babble nervously until the guy you're with suddenly gets a phone call informing him that his best friend has been in a helicopter accident and needs him to be there right that second to whisper faintly where a hidden treasure has been buried before he dies."

"Has that ever actually happened?"

"Maybe not verbatim. I might have added the helicopter crash part to make myself feel better."

Law purses his lips. "On a good date, you'll have fun," he says with a solemn nod. "I'll prove it to you."

Law takes the lead and starts asking me about school and my studies, and before I know it, I'm so into the conversation that any nervousness I might have felt has disappeared.

I feel comfortable with Law. He's seen me freak out over tutoring. He's seen me embarrass myself. He's seen me first thing in the morning. He's seen me late at night. We've seen each other naked, for crying out loud. This guy knows me, the good and the bad, so I don't have to try to be something I'm not.

"MIT," he repeats and lets out a low whistle. "Impressive."

I shrug one shoulder. I haven't told anybody about that dream, even though I've been preparing for it for close to a year already. Not even my family knows, but telling Law feels natural and easy.

"What about you?" I ask. "What happens next year?"

"I want to coach. Playing in NHL will never happen, obviously, but I can't imagine taking an office job. Hockey has been my life for over ten years, and I don't want to give it up. I guess I could do it on the side. My parents would prefer it, but it seems I'll just have to disappoint them yet again."

"For what it's worth, I think you make a hell of a coach," I say, and I mean it. Law has been so dedicated to his team, and I have no doubt he'll eventually end up in the NHL, just like he's been dreaming about.

Law smiles, but the next time he looks at me, he's biting his lip, looking uncharacteristically nervous. "Coach Williams has been... I mean, I guess he likes me. He says he sees potential in me, so he's trying to help me plan for the future. He has a lot of connections, and he used to work in Boston." Law looks to the side, refusing to meet my eyes. "I'd love to end up in Boston. College hockey is unbelievable there, so it would be amazing to get a position in that city. I mean, there's a chance I'll end up working in the minors somewhere in the middle of nowhere." He chuckles. "Fuck it, I guess what I'm saying is that, if by some miracle I end up in Boston, I'd like it if we could still... hang out."

My heart skips a beat and then starts working overtime. It feels like sunshine has burst into my stomach. I've never seen Law so nervous before, which is kind of cute and very unnecessary because hell yes I want to keep hanging out with him. I've been dreading the fall because, once tutoring is over, I can't help but fear that Law will just... drop me. But it seems I've been wrong to doubt him.

I nod vigorously, totally forgetting to be cool about it, but then again, who cares? Law already knows what I'm like, so there's no need to put on a show. Maybe that's why this date is going so well? I'm not trying to be something that I'm not. Sure, I'm dressed better than usual, and my hair is not as wild, but that's all just packaging. It takes me a second to put my finger on it, but then it dawns on me—with Law, I don't feel like I'm the sidekick. He doesn't make me feel like I'm a hero either, but the thing is, with Law, I don't really care about *being* a hero at all. With Law, I'm just me. Just Andy. And with Law, it's enough.

"I'd love it if we both ended up in Boston."

Law beams at me, relieved and happy, and I smile back.

We arrive at my apartment a little after eleven. We were kicked out of the restaurant. The hostess politely hinted that they were closing, and that maybe we could be so kind as to get the hell out of there so that all of them could go home.

Law turns the engine off and we sit silently for a moment. I look up at the dark windows of my apartment. I turn to Law.

Dry. My throat is dry like all the saliva has been wiped up with an extra-absorbent cloth, which means that my first attempt to say anything comes out like more of a croak. Law looks at me with raised brows, so I clear my throat and try again.

"Do you want to come upstairs?" I ask. "For a nightcap. Is that a thing? I should warn you, though, I don't have anything alcoholic in there. I mean, there's an open bottle of orange juice that has been in the corner of the fridge for months, so that probably has some kick to it? So I guess I'm asking if you want to come up for"—I try to think of some kind of a beverage I might have in there—"milk," I finish. "Or water." I make a wave motion with my hand. "Some good old-fashioned H2O?"

I would probably have continued babbling, but Law stops me with a palm on my thigh. "I'd love to come up," he says in that low and sure voice of his that always seems to calm me down. I take a deep breath and nod before we get out of the car.

Law walks behind me as we go up. I'm not sure if I should put an extra swivel in my hips or shake my ass in silent flirtation, but I eventually opt out of both options. I'd probably make a fool out of myself and fall down the stairs.

We stop in front of my door, and I lean against it. "So, this is me," I say. Silence follows. So much silence.

"I remember," Law says with a barely held back smile. "I was here four hours ago."

"Ah." I feel my cheeks heat. "That's good. That was a test, and you passed. No early signs of Alzheimer's for you, mister."

Law looks down at his feet to hide his smile. "Should we go inside?" he asks after we've stood there for another couple of moments.

"Shit," I say as I remember that we're at my apartment, and I'm the one with the keys. I don't know what's wrong with me. Why can't I be normal for just an hour?

I fumble with the lock but we get inside with no further embarrassing incidents. "So how about that… milk, then?" I ask because I'm nothing if not a gracious host. "Athletes need their calcium, right?" *Oh good. We're back to babbling.*

"Sure."

We make our way to the kitchen, and I pour two glasses of milk. The carton is almost empty, so I manage one half-full glass and the other glass only has like an ounce at the bottom. I grab that one and push the other one toward Law before I raise my glass.

"Cheers," I announce loudly because I haven't embarrassed myself enough yet.

"No cookies?" Law teases as I down my shot of milk.

I jump at the prospect of having something to do with my hands. "I have some! Do you want some? I'll get you some."

I drag the chair to my secret stash cabinet and start rummaging around. I push aside potato chips and candy and chocolate bars, all of which I haven't touched in a while, since I've been so busy and all these gym sessions Law has forced on me are wreaking havoc on my sweet tooth. I haven't eaten a candy bar in days. Something inside me must be broken.

I'm still busy sorting through the contents of the cabinet when I feel somebody's hands on my hips. "I think I'll pass on the cookies," Law murmurs as his palms travel from my hips to my ass.

"You sure? I swear I have some somewhere," I say in a choked voice as Law squeezes my ass cheeks and pulls me against him.

He presses his forehead against my back. "I'm sure."

He places his hands back on my hips and nudges me until I turn around. I'm standing on a chair in the middle of my kitchen with Law pressed against me. My cock has already perked up, liking the way Law's chest rubs against it as he moves.

Law's gaze is trained on mine as he locks his fingers around my thighs and pulls me toward him. It takes me a moment to realize his intent, but once I catch up, it's easy for me to slide against him and wrap my legs around his waist.

I swallow and lick my lips before I slide my hands upward until my palms are on his cheeks. Slowly, I lower my mouth to his. The kiss is slow and seductive. We take our time exploring and tasting.

Law's teeth nip my bottom lip, and I push my tongue into his mouth. I've kissed Law more than once by now, but every time I do, it just seems to get better. I love it. I'm plastered against him, but I still want more.

I can't get enough of Law, and in moments like this, when it's just the two of us, I don't think it's possible to ever get my fill of Law.

"Hold on," he mumbles through the kiss as he grabs my ass, pulls me even closer, and walks out of the kitchen with me still wrapped around him like a vine. Law heads toward my bedroom with purposeful strides, and in seemingly no time at all, I'm flat on my back in the middle of my bed.

It takes another minute, and we're both naked, courtesy of Law, who's stripped us both so quickly firemen would be proud.

He then climbs on my bed, pressing his naked body against mine, and I moan at the sensations that course through me. I'm already crazy with need and ready to combust, and Law hasn't even gotten started yet.

His palm slides up my side, leaving goosebumps in its wake. Law's lips cover my nipple as he licks and sucks at it before leaning over me to bestow the same attention to my other nipple. All the while, his hands keep roaming over my skin, touching everywhere.

Law slides his tongue up, moving from my nipple to my neck, where he dips his tongue into the hollow of my throat, licks upward to the tip of my chin. His tongue touches my lower lip and tracks the contour.

I'm panting like I've just run a 10K, and I haven't even done anything. Our breaths mingle as Law presses his forehead to mine. He closes his eyes for a second like he's trying to gather himself. Then, those impossibly green orbs focus on me, and I feel a jolt inside.

"What do you want, Andy?" he whispers.

It's a complicated question. *You*, is the answer that everything in me wants to scream out at the top of my lungs, but that goes against everything that I promised Law at the beginning of this... whatever it is we're doing here. I told him I wouldn't get attached, so I can't ruin everything by doing just that.

"I want you to"—*make love to me*—"fuck me." I stumble over the last words.

Law's breath hitches. He swallows hard, like he's not convinced it's something I really want, but he couldn't be more wrong. I've thought about it ever since I first realized how deeply I trusted him. I can't imagine doing this with anybody else.

"Are you sure?" Law asks.

I nod. "As death."

Law's lips twitch. "Well, that's romantic."

I push at his shoulder. "I was trying to illustrate my level of commitment."

"You really are one of a kind." The way Law says it, it's not a bad thing, but I can't let it mean too much. I need things to remain light and easy between us. That's the only way I can keep my promise to him.

"Stop trying to butter me up and just do me."

He snorts. "Yes, sir."

He kisses me again, and I quickly lose myself to the sensation of his lips and tongue on my body. Law moves back down, planting kisses as he goes, until my rock-hard dick taps against his chin. He looks up at me with a wicked grin as he wraps his hand around the root of my cock. Instead of putting me in his mouth, though, he blows a warm breath over the head. I shiver and close my eyes as he does it over and over again until I feel like I'm about to claw my way out of my skin. My hips are twitching with the effort to stay still. Law slides his palm up and then down. It's agonizingly slow, but he keeps it up for several minutes.

"Please," I finally rasp when I can't take it any longer. Precum is sliding down my cock, and I need more. More friction. More everything.

Law smiles, satisfied with whatever he sees on my face—desperation, most likely—and lower his head, taking me into his mouth. His lips wrap around the crown of my dick, and he goes lower and lower and doesn't stop until he's engulfed my whole cock.

"Fuck!" I gasp. That is an extremely good use of Law's mouth. And then he swallows. The tip of my cock presses against the back of his throat, and the feeling is too sensational for words. He slides up, sucking all the way to the tip, cheeks hollowed and a wicked glint in his eyes, and then he does it all over again.

I think I'm going to die. My toes curl and every inch of my skin buzzes with mind-numbing pleasure. I've never felt anything like this before.

I can't take much more. It's been mere minutes, and I'm ready to come. My balls are tight and shivers wrack my body as I try to hold back. Law pulls off with a pop, but before I can protest, he moves even lower. My hazy mind has trouble registering what he's doing, and my ability to think about anything at all is completely thrown out the window as Law sucks my balls into his mouth. He's not done, though. Far from it.

With easy confidence, he pushes my legs up, exposing every inch of me. It's intimate as fuck to be so open in front of somebody like this, and it should feel like too much, but it's Law, and with him, there's no embarrassment or insecurity. Only need. All-consuming and limitless need.

Law licks his lips, and then—sweet Jesus—he licks over my hole. I've seen it in porn, but to be the actual recipient of this treatment is overwhelming as fuck. Nerve endings sizzle and zing, and I gasp, unable to do anything but hold still and pray that this won't turn out to be a dream.

The tip of Law's tongue prods at my entrance, slowly and patiently loosening the tight muscle until I'm relaxed enough that he can push the tip of his tongue inside. I grapple with the sheets to have something to hold on to because I'm about to fly off the bed. Or at least that's what it feels like.

The blissful high keeps building and building as Law licks and fucks me with his tongue. Everything tingles and I'm simultaneously loose and taut as a wire, ready to combust but desperately holding back.

I watch as he pulls open the drawer of my nightstand and grabs the bottle of lube I keep there. He flicks the cap open and drizzles some on my hole.

Things only get harder, literally, when Law pushes the tip of his finger inside. I tense up for a second, but Law's tongue is back immediately, so it doesn't take long for me to relax again, and soon he's worked his whole finger inside me.

Law takes things extra slowly, so by the time we're on the second finger, I'm a mess. It's not like he's purposely edging me, but I've been close to coming so many times by now that it damn well feels like he's doing just that.

It's not the first time I've had something in my ass. I've done extensive research, and I've learnt that the key to anal sex is definitely practice. A while back, even before Project Hero started, I ordered myself some toys, and I've used them on myself, but it's a whole different ball game to have somebody else's hands give you pleasure.

Law pushes a third finger inside and sucks my cock into his mouth. My hips come off the bed as I push up to meet him. I'm teetering on the edge again, but just as before, Law must sense what's about to happen because he stops and straightens himself. He grabs one of the condoms he threw on the bed earlier and rolls it down his very impressive erection.

His eyes flitter between my face and my ass. It takes some fumbling on my part to shove a pillow beneath my hips, but then Law lines himself up. He adds more lube, and the slippery sensation is hot as fuck as he rubs it in and around my hole, and then it gets even better as I get to watch him slather his cock in lube as well.

"Breathe," he mutters, and I forcefully exhale, not even realizing that I've been holding my breath. Law starts working himself inside me, and I try to relax, but it's not going that well because Law's dick is definitely bigger than the dildo I've been practicing with.

The crown slides in, and I gasp. Law adds more lube and kisses me, nipping at the place where my neck meets my shoulder, making tingles run over my skin. He rolls my nipple between his fingers and keeps kissing me. My tense muscles relax slowly but surely.

"Fuck," I gasp.

Law is panting like crazy. He's holding himself back as he lets me adjust to the intrusion.

"Keep going," I finally get out in a choked voice.

He gives me a strained nod as he slowly starts to sink further inside me. It feels a bit strange, but there are undercurrents of pleasure there, waiting to be unleashed. I can feel it.

"Jesus," Law gasps once he's all the way inside me.

I can't speak. I've never felt so full. The feeling is almost unbearable in its intensity. I grab Law's ass. My grip will probably leave bruises behind, but I need to hold on to him. Law doesn't seem to mind as I pull him, impossibly, even deeper.

"Please," I say not sure what I'm asking of him, but as always, Law understands what I need as he slowly draws out, making every one of my nerve endings sing.

It's too much.

It's not enough.

I never want this to stop.

Slowly but surely, we build up to a steady rhythm, Law's hips snapping as he pushes into me. Our loud gasps, muttered curses, and the slap of skin against skin are the only sounds in the room.

Law takes hold of my ankle and pushes my leg up. I'm about to make a quip about not bending that way, but Law pushes inside me, and holy fucking shit, he hits the bullseye.

He glances at me and a wicked smirk appears on his lips as he does it again and again until I can't take it anymore. I push my hand between our bodies and grab onto my dick. It only takes one squeeze before I gasp, "Coming."

My orgasm slams into me, and that's that. I come so hard that there are black spots dotting my vision. Nothing has ever felt like that before, and it only gets better when Law presses his palms on either side of my head, and lets loose on me. His hips snap as he drives into me wildly, chasing his release. It doesn't take long, just a couple of thrusts before he pulls out. He has a wild look on his face as he tears the condom off and grabs his dick. With a loud roar, he comes all over my stomach and chest, before promptly collapsing on top of me.

"Jesus Christ," he mutters when we've lain still for so long that we're stuck together. He pries himself off me. We're a sticky, sweaty mess, but I love every single thing about this moment.

It's much later, after we've showered and are lying together in my bed, wrapped around each other, that I say, "The Fourth of July weekend is coming up. Any big plans?"

Law yawns and snuggles in closer. "Not really. My parents are not big on celebrations, so they'll probably have a fancy dinner with some of Dad's business buddies on Thursday, and from then on, it's just business as usual."

My hand, that has been tracking the ridges of Law's spine, stops. "You're not going home?"

"There's no point. The traffic will suck, and it's not much of a celebration in the middle of New York."

"But... you'll be all alone, then." In my family, the Fourth of July has never only been about celebrating independence. For us, it's a day for our family. We all come home and just spend the day together. Dad grills burgers, we go swimming at the lake, and later we watch fireworks. It's a day for the family, and suddenly, I can't seem to get the thought out of my head: Law should be there too.

Law frowns. "It's not a big deal. It's not like I spend the day crying into the pillow," he jokes.

"No, you'll just end up at the gym, and I'm sorry, I kind of tolerate exercise now, but that is no way to spend a holiday. You're coming home with me," I announce grandly.

He shakes his head and flops onto his back. "No, I'm not."

I push myself up on my elbow. "But... you have to come with me."

"No, I don't," he says, and before I can argue, he continues, "Think about it. Who else is going to be there for the holidays?" He gives me one of those raised-brow, meaningful looks, and I just stare back with a blank face because I have zero clue what he's talking about.

"My siblings?" I offer with all the confidence of a kid who's just been asked a question about the homework he hasn't even opened.

Law looks like he isn't sure if I'm kidding or not. "No. Asola," he says. "I mean, I assume he'll be there?"

"Oh." Now I feel stupid because Falcon will definitely be there. His family lives next door. Ever since the summer we became friends we've been moving between the two houses with very little thought about who lives where. I've eaten countless meals at the Asolas' dinner table, and Falcon was responsible for convincing my mom to incorporate such horrors as asparagus, sardines, and lentils into her cooking. I don't think Ian ever forgave him for the lentils. Our dads go fishing together and our moms go out on margarita nights, and the Fourth of July family gathering will most definitely include the Asolas.

"Yeah," Law says, but it sounds more like, *Duh*. The inch that separates our naked bodies feels like a mile now. Law stares out the window, refusing to meet my gaze. "If you think about it, it's kind of the perfect moment to, you know, let him know about your feelings."

My stomach drops. "Oh." I can't seem to form any coherent sentences.

Law still refuses to look me in the eye, but he nods and smiles. "Absolutely. It's a festive and happy day. You couldn't find a better opportunity."

"Hmm," I mumble noncommittally. Telling Falcon how I feel about him has always been the plan. The end goal. It's what started this whole transformation business of mine. But I always thought I'd have an overwhelming feeling of rightness when the time came. Something that would make me go, *Yes! This is it! This is the moment*. I don't feel like that right now, though. It feels unreal, but not in a good way. The thought of talking to Falcon does not fill me with excitement.

*I don't want to do this.*

The feeling is sudden and alarming. I've changed my looks and the way I dress. I've been trying to change myself into somebody who's worthy of being with Falcon. It's not like he's asked me to do it, but because I'm obviously a bit crazy—it might be that all those products and gels I've been using to tame my hair have gone to my head—because I feel something like resentment toward Falcon.

And to top off the overflowing bucket of crazy, I kind of don't mind that I don't look like a slob anymore. In fact, I feel a bit relieved that I now have clothes I can wear when I need to look a bit more put together.

My inner turmoil must look like worry because Law swallows and turns to me for the first time since the topic of Falcon came up. He takes my hand in his and links our fingers as he pulls me to him.

"Andy, you have nothing to worry about. You never did. Asola... he'll be lucky to have somebody like you in his life because... you're perfect. You've always been perfect."

Butterflies. My stomach is full of them. They're like battering rams, slamming into the walls of my belly and chest.

"I..." I have no words. Everything that I can think of to say feels inadequate.

"So chin up," he says, but the smile that follows looks forced. "He'd be crazy to turn you down."

Only then do I remember that we were talking about Falcon because my mind is still stuck on Law's previous words.

*You're perfect. You've always been perfect.*

"Besides, I'm used to spending the holiday away from family," Law continues, unaware of my inner turmoil. "It's not a big deal. I'm not sitting at home and moping. I usually go out and it'll distract me just fine."

My throat goes dry. What the hell does he mean by *go out and it'll distract me just fine*? Does that mean he's finding a hook-up? Because it sounds like he's planning to find a hook-up. An uncomfortable feeling settles in my stomach like a weight that is dragging me down.

I'm not jealous. Not at all. Law doesn't owe me anything, and he can go and have sex with whoever he wants to, whenever he wants to. I have no problem with that. Absolutely none. It's not like the two of us are exclusive. Hell, there isn't an us to speak of. I practically begged the guy to have sex with me because I was inexperienced. As far as I know, maybe Law just wants some *good* sex for a change, instead of my fumbling. A good friend would encourage him to go out.

I'm not a good friend, though.

"You have to come," I say resolutely. "I'm not ready to talk to Falcon yet, so if you think that's something that should keep you away, you're wrong. Besides, we've been spending so much time together lately that you can't just cut me off like that. I might go into withdrawal. And don't even get me started on the fact that we're not even halfway done with my sex lessons."

Law stares at me like I've lost my mind. "Sex lessons," he repeats flatly.

"Hey, you're the one that committed yourself to teaching me the intricacies of sex, buddy, so you can't just quit halfway through. I mean, I didn't wait for the results of the physics test, and then go all, *Ah, well, they passed. I'm off to the beach.*"

"You didn't," he agrees with the same monotonous tone, but I'm not letting it stop me. Karma will probably come and bite me in the ass, but while I'm still breathing, Law is not staying in town to have lots of sex with festive party-goers. I'm sorry, he's just not.

"And that means you can't either. You're stuck with me 'til the bitter end."

Law stares at me for a moment, but then he shakes his head and smiles. "I guess I need to pack a bag, then."

## 18

## LAW

Andy's hometown is beautiful. Situated near the state line, it's got a little bit of everything, so it could easily be in a tourism ad. There's a view of the mountains. There are maples. There's a lake. It's downright idyllic.

The town itself is tiny. One of those places where your teachers have also taught your father, your mother, or both when they were in high school, and everybody knows everybody. It's probably a nice place for raising kids. I imagine that children around here are free to play with the neighborhood kids with no need for their parents to chaperone. They can go swimming in the lake and run around in the forest. Wild and free. I can almost picture little Andy doing just that.

Andy's childhood home is on a quiet street, surrounded by massive trees. The house itself is a two-story, gray colonial. Andy smiles as he looks at it before climbing out of the car.

"Home sweet home," he says, and he really means it. My parents' Manhattan apartment has never made me feel nostalgic or warm inside when I visit. They still have my room, but it's in name only. Mom redecorated last year, so it's more like a guest room now. Not that it really matters, I hardly visit for longer than two days at a time anymore.

"So this is where you grew up." I get out of the car and open the trunk to grab our bags.

Andy grabs his duffel from me and grins. "Yup. This is where the magic happened."

Just then, the front door opens, and a woman comes out. "Hi, baby," she says cheerfully as she comes down the porch steps and pulls Andy into a hug. She's almost the same height as Andy, but where he is sinewy, she's slender and graceful. Andy's mom has the same dark brown hair as her son, but her eyes are blue instead of gray, and her features are softer than Andy's.

When Andy's father comes out to greet us, it's clear Andy takes after his mom, since Andy's nothing like his giant of a father. The man is at least a foot taller than me, and I'm not short by any stretch of imagination. Also, Andy's dad is blond. He's like a Viking or a Norse god.

Andy hugs his dad, and then looks at me with a giant smile on his face. "Mom, Dad, this is Law. Law, these are my parents, Jane and Mark."

I reach out my hand, but Andy's mom just pulls me into a hug as well. "We're so happy to finally meet you!"

"It's good to put a face to the name," Andy's dad says. "All we hear lately when we talk to Andy is *Law this* and *Law that*."

Now that's interesting. I turn to Andy. "You've been talking about me?" Andy's cheeks have gone bright red as he glares at his parents. "I may have mentioned you once or twice. Mom and Dad are pathological liars, though. A family curse."

"I resent that," Andy's dad says. "I'm honest to a fault, except for a tiny white lie here and there." He snaps his fingers. "Like when we told you they didn't sell replacement batteries for that god-awful keyboard you loved so much." The man looks at me and speaks from the corner of his mouth. "God love him, but Andy has no musical gifts."

"The TV only works when it rains," Jane says.

"Swallowing your gum makes your poop bounce out of the toilet."

Andy groans at that and hides his face, but that doesn't stop his parents.

"The security cameras are actually Santa cams, and he's always watching," Mark adds to the growing pile of lies. He smirks as he catches my eye. "Andy believed that one 'til he was nine."

"Eating green beans will make your muscles grow." Andy's mom keeps listing, ticking stuff off on her fingers.

"Somebody broke into our house, but they only took the... what was that DVD again?"

*"Finding Nemo,"* Andy's mom supplies.

"Enough!" Andy cries. "Can we just once pretend that we're a normal family? Just for this one weekend?"

Jane and Mark look at each other and shrug at the exact same time. "Sure honey. We can definitely give it our best shot," they say in unison.

Andy sighs and shakes his head at that. "Are the others here already?" he asks, changing the topic.

"Ian took the twins to the store to pick up the new patio table, since somebody"—Jane looks at her husband pointedly—"thought a DIY project was a good idea and tried to turn the old one into a ping-pong table. The girls are coming later today."

"In my defense, Pinterest made it seem so easy."

Andy's mom pats her husband on the cheek. "It always does, hon. It always does."

We grab our bags and head inside. "You two get the attic room," Jane says as Andy groans, but his mom doesn't seem the least bit affected by the expression of misery on her son's face.

"How come I always get shipped off to the attic? It gets unbearably hot there in the summer," Andy complains.

"It's not my fault you don't book a room in advance," Jane says with a shrug.

Andy stops mid-stride. "I'm sorry, what?"

Jane cocks her head to the side. "Everybody else calls me before the big holidays and tells me which room they want."

Andy gapes at her with raised brows. "But... why has nobody told me it's a thing we do?" he finally asks.

"I don't think anybody's been told specifically. The others just caught on a lot sooner that you could call dibs on the better rooms," Jane says with a shrug of her shoulder.

"So this is what betrayal feels like," Andy mutters as we follow his mom up the two flights of stairs until we get to the small door that leads to the attic.

"Here we are," she says cheerfully. "There's a bathroom behind that door, Law. You two will have to share with the twins."

Andy groans. "And the hits just keep coming."

"I forced them to clean it, so you can relax. It looked fine this morning," Jane reassures Andy, but Andy doesn't seem to believe the bathroom could be in decent shape. "I put the sheets and pillows on the bed already, so just drop off your stuff and come back down, so I can put you to work."

"So that's why you were so excited to have us all home. You missed the free labor."

Jane laughs. "That's it. I endured thirty-six hours of increasingly painful contractions with you just so I would have somebody who'd peel the potatoes. You've cracked my evil masterplan. And here I thought Mrs. Patterson was crazy when she tried to tell me that you're a genius in the seventh grade. It obviously took me some time to catch on, but now I can really see it."

I can't help but laugh, especially after Andy gives Jane an exaggerated frown. I like Andy's parents. They don't seem to take life too seriously, which is a contrast to my own parents. I'm already looking forward to meeting the rest of the Carters.

———

Andy's family is loud. It shouldn't exactly come as a surprise, since a) there's a lot of them, even if we're not counting the aunts, uncles and grandparents that will arrive at some point tomorrow, and b) Andy has told me about it and warned me in advance on the drive over. Still, compared to my own family gatherings, which mostly entail a quiet dinner at a fancy restaurant, the Carter family takes me by surprise.

I've been keeping to the background. I want to make a good impression, so it would be embarrassing as hell to call somebody by the wrong name or joke about something that turns out to be a sensitive topic among the Carter clan. I feel like I know these people because Andy has talked about his family a lot. Still, I'm uncharacteristically apprehensive, and a bit nervous.

Just in case, I quiz myself quickly as I stand before a wall of family photographs.

Andy's older brother Ian takes after their dad. He has the same blond Thor look with his large frame and long hair.

The two older sisters, Cecilia and Emily, are also blonde, but where their brother and dad are hulking giants, the women are tall and slender.

Ryan and Landon, or the twins, as everybody refers to them, are slightly shorter than Ian and their dad, but still taller than Andy. They have the same hair color as Andy, but nobody else in the family has the crazy locks Andy sports on his head.

There's also Cecilia's husband, Matt, a self-admitted recovering workaholic, and their daughter, Lily, a shy ten-year-old who mostly just ignores me and has inherited the same love for science her uncle has. In Lily's case, it seems to be astronomy that interests her most.

The wall holds a staggering number of pictures, documenting the history of the Carter family. It's interesting to see their life play out in front of me, but mostly, my eyes are drawn to pictures of Andy. I start with the photos of him when he was a chubby baby, with large, serious, gray eyes, then move on to the ones of the toddler Andy with his mop of already untamable, curly hair. I move on to the teenage Andy, holding up a trophy at what looks to be a science fair, then to Andy on his graduation. I keep staring at that picture the longest. Next to Andy, there's Asola. The guy looks the same as now, except for the wide smile that I've never seen on his face, since he usually glares at me when we're in the same room. What stops me, though, is the fact that Andy isn't looking at the camera. Instead, his eyes are fixated on Asola, and the look in Andy's eyes... it's part worship, part longing.

It's like a sucker punch to the gut.

It registers only now that somewhere down the line, somewhere deep inside me, I've started to entertain a foolish hope that maybe, just maybe, there could be something more between Andy and me.

It's something only a complete idiot would think, considering I promised Andy I'd help him woo Asola. My only excuse is that it has been damn easy to forget Asola even exists. He hasn't really been around this summer, so I've conveniently pushed him out of my mind while I've been steadily falling for Andy myself.

It feels like my heart is jumping into my throat as the thought registers and settles.

Falling for Andy.

Is that what I've been doing?

I want to say no. I want to laugh at the ridiculousness of the thought, but then images jump into my head. Andy gesticulating wildly as he talks about the probability of the existence of dark energy. Andy trying to debate with himself about who should receive the Nobel Prize this year. Andy completing a 5K run without stopping once and the dorky victory dance that followed the achievement. Andy yelling at the TV when he happened to come upon a game of Jeopardy that had questions about National Marine Sanctuaries.

Andy throwing his head back as I suck him into my mouth. Andy letting out a shuddering breath as I push my fingers inside him. Andy arching his back as he comes with a shout, squeezing around me.

I stare at the frames with unblinking eyes.

*Well, shit.*

*I'm in love with Andy Carter.*

I'm so deep inside my head that I almost scream like a little girl as a hand lands on my shoulder and I see Andy's dad standing next to me.

"Fu— fudge," I say. "Mr. Carter."

"Sorry," he says with a grin, but he doesn't really look that apologetic. "And, please, call me Mark." He stuffs his hands in the pockets of his pants. "I see you got lost in the Wall of Shame."

I must look perplexed because Andy's dad chuckles and lets his gaze wander over the frames. "It's what Cecilia used to call it when she was an overdramatic thirteen-year-old." He cocks his head to the side. "In all fairness, we had a picture here of the time she tried to dye her hair platinum blonde and ended up accidentally dying it gray." The man smiles like it's a fond memory. "Good times."

"I'm guessing it worked as an effective punishment."

"Oh yeah, no other crazy hair experiments as far as I know."

We're both quiet for a little while. I keep giving Andy's dad glances out of the corner of my eye. I'm trying to find the resemblance to Andy. I want to know everything about Andy. How he became interested in physics. Where he got his sense of humor. What he was like when he was in preschool.

I want to find out every little detail about Andy because I have an addiction that needs feeding, and this man holds the keys to a vault of information, so I don't know where to start.

"Andy's always been a bit of an odd duck," Mark says. It's almost as if he's sensed my curiosity. "My other kids, they're a lot like me. Athletic, rowdy, loud, outgoing. Andy was never like that. He even *looks* different with that crazy hair of his, and the pale skin. We'd all be out together on a family outing, and people would look at my other kids and then look at Andy, and then they'd give me those sympathetic glances, like, *Oh, that poor schmuck is probably raising the neighbor's kid.*" Mark chuckles and shakes his head at the memory. "Andy looks just like his grandpa, Jane's dad. The guy was a farmer and a real bookworm. Always had a book in hand or tucked in the back pocket of his jeans. Read odd paragraphs here and there whenever he had a free moment. I guess Andy takes after him."

"Genetics are weird," I conclude.

Mark smiles. "Exactly." He looks back at the wall. "I used to worry about Andy," he confesses. "Well, I worry about all my children, it comes with the job of being a dad, but Andy... he didn't have it as easy as my other kids. I suspect he didn't tell anybody how bad school got for him, but for a while there, he just seemed to lose all his spark. It got a bit better for Andy when the Asolas moved next door, and Falcon took Andy under his wing."

I'm not sure where Mark is going with this, but I get an uncomfortable feeling in my stomach. What if he's detected my feelings and is now trying to warn me off because he wants to see his son with Falcon?

*Aaand I'm officially nuts. Great.*

"This summer, though?" Mark continues, blissfully unaware of my inner turmoil. "Andy's... it's almost like he's coming out of his shell. There's this wonderful, magnificent person hidden inside of Andy, but it was as if he was afraid to let anybody see it. He was holding back, even with his family, and I think he's been doing it for so long that he doesn't even realize the extent of it himself." Mark touches my arm, prompting me to look at him. "And then he suddenly mentions this guy he's helping in his free time. And then he starts skipping our Monday night calls because he's busy tutoring. And then he mentions the name Law more and more frequently, with each conversation. He has all these new things he's trying: the gym, hiking, tutoring. And he sounds so damn happy."

It sounds like Mark is giving me a lot of credit for something that I don't think I've had that big of a part in, so I say nothing and keep my eyes trained on the wall of photographs.

"I guess I'm just trying to say that... we're all glad Andy found you," Mark says before he claps me on the back and heads toward the kitchen, leaving me standing there, more confused than ever.

# 19

## ANDY

Friday flies by in a flurry of preparations. We've never been one of those families where the mom has to slave away for a week before the holidays to cook and clean for the family. Instead, for as long as I can remember, we've all come in a day early and spent that day preparing for the next day's festivities.

"It's because Dad is such a feminist," Mom always says with an affectionate smile.

I've chopped and diced and minced everything Mom has pushed in front of me over the last several hours. Law has been next to me the whole time. He's been relegated to peeling duties since Mom wasn't impressed with what Law did to the garlic he was supposed to mince.

It's Ryan and Ian's turn to tackle the cake this year, while Cecilia, Emily, Landon and Dad deal with the yard. We have a huge backyard, which is in a perpetual state of disarray. None of us mind, but in the spirit of holidays, we usually mow the lawn and clean it up a bit.

By six o'clock, we're done for the day. We've prepped the food for tomorrow's garden party. The yard doesn't look as overgrown as it usually does, and Law, my siblings, and I are chilling out on the back porch, watching Ian and Landon bicker as they try to hang up the string lights Mom bought.

"Can you not pull it?" Ian grouses from his spot on the porch.

"Oh, I'm sorry," Landon says sweetly. "I thought you wanted the lights to hang. Didn't realize you were planning to just lay them on the ground." Ian yanks at the cord and Landon stumbles a few steps forward.

"Hey!" he protests and immediately retaliates by pulling the cord himself. Ian loses his balance and steps on one of the bulbs. It's a miracle it took so long for the first casualty.

"You little shit," Ian says matter-of-factly as he lets go of the cord and steps over the mess of lights on the ground in front of him. Landon's eyes flitter left and right as Ian approaches. Without warning, Landon takes off toward the trees at the back of the yard. Ian jumps over the railing and follows him until they both disappear into the forest and only an occasional shout informs us they're both still alive out there.

Cecilia shakes her head as she leans against her husband. "We should have done it ourselves. Less blood to clean up later."

Ryan stretches out on the porch, totally unconcerned about the well-being of his twin. "It wouldn't have been as entertaining. Watching Ian and Landon try and hang the lights is the highlight of my month."

Law cocks his head to the side and smiles. "That happens every year?" he asks, pointing to the trees where Ian is still, presumably, chasing after Landon. Unless one of them has already killed the other.

"Oh yeah." Emily chuckles. "It's part of the plan. Prepare the food. Clean up the garden. Watch Ian and Landon duke it out over hanging the lights. When you think about it, it's like a tradition."

"You guys are a strange bunch," Law says, but with an affectionate smile, like he doesn't mind at all.

"Thank you," Cecilia replies and grins.

Matt looks at Law. "Don't worry, you'll get used to the weirdness."

"We'll turn you into one of us," Ryan says from his spot on the ground. "We thought Matt would never get rid of that stick up his ass when Cecilia started bringing him around, but look at him now.

We've been sitting here for at least an hour, and he hasn't brought up work once."

Emily straightens herself. "That's a good point. Now that you've mentioned it, I haven't seen him on the phone once all day. What gives, Mattie? Did you crash the stock market and are in hiding?"

"Hey! I'll let you know, I can relax and not work just fine," Matt protests.

"Says the guy who threw a hissy fit in the airport when his luggage got lost."

"To be fair," Law says diplomatically, "it sucks when that happens."

"They were on their way to their honeymoon, and Matt had hidden his laptop in his suitcase," Emily says, and everybody starts laughing. "According to Cecilia, Matt had an epic meltdown."

"If you must know, I've decided to reevaluate my work-life balance," Matt says primly, before he looks to the side and mutters, "and Cee confiscated my phone because I was using it at the dinner table. I've got a one-week penalty."

There's a beat of silence before everybody erupts into laughter again. Matt and Cecilia are one of those couples who seem like they come from two different planets. But they just fit, even though my hippy, music teacher sister is Matt's polar opposite in nearly everything.

My eyes search out Law. He's leaning against the porch railing, legs stretched out in front of him, laughing with my brothers and sisters. He's seamlessly merged into the family dynamic, and everybody treats him like he's not a guest, but a member of the family. Law's quick wit and good sense of humor mean that he can give it as good as he gets when it comes to teasing and bantering, which is a skill as necessary as breathing when it comes to this bunch.

The French doors that lead to the porch from the living room open, and Mom slips out with a cup of coffee. She looks at us and then at the discarded lights on the porch. "Ian and Landon?" she asks.

"Ian and Landon," we all confirm in unison and laugh again.

"Where's Dad?" Emily asks.

"He fell asleep in front of the TV when Lily coerced him into watching one of her space documentaries," Mom says distractedly. "Should I bring the first aid kit?" She angles her head in the direction Ian and Landon had disappeared in.

Cecilia shrugs. "Might come in handy, but I say let them doctor each other. It'll be a teaching moment."

Mom fist bumps Cecilia and takes a seat.

It's a nice evening. It's barely seven o'clock. The air is muggy and hot, and it makes everybody feel lazy. I wouldn't mind a cold shower, but I don't feel like going upstairs yet. I look around and smile. It's one of those perfect moments where absolutely everything in the world feels right. I'm surrounded by people I love, and for once, I feel completely at peace. I don't feel like I have to impress anybody or change myself to fit in. I can just *be*, because these people right here are the ones who know me best in the whole world, and they like me just the way I am. No pressure and no expectations, just unconditional love.

My gaze lands on Law, and for a moment, I'm stumped. When I was thinking about the people nearest and dearest to me, I counted Law in without even having to think about it. I don't think I've ever trusted another person so quickly and easily, but then again, I've never met anybody like Law either. Law turns his head and looks at me. He cocks his head to the side and mouths, "All right?"

I smile and nod. "Perfect," I mouth back.

That's the moment when Emily asks, "Hey, where's Falcon?" and I feel like a balloon has been popped inside me because, *Oh yeah, Falcon.* The guy I've been crushing on for years... and that I haven't thought about in days.

"Earth to Andy."

I flip my head toward my sister. "What?"

She looks at me with raised brows. "I asked you where Falcon was. I would have thought the two of you would be joined at the hip now that you've been forced to spend so much time apart."

"Ha ha." I roll my eyes at Emily.

"No, but seriously, where is he?" Ryan straightens himself and looks around like he suspects Falcon might be hiding in the bushes.

I shrug. "Home, I guess?"

"You don't know?" All my siblings are looking at me like I've said something unthinkable. I'm saved from further discussion about Falcon by Ian and Landon, who walk out of the forest and sit down on the porch.

"We decided that we don't need the lights," Landon announces and flops down next to Ryan.

"It's summer. It doesn't get dark until late into the night," Ian adds.

"Lights are more of a Christmas thing," Landon says.

"Forgoing lights in the summer helps reduce our carbon footprint," Ian says.

Mom rolls her eyes. "I really need to just hire somebody," she mutters as she gets up from her chair. "I need to get ready. Dad and I are going out for drinks with the Asolas."

Cecilia pats Matt's leg. "We should get ready too. I said we'd meet Chloe and the others at seven thirty, and we need to get Lily ready."

One by one, people get up and go into the house. Most of my family has made plans to meet up with friends while they're in town, so they'll be going to bars, barbecues, parties—all of them have plans. Soon, it's just me and Law sitting on the porch in the fading light of the day.

Law has his head leaned back, and he's tapping out a rhythm with his fingers. I smile as I look at him. A strand of hair has fallen over his left eye, and without giving any thought to what I'm about to do, I lean forward and push it away. I don't stop there, though. Mesmerized, I let my fingertips slide over Law's cheeks and nose. I caress over every ridge and valley of his face. Our gazes lock as my fingers continue their exploration. Law's lips are slightly parted, and I skate the pad of my thumb over his lower lip. He pushes the tip of his tongue against my thumb and my breath hitches as he slowly licks over the skin, making my whole body tingle.

Law's palm rests on my thigh, and I'm hovering above him. There's an overwhelming sense of rightness in what I'm about to do—kiss a boy in my parents' backyard.

I'm just about to lower my lips to Law's when I hear the metallic clank of the foot gate that connects our yard with Asolas' backyard.

"Hello? Anybody home?" I snap up my head at Falcon's voice. The moment is broken into so many tiny pieces that I couldn't even begin to count them. I look up, tearing my eyes away from Law. At the sight of Falcon's battered flip flops, which are the first thing I see from behind the overgrown Magnolia bush, reality snaps into place, and I scramble off of Law.

This moment between Law and me is too intimate and precious to share with anybody, not even my best friend.

Falcon emerges from the bushes and freezes when he sees us on the porch. He blinks and his brow furrows as he slowly comes closer. "Hey," he says. "When did you get here?"

"This morning." I glance at Law who is staring at me with an inscrutable expression. "Around nine?" Law nods. "About that, yeah."

Falcon raises his brows. "Oh, well thanks for the heads up." He sounds hurt, which I get since, even if I didn't appreciate the earlier teasing, my siblings were right. Falcon has been my best friend for years, and we have always spent most of our free time together.

"I meant to text." The excuse is weak, my guilt shining through brightly.

"And what's he doing here?" Falcon glares at Law.

"I invited him."

Falcon looks gobsmacked. "Why?"

He's being really rude, but Law doesn't seem that bothered by Falcon's attitude. It takes me a moment to remember that, *Oh yeah, there was that whole deal with the feud.*

"He's my friend." I take a step toward Law.

That makes Falcon purse his lips. "Since when?"

"A while now," I say evasively. It's not the right time to talk about my and Law's friendship. I don't feel like listening to a lecture right now, and I can see from Falcon's expression that that's the way he's heading.

"So, what's up?" I ask in a poor attempt to move the conversation to another topic.

For a moment, I'm afraid I'm going to get the lecture anyway, but eventually, Falcon looks away from Law and concentrates all his attention on me. "There's a bonfire with some of the high school gang. You should come."

"Oh." I glance at Law. It's a chance to spend time with Falcon, so I should take it, but the truth is, I'd rather stay here with Law. This whole situation has my head spinning with confusion. I've loved Falcon for years, but this summer, every time I'm put in a situation where I have to choose between him and Law, I find myself leaning toward Law.

I've never been impulsive or quick to change my mind. All my decisions are the result of a long and thorough thought process. I weigh all my options and try to leave emotions out of the equation. I've applied the same logic to Falcon as well. I mean, yeah, there's love, sure, but more than that, the two of us together just make sense. I don't see any big hurdles in our way, except for that telling-Falcon-about-my-feelings part, but after that, it should be smooth sailing from there on. It's what I want. Always have. Because that's the plan.

My gaze lands on Law, and the already familiar fluttering feeling inside makes me press my palm against my stomach. It kind of feels like my internal organs are trying to escape, but not in a disgusting, painful way. More like I'm slowly gaining the ability to fly, and my lungs, liver and all that other stuff inside me has just gotten a head start.

I don't know what to do with that, though. Whatever it is I feel for Law, it's not the same regular warmth Falcon elicits in me. Far from it. It's kind of uncomfortable, to be honest. What I feel for Falcon is like a nice, cozy blanket on a cold evening, whereas what I feel for Law is like a cold shower early in the morning—impossible not to notice and it eventually makes you feel so damn alive. But then again, it's not generally considered pleasurable being blasted with icy water, is it?

Law makes me step outside of my comfort zone, and it's not enjoyable. There's been blood and anxiety and sleep deprivation. I still don't think six a.m. is an acceptable time to wake up, but I can't really deny that, thanks to Law, I don't feel like I'm standing still anymore.

"So?" Falcon asks. "Are we doing this or not?"

I'm still not sure what to do, so I glance at Law, hoping he'll give me a sign about what *he* wants to do. He stares at Falcon's profile for a long moment before he looks down and then at me. He has a weird expression on his face, but it's quickly replaced by a smile. It looks forced and unnatural, but Law nods at me encouragingly and gives Falcon a pointed look. *Go for it*, he seems to say. *Catch the ball or puck or insert your own sports metaphor here.*

I'm basing a lot of it on his body language, and we've already established that I'm shit at interpreting other people's gestures and facial expressions. For all I know Law is begging me with his eyes to never leave him. All in all, this silent exchange does a fat lot of good for me right now.

Law must be sensing my hesitation because he leans forward. "That sounds like fun."

I guess we're going out.

And I have the answer to what I want to do, because I'm definitely disappointed about the direction my night is taking.

# LAW

I am in hell.

Not the literal kind, although there is a fire, albeit a small one. There are also people around me yelling and shouting. Again, it's not because they're burning alive for their sins, more like a lot of them are drunk and just happy. But if we follow the logic that hell is a place of suffering and torture, I'm definitely in it.

I'm by the bonfire, and I'm forced to watch Andy with Falcon. I am the third wheel here, and not like, say, on a tricycle. Nope. I'm the third wheel on a racing bike. Unnecessary and useless.

Andy laughs at something that Falcon says, and I give Asola the stink eye, even though he doesn't notice it and most likely doesn't care. And why should he? He gets Andy all to himself.

There are people around me talking about... something. I'm really not following the conversation since I'm too busy staring at Andy. And trying to ignore the inside jokes and stories of camping trips and sleepovers and every other fantastic activity that Andy has done with Asola over the years.

All this night has done is hammer home how monumentally stupid I've been in my hope that Andy could just shake off his feelings for Asola and choose me instead. Without Asola anywhere in sight, it has been easy to forget he even exists, but now when I get to watch the two of them sitting here, shoulders pressing together, laughing, joking, swapping stories, it's becoming increasingly obvious how arrogant I've been in thinking that I could somehow challenge the connection between them.

I rub my fingertips over my forehead. Asola says something about being able to run faster than wasps, which is impossible to understand without knowing any background of the story, and Andy throws his head back and laughs.

I stand up so quickly that I almost lose my balance. Andy looks up and smiles. "Whoa there," he says and places his palm on my thigh to steady me, and I almost fall again in my haste to back away from his touch. Andy looks at me questioningly, and I give him a tight smile.

"Bathroom," I say as an explanation and hightail it out of there.

I need a second to gather myself. Otherwise I'll probably do something idiotic like beg Andy to choose me. I walk away from the bonfire and wander around until I end up by the river. I take a seat on the ground and try to put things into perspective.

I promised Andy I'd help him with Falcon, and I'm going to. Andy has become my best friend, so I have to push my feelings aside and do what I promised—help Andy with Falcon, even if it makes my insides feel like they've been put through a shredder.

I drop onto the ground on my back and stare at the sky. There are a lot of stars, and for a while, I feel a tiny bit calmer.

That lasts a good fifteen minutes, and then Andy walks out of the forest and plunks down next to me.

"I was starting to think you got lost," he says.

I try for a smile, but it ends up feeling like a grimace on my lips. I motion vaguely to the stars. "I needed a moment to myself. I'm not used to loud parties anymore, I guess."

"You? The big, strapping hockey god?"

"Phew, finally somebody gets my title right."

Andy pushes at my shoulder and laughs, and I feel lighter already. When Asola is nowhere in the vicinity, everything is perfect.

"You're not having fun at the party," Andy observes. I can feel his gaze on me, but I just stare at the stars. It's hard enough that I have to let him go, I don't need to see him while I do it.

"I'm just having an off night."

"Why didn't you say anything? We can go back home and just chill." I glance at Andy, who looks at me with concern and sort of like he'd be willing to steal a car if I needed to get out of here right this second. Why does he have to be so perfect?

I grit my teeth and slam a lid on my feelings. Andy's happiness is the most important thing.

"I'm fine," I say. "Besides, you can't leave yet. I've been thinking about you and Asola, and I think you should tell him how you feel. Just rip the Band-Aid off, you know?"

Andy stares at me without blinking. A small wrinkle appears between his eyebrows, but I just keep going, because if I stop I might lose what little determination I've gathered. "I know it feels scary, but that's okay. You're going to put yourself out there, so it's normal to be nervous."

Jesus Christ, I sound like a doctor who's trying to talk a kid into getting his shots. I try again. "Andy, you're great. Asola would be a real idiot not to want you. I mean, he actually *is* an idiot"—Andy shoves me—"but I'd be willing to bet that this is the one time he'll use the few brain cells he has and, you know, see what's been right in front of him the whole time."

Andy still looks unsure, so I amp it up another notch.

"You two are perfect together."

*Somebody shoot me.*

"Practically childhood sweethearts."

*I'm going to puke.*

"He's going to be happy about this."

*And I will want to die.*

"It's time, Andy," I say firmly, and finally, he nods.

*Huh.*

I guess now I know what heartbreak feels like.

# ANDY

I walk through the darkness toward the bonfire that is flickering somewhere behind the trees. I feel like I'm free falling, or at least I suppose the hollow feeling inside me resembles the sensation of jumping off a cliff and hurtling rapidly toward the ground.

Social interactions have always posed some difficulties for me, but now more than ever, I feel like I'm stumped.

I had sex with Law. Even the thought of it seems unreal, and if it weren't for that faint hickey right under my collarbone to remind me of what happened, I would probably think I made it all up in my head.

The sex itself was perfect. Every moment of it. And fucking hot, and I really want to do it again and again and again. But judging by how Law has steadily pulled away from me ever since we got out of bed the next morning, I don't think Law is going to volunteer as tribute.

He's been distant and serious and he keeps giving me those looks when he thinks I won't notice. I feel like he's pulling away from me, and I don't know what to do about it.

Things have only gotten more complicated with the addition of Falcon into the mix. The thing is, right now, I should be sitting by that damn bonfire next to Falcon, trying to figure out how to get him alone to tell the man that I love him, and that we should shack up for real and have lots of sex and be happy forever.

It sounds like a solid plan.

In theory.

In reality, I'm dragging my feet, trying to come up with a reason to turn around and go back to Law. I can't make sense of what I'm feeling anymore. It feels like I'm standing at a crossroads, but I'm not sure how I got here, and if it's even really a crossroads.

The fact is that over the last few weeks, I've slowly started to see Law differently. What started out with Law seeming like an annoyance and a borderline stalker, turned into a genuine friendship and now... Shit! I don't know what's going on between us now, but I think it's safe to say that the things I've done with Law and the things I feel for him have firmly jumped past the friendship zone and landed in the territory of confusion, which is exactly what I promised Law would not happen.

What makes this whole situation even worse is the fact that I'm almost a hundred percent sure Law knows about my developing feelings. He started to push me toward Falcon the moment the guy made an appearance, and now he's given me a pep talk about how I should go and tell Falcon that I love him. Law has all but tied a ribbon around my naked body and placed me on Falcon's doorstep, but instead of embracing the opportunity, I'm struggling to get free.

I groan and thump my forehead against the trunk of the big maple next to me. The only good it does me is leaving a scratch above my left eyebrow. I should never have started scheming in the first place. I should have continued being the sweats-wearing, awkward, nerdy sidekick. But no. I just had to ruin it by thinking I could be a hero. I could have just nursed my crush on Falcon without the added complication of ever telling him.

"What a fucking idiot," I say out loud.

"Andy?" I nearly jump out of my skin at Falcon's voice on my right.

"Eep!" I'm not proud of the high-pitched voice that escapes my mouth.

"What are you doing here?" Falcon asks. Already there's a familiar, concerned look on his face. "What's wrong? Whose ass do I have to kick?" He looks around, ready to stand up and face the enemy. He gets that way a lot when he's near me. I've never been bothered by it. It has always felt caring, but now, I can't stop comparing Falcon with Law.

Falcon always seems to want to do all the fighting for me, whereas Law supports me while I fight. Sometimes he even pushes me toward the confrontation. The contrast between the two is so sharp, and it's not to the benefit of Falcon. I understand why he's like that, considering our history, but it can't go on like this. The realization, which now feels like it's been a long time coming, is like a puzzle piece, clicking into place.

I wonder if I would be so keenly aware of the unhealthiness of the dynamic between me and Falcon if it weren't for Law.

"Andy?" Falcon sounds impatient. "Was somebody giving you trouble?"

"There's no one here." It comes out more sharply than I intend.

Falcon raises his brows. "Easy there, tiger. I was just trying to help."

"I can handle myself."

He frowns. "Okay."

I take a deep breath and blow it out through my teeth. "Sorry," I mutter.

"It's fine." He waves me off. "What are you doing here?"

"I wanted some peace and quiet."

"Okay. Are you coming back to the party?"

"Sure." I nod. "I just needed a breather."

Falcon leans his shoulder against the tree and settles in.

"You don't have to stay because of me," I say.

"It's fine. We haven't hung out at all lately. I miss you."

My heart gives a loud thud. It's nice to hear it. It's nice to be missed, I guess. I don't have a lot of people outside of my family who feel that way about me, and despite my mind being all messed up, Falcon is still one of my best friends. Has been for years.

"I've missed you too," I say.

"This summer has been weird," he says. "We haven't really spoken at all, and it's not like it's the first summer we've lived in different places, but this one feels different."

I nod. He's right. We used to text and call all the time, but this year, that hasn't happened. I've been busy with Law, and tutoring, and work, and I've only been home once, even though last year I drove back all the time, even finding excuses to stretch some of the weekends longer whenever I could.

Maybe that's the problem? What if I'm not questioning my feelings about Falcon? What if it's just the general weirdness of being apart for such a long time? That seems plausible, doesn't it? Ian once dated a girl who lived in Toronto, and since neither of them wanted to move, they did the long-distance thing. Ian said that the first day they met up after spending time apart was always super weird.

That sounds like a plausible theory, to be honest. Falcon and I are in a long-distance relationship, and now we're in the weird phase.

So I've got my theory, and now I just need to confirm the hypothesis. We sit in silence, and at least that's not weird. I ponder the situation. What if I do nothing? We'd just go on as we always have. Falcon and I would be friends, and Law and I... well, I'm not sure what Law and I would be. Also friends? Somehow I don't see the three of us all hanging out together.

The more I think about it, though, the more I realize that going back to the way things were is just not an option. Maybe I've failed in my quest to turn myself into a hero, but I *have* changed. I've stepped out of my comfort zone so many times over the course of the summer, and all in all, I'm still alive. Sure, there have been moments of embarrassment, anxiety, and stupidity while I was trying to face my fears, but I haven't let them drag me down. Instead, I moved on, and this summer has been one of the best in my life because, for the first time in my life, I don't feel like a pathetic loser when I look at myself. I feel... tentatively confident, which doesn't sound like something to brag about, but for me, it's a big improvement. So fuck what everybody else might think, I'm going to be proud of myself.

Fired up by my own thoughts, I turn toward Falcon, who's still leaning against the tree, hands in his pockets, a dreamy smile on his face as he looks up at the clear night sky. Maybe one more step out of the comfort zone will bring even better results?

"I need to tell you something."

"Shoot." He straightens himself, and almost immediately starts fidgeting, hopping from one foot to the other. "Or wait a sec. My bladder is about to burst." He moves a couple of trees over, and I can hear the distinct sound of zipper being pulled down. Then I hear piss hitting the leaves.

Okay, so it's not exactly romantic, and it's not going as I planned, but whatever, I'm determined now. I'll do it. Law believes in me, and I'm not going to let him down.

Falcon moves back over to me and looks at me expectantly.

So… I'm just gonna go for it. Heart in my throat, I press my nails into the soft part of my palm.

"I love you."

Falcon cocks his head curiously to the side and smiles. "That's nice. Love you, too."

Again, not exactly how I imagined this going. I thought there'd be more confusion, and I'd have to explain myself, but Falcon is smiling at me and doesn't look that shocked by my admission.

It takes an embarrassing amount of time to realize that Falcon hasn't gotten what I meant.

For a moment, I'm tempted to leave it at that, but then I hear Law's voice in my head, urging me on. *You can do it, Andy.*

I guess it's time for the second take. "No, what I mean is, I…" *I am in love with you.* The words refuse to leave my mouth. They don't feel right. It's like I'm juggling with the words and they refuse to align perfectly. I fumble for a second before I blurt out, "I have feelings for you."

Falcon frowns. "What do you mean?"

"I have feelings," I repeat. "Feelings that are not entirely friendly anymore. I guess what I'm trying to say is that I have unfriendly feelings for you?" So much for my staggering confidence.

"I'm not sure anymore if you're pissed at me or the other way around," Falcon says slowly.

I replay what I've said in my mind. Yeah, I see how that might have been confusing.

"I have a crush on you." I bite my lip as I stare at Falcon. It feels like an out-of-body experience. This moment isn't real. Somebody else is telling those things to Falcon through my mouth because it can't possibly be me.

Falcon doesn't exactly look ecstatic about my revelation. At the same time, he doesn't seem totally put off either, so I guess that's a win?

"Andy…" He says nothing else.

I don't know what to do with that.

"Yeah," I say, and then we're both just staring each other. It's not awkward, and I'm not embarrassed or anything. As far as feelings go, I don't seem to have anything to offer. I'm a bit indifferent about the outcome of my big revelation, which is extremely underwhelming, seeing as I've harbored this crush for years. It's all very anticlimactic, to be honest.

"Right," Falcon says. He's all businesslike now. "Kiss me."

I take a step back. "W-w-what?"

"Kiss me," Falcon repeats and takes a step closer. "You have a crush on me, so let's test it out."

I shove my palms out in front of me. "Whoa there, buddy."

He stops his advance and frowns. "What?"

"Nothing. Just… give me a moment."

He stands still and waits. I take a deep breath and step closer. I can do this. Kissing is easy. I've had plenty of practice over the last few weeks.

It takes no time for the toes of my sneakers to bump against Falcon's. I look up at him, startled for a moment not to encounter the bright green gaze I've become used to over the summer.

*Falcon. That's Falcon you're about to kiss, and that's what you've wanted for years now, Andy,* I lecture myself.

I take a deep breath as if to reassure myself and then I go for it. I press my mouth to Falcon's. For a second, nothing happens. Then, Falcon tilts his head to the side and kisses me. Objectively speaking, it's a nice kiss. No tongue. His lips are soft and warm. He doesn't slobber all over my face.

Falcon is a decent kisser.

And there's something seriously wrong with me because I'm kissing the guy of my dreams, and yet I have time to critique his technique.

"This isn't doing anything for you, is it?" Falcon asks against my lips.

I shake my head, sliding our lips against each other as my head moves from side to side.

Falcon pulls away and wipes the back of his hand over his lips. "So… was it earth shattering for you, too?" he asks drolly.

I push him, and he laughs as he stumbles back until he hits the big maple with his back.

"It was…" I say, not sure how to finish it politely.

"Gross?" Falcon offers.

"Wow," I say, pretending to be offended. "I guess the fireworks were just on my end, then."

Falcon laughs. "Oh please. I could practically hear you thinking while we were smashing our lips together." He rolls his eyes. "Fireworks, my ass."

I sit down like a deflated balloon man. "It was not what I was expecting," I mutter. "I kept thinking, *This is weird.*"

Falcon drops down next to me. "Exactly. Don't ever make me do that again."

"I don't think you have to worry about that." I shoot him a strained smile. "I'm sorry."

Falcon shrugs one shoulder. "No biggie. At least now I know what it'd feel like to kiss my own brother, so I guess thanks for the experience? I mean, as an only child, how would I have known otherwise?"

"If only all the people who think you're so cool knew what a weirdo you actually are."

Falcon motions toward the bonfire. "By all means, go educate the masses."

I snort. "Like any of them would believe me."

"You can take it as a compliment, you know? You're the only one that gets to see me when I let my freak flag fly."

"I'm honored."

"As well you should be."

We both laugh, but then Falcon turns serious. "So... want to tell me what brought that whole unfriendly crush forward?"

I rub my palm over my face. "Not really."

Silence descends between us again before Falcon drops a bomb. "I kind of thought you were sleeping with Anderson." He makes a face as he says Law's name, and I gape at him because, *What the hell?* I mean, it's true, but still, *What the hell?*

"You two seemed awfully cozy on your parents' porch earlier," Falcon continues, unbothered by my unsuccessful attempts at speaking.

"What?"

"Dude, you were straddling him."

"You saw that?" I croak.

"It's not like that magnolia bush is a concrete wall." He rolls his eyes.

"Well, shit." I laugh. What else is there to do?

"Yeah," he says thoughtfully. "Which was why I was kind of surprised about the whole feelings thing you just spouted at me. You've never once looked at me the way you look at him."

I swallow hard. "What way is that?"

"Like he's the best thing that's ever happened to you," he says simply. Falcon studies me for a bit. "He looks at you the same way, you know?"

I groan and drag my hands through my hair. "I don't know what happens now," I admit.

"Well," Falcon says, cool as a cucumber. "I'd suggest making that speech again, but to a different audience."

Then he looks at me and purses his lips. "Scratch that. You need to say everything differently. The fuck was the unfriendly feelings crap?"

"I got nervous," I grumble. "You try and say romantic shit when you're about to pee your pants from nerves."

"Okay, add *go to the bathroom before talking to Law* to your to-do list," Falcon says.

I smack him up the back of his head. "Shut up."

Falcon jumps up and reaches out his hand. "Right. Come on."

I let him pull me to my feet. "Where are we going?"

"*We* are going to come up with a plan." He starts walking. "God knows without me you're going to start with the peeing line."

"I heard that," I yell after him.

"You were meant to," he shoots back over his shoulder.

I shake my head and chuckle as I follow Falcon through the trees. Once again, Falcon has taken the lead, but this time, I catch up to him quickly, and we continue our walk side by side.

I guess it's the start of a new chapter.

# LAW

It's official.

I'm a coward.

And an asshole.

I ran away. Sent a text to Andy with a bogus excuse of a sudden work emergency and took off in the middle of the night like the gutless asshole that I am. I pushed Andy into Falcon's arms and then got the hell out of there because watching those two make googly eyes at each other during the Fourth of July celebration sounded about as delightful as volunteering to let somebody demonstrate the use of experimental torture devices on me.

So here I am, in the afternoon of a national holiday that people usually spend with family, and I'm one hundred percent alone. My only companion is the bag of takeout from the Chinese place down the street.

The streets of Montpelier have been decked out with flags and balloons. There was a parade earlier, but I wasn't in the mood to go and celebrate. All the happy people make my loneliness more pronounced, so I hurry toward my apartment, avoiding eye contact and ignoring the cheerful shouts and waves.

I have a plan. I'll give myself exactly two days to wallow, and then, come Monday, I'll fix a fucking smile on my face and continue on like nothing has happened. For now, though, it's Netflix and junk food.

I speed walk to my apartment to limit my exposure to the holiday cheer. I try to wrestle my keys out of my pocket while jogging up the stairs and almost lose my balance on the landing. I let out a curse as I steady myself. I'm so damn occupied with the keys I don't notice the next obstacle, so I unceremoniously trip on somebody's feet.

"What the—" I lift my eyes, and I must be seeing things because there, in front of my door, sits Andy.

"Hi," he says cheerfully as I gape at him.

"Hi."

My heart soars at the sight of Andy, sweats and messy hair and all. He looks just like he did the first time I found him waiting on my doorstep, and I take a step toward him, ready to kiss him before I remember that we're not doing that anymore.

I lick my lips and stuff the hand that isn't holding the takeout bag into my pocket. "What are you doing here?"

I pull out my key. Andy moves to the side, and I step forward, inhaling deeply as I pass him on my way to the door. I don't know what he bathes in, but Andy smells better than anybody else I've ever met.

He shrugs. "I was in the neighborhood." Andy follows me inside and closes the door behind him.

I toe off my sneakers and place the paper bag of food on the kitchen table. "And you just happened to stop by?" I ask. My hands are shaking as I unpack the food.

Andy drops his laptop bag on the couch and turns toward me. "We have unfinished business," he says as he opens his bag. He places his laptop on my coffee table. Then he pulls out a small projector and turns in a circle, inspecting his surroundings as he mumbles under his breath about *the right wall*.

I step closer. "What's all this?"

Andy looks up from where he's kneeling on the floor, connecting the projector to his laptop. "We have a tutoring session." He aims the projector toward the white wall behind my TV and nods, satisfied with his work. "Take a seat," he tells me and points toward the couch.

"You don't need to tutor me anymore," I remind him, but already, my feet are moving toward the couch.

"It's one of those buy-one-get-one-free deals," Andy says. "Just go with it."

I zip my lips and concentrate all my attention on Andy. Hah! Like I'm even capable of looking at anything or anyone else when Andy is in the room. I take advantage of the moment and look my fill. Fuck knows if I'll ever get the chance again.

There are shadows underneath Andy's eyes. They're barely there, but I notice them because I know Andy's face. I love Andy's face. I love the tiny dimple that becomes visible only when he laughs out loud. I love the bow of his lips. I love the silvery-gray eyes that are now aimed at me.

Andy raises one eyebrow. "Ready?"

I nod. I don't know what's happening, and I have no idea how Andy is even here, but I'm going to enjoy the fact that Andy is in front of me. It might be the last time.

"I thought we'd spice it up a bit, and I've added a slide show to today's lesson," Andy says and presses a key on his laptop, bringing the projector alive.

*Magnetism*, the title reads in big, bold letters.

"Magnetism," Andy says. He looks nervous for some reason as he looks at the screen, then at me, then at the wall, and then he makes a stiff hand gesture toward the title. "Magnets," he says, "have this fun little quirk. They can snap together and then stick like that until you pry them apart.

"Not always, though," Andy continues. "Sometimes magnets repel each other." He glances at me quickly, and his hand is shaking a bit as he clicks a key on his laptop. The title slide is replaced by the next slide.

I stare at the wall. There, on my living room wall, are two pictures. Not of magnets, as the title would suggest. Instead, it's a selfie of Andy and a picture of me that looks like it's taken from the hockey team's website, where they have headshots of all of us. In between the photos, somebody has drawn some arrows that point away from each other.

My gaze shoots toward Andy. He looks away from me quickly, licks his lips, swallows, and continues. "Magnets have poles—a north pole and a south pole—and when you try to push together, say, two north poles, the two magnets push away from each other because their forces are not compatible."

The slide changes again. This time, there's a photo of a... pizza? I'm guessing it's a reference to the Italian restaurant we were at when I convinced Andy to coach me in tutoring.

Andy continues speaking and clicking through slides. There are all sorts of pictures that look random at a first glance but actually are all related to my and Andy's history. All the while, Andy continues talking about magnets. Magnetization. Magnetic fields. Permanent magnets. Electromagnets. Only he's not really talking about magnets.

Picture after picture appears on my wall. All of them telling our story.

Only in this version, it's not only me who feels the attraction. According to the pictures on my wall, Andy has spent these last few weeks falling in love with me too. Andy stops at a slide that has a photo I've never seen before. It's Andy and I in Andy's parents' backyard. We're sitting next to each other and we're smiling. If the look on my face doesn't scream *love*, then I'm a blob fish.

"Attraction," Andy says.

Of course, right as my heart soars with hope, there's another picture change, and now there's a photo of Falcon.

He clicks again and the slide changes. This time it's two stick figures. One of them has a crazy head of hair. The stick figures are drawn standing close together. They're kissing. I rear back like I've been slapped.

Man, that's a cruel and unusual way to find out that the guy you're in love with does *not*, in fact, feel the same way about you. The pain I'm feeling inside must be all over my face because Andy shouts, "No! Wait. Please, you have to watch the whole thing." He clicks and a thought bubble appears above their heads with just one word in capital letters: *EWW!*

Andy clicks again, and… that's the end of the slideshow.

I blink a couple of times at the abrupt conclusion.

He bites his lower lip as he ends the presentation with elaborate, magician-like hand gestures and says, "Ooh, a cliffhanger!"

Andy bends down and takes something from his bag. He walks toward me, his fingers wrapped in a fist to conceal whatever he's hiding in his palm. He stops in front of me and shoves his hand toward me. I cock my head to the side and slowly raise my hand, palm up. I study the small magnet that lands in my hand.

"Hold it up," Andy instructs me.

I do as he says, and he kneels in front of me so that we're at eye level with each other. Between Andy's fingers, there's another magnet. He brings it forward until the two click together.

"I find myself strangely attracted to you," Andy says with a shrug. Then he winces. "Shit! That was the wrong one. Umm. Soul mates attract each other like magnets?" he says like he's not sure of himself. Then he scrunches his nose. "Man, that sounds even cheesier than it did when we practiced it. Damnit, I'm fucking it all up." He swipes his palm over his forehead. "Did you swallow magnets because you're so attractive?" he rushes out and then slams his eyes shut and groans.

I think I'm in a state of shock. One that even extremely bad puns can't seem to bring me out of.

Andy peeks at me through his curls. "Did any of that make you want to bang me with undying passion?" he asks and scrunches his nose.

Well, that does it.

"What?" I ask.

"Ah, fuck it," Andy says and throws his magnet on the floor. "Okay. Here's the thing. I'm going to tell you something, but you've got to promise you won't freak out."

He pauses dramatically, and it kind of looks like he's about to pass out before he blurts out, "I'm in love with you. And I know I promised there wouldn't be any feelings and shit, but I failed. So… oops?

Although, I'd like for you to take into consideration that it wouldn't have happened if you weren't so goddamn irresistible and funny and smart and great, so if you think about it, really, it's your fault that we're in this pickle to begin with." He raises his palms like he expects me to argue. "Now, I'm prepared to take half the blame. Well, maybe we'll split it forty-sixty. Anyway, the point is that, yeah, there's love. Inside me."

Andy takes a deep breath, which is good because the guy looks like he's about to pass out. Me, on the other hand? Well, I'm speechless. Happiness settles over me, deep and all-encompassing. It feels like there's sunshine inside me. I feel lighter than I've ever felt before and holding my smile back is impossible.

"Would you say," I start as I slide down on the floor in front of Andy, "that what you feel for me is like an impenetrable stone wall of feelings?" I ask because it wouldn't be us without a bit of teasing.

Andy's eyes widen as he remembers the rambling from when he was trying to convince me that sleeping together was a good idea.

"Shut up," he says with a laugh and pushes at my shoulder.

He looks so damn cute and sexy, and I've missed him so much that I can't do anything other than grab his face between my palms and slam my mouth down on his.

Andy's familiar taste and smell surround me, and it feels like home. I sink into the kiss until we're both breathless. A low hum of desire mixed with love runs through me, but before I'm going to address that, I need to know what happened with Asola.

Andy makes a face at the mention of his former crush. "Uh, well, I kissed him, and it was easily the most horrifying experience of my life. I mean, I can now safely say that I know what incest feels like."

Relief rushes through me. It's as if those words chase away the last of the doubts that were hiding inside me.

"I was never in love with Falcon," Andy continues. "It was just a case of hero worship that got out of hand. He's been my best friend, hell, my only friend, for a long time, and I guess I twisted that friend-ship in my head until I started to think it was love, but the more I fell for you, the more I started to realize that what I felt for Falcon didn't compare in any way." He shrugs. "But then you told me to go to Falcon, and I started doubting myself, and I told Falcon that I had a crush on him in the most awkward speech ever made. It included references to peeing, so you can try and imagine the magnitude of awful I was spewing out."

That... sounds like something Andy would do, actually.

"Anyway," Andy continues. "I kissed him. It was traumatizing. We'll continue being friends. Now *you* kiss me, because with you, I plan to be a lot more than friends."

I can't help but laugh at that. "Is that so?"

"Oh yeah. I bet you didn't expect that outcome when you came to the library to talk me into tutoring your team. Man, you got a lot more than you bargained for that day."

"You won't hear any complaints from me."

"You say that now, but just you wait unt—"

I shut him up with a kiss, and he laughs. Andy wraps his arms around my neck and pulls me closer.

I should probably get used to the surge of happiness. I have a feeling it will be a permanent part of my life from now on.

# EPILOGUE

## LAW

*10 years later*

I push the door open a crack and slide in. The goal is to go unnoticed. It's like a game. I try every time I'm here, but it's as if Andy has planted a bug somewhere on my person because he notices me almost every single time.

Today is one of the days I get lucky. Andy's back is toward the class as I slide into a seat at the back.

"Okay, people," Andy says. "Let's revise. What is acceleration?"

He points to a blonde girl in front of him. "Change in velocity over time," she shoots back immediately.

"Okay, now, an object is traveling in a straight line. Its acceleration is given by"—Andy scribbles a formula on the whiteboard—"C is a constant, n is a real number…"

Andy tells his students the rest of the problem and after a couple of minutes, the students start calling out answers. The thing that makes Andy such a great teacher is that he's so damn enthusiastic and invested in making the topic clear for everybody who sets foot in his classroom. No wonder he's insanely popular in his department.

The class continues for a while longer. Andy goes over the lecture until he's satisfied everybody's got it. He is animated and alive in front of the class. So unlike the timid guy I hired to tutor my college hockey team a decade ago. It's been an honor watching the transformation. I was next to him for every late-night freak out and session of self-doubt when he first started teaching classes after enrolling at MIT for his PhD. Looking at Andy now, you'd never guess that, once upon a time, he found a group of seven to be too intimidating to teach.

At front of the room, Andy smiles and nods. "We're done here, guys. Good job today. Don't forget that we have an exam coming up, and I'll see you on Wednesday."

Chairs scrape as the classroom empties, people calling out their goodbyes as they leave. Some of them smile and wave at me as they pass. I'm a regular, and from time to time, some of Andy's students recognize me. I'm not famous by any stretch of imagination, but the hardcore hockey fans recognize people from the coaching staff as well, I guess.

Now that the room has emptied, it isn't hard for Andy to spot me. He doesn't come to me, though. Instead, he leans his ass against his desk and a sexy smile curves his lips. "Mr. Carter," he calls. A shiver of pleasure runs over my skin at the sound of my married name on his lips. I've had the privilege of calling Andy my husband for five years now, and it feels just as good as it did the first time.

My mom and dad were disappointed when I chose to change my name, but using the same name felt right for me and Andy, and since Andy refused to be Andy Anderson, the choice of which name to use wasn't that difficult.

Andy smiles, like he knows exactly what's going on inside my head. "Did you have a question about the lecture?" he asks with a raised brow.

*Oh fuck, yeah. Hot professor fantasy is live, ladies and gentlemen.*

I nod my head. "Yes. I was hoping we could discuss the problems

I'm having in your class." I leave a short pause before I add, "Professor."

Andy sucks in a breath and a spark of heat ignites between us as he slowly walks toward me.

"And what might those problems be, Mr. Carter?" he asks as he stops in front of the desk I'm occupying.

My gaze travels over my husband's body as he stands there. In his dark gray slacks, black T-shirt with a science pun on it, and tweed blazer, he is the personification of a hot professor. And he's all mine.

It's getting difficult to think clearly through the haze of desire that is clouding my brain, but I persevere. Somebody should give me a fucking prize for the self-restraint I'm displaying.

"It's a large class," I say.

Andy smirks but plays along. "Twenty people isn't that many."

"I think you'll find I respond better to a more personal approach," I say and slide my foot against his. Andy looks down at our connected shoes, my battered sneaker against his proper Oxford, and smiles.

Andy stays in character, though, as he taps his forefinger against his chin. "Have you considered private lessons?"

"I have, but finding a good teacher is so difficult. Would you maybe consider teaching me yourself?"

He pretends to think about it for a second, and at the same time, slides his hand in the pockets of his slacks and cups his cock. My breathing picks up.

"I would," Andy says. "But I have to warn you. My services are not cheap, and I demand your full attention at all times."

I worry my lower lip between my teeth and shake my head. "I don't have much money."

"I think we can come to a mutually beneficial agreement." Andy slides his palm over my forearm. "Don't you think?"

I throw my head back and groan. "Okay. You're getting way too good at this game."

Andy's eyes light up and he whoops. "And that's. How. It's. Done!"

He follows each word with very questionable dance moves. I

mean, I love my husband, but the first dance in our wedding went viral and not for the right reasons.

"Yes, yes, I got hard before you. Congratulations."

Andy laughs and sits in my lap.

"Don't be a sore loser," he chides as he kisses me, not helping the erection situation one bit.

I slide my palms over his back and down his ass to squeeze. "I think we're both winners here."

I rub my hard dick against Andy's ass, and he closes his eyes and presses our foreheads together.

"We should go home and have sex," I say.

Andy groans. "You know we can't. We're supposed to have dinner with your parents in an hour."

"You can call them and say that we're busy doing science. You don't have to specify what kind. You know they'll believe you."

And they definitely will. My parents adore Andy. Have loved him ever since they first met him. In a way, he's the son they always wanted. My dad has long conversations with Andy about the business. Dad still runs it himself and has finally given up hope that I'll take over one day. Right now, the plan is to sell it at some point in the future. My mom has long phone conversations with Andy, where they discuss anything and everything, starting with Andy's research and ending with Mom's court cases.

Andy laughs and gets up. "Nice try, but we need all the bonus points we can get if we're going to announce the big move."

Setting all the jokes aside, I get up as well and take Andy's hand in mine. "You sure you're okay with it?" I ask.

Andy has been incredibly supportive about the whole thing but leaving Boston is still going to be hard, and if he's not okay with it, we're not going to do it.

"For the hundredth time, yes." Andy throws his arms around my neck. "Babe, we've talked about it. A lot. I'm one hundred percent on board with living in Chicago." He gives me a quick peck on the lips. Andy pulls away way too quickly for my liking and turns serious. "Law, you got offered the position of head coach for a university hockey team. A great team. Chicago has been on fire recently, and they want you. It's the next step toward making your dream come true."

"But you love Boston. You said it felt like coming home when we first moved here."

Andy nods before I'm even finished talking. "I do love Boston, but the home thing? That's all you. *You're* my home. With you by my side, I'd move to Timbuktu, if I had to."

"Thank God they don't have an NHL team," I joke and Andy laughs.

He turns serious again a moment later. "It's your dream. I will do anything to make it happen for you. Besides, University of Chicago offered me a great position." He nods his head once and smirks. "Change will be good. It'll shake things up. I mean, I might get bored of you otherwise."

I pull him against me. "Oh you might?"

"Well, we've been together for ten years. Let's face it, we're an old, married couple. Who knows? Maybe it's time to exchange you for a younger model?"

"Did I tell you I'll get a huge raise?" I ask.

"Then again, the old one is good for a few more years," Andy continues smoothly, and I snort out a laugh.

"What?" Andy asks. "I'm only with you because of your money."

"Oh good. I've always wanted a gold digger of my own, so you've made another one of my dreams come true."

"That is the goal." Andy presses another kiss to my lips. "And Chicago will also be a dream come true. I'll rock the University of Chicago with my awesomeness, and you'll win the Frozen Four and become a college hockey legend and before you know it, the NHL will be scrambling to hire you. Plus, we'll make some great memories in Chicago in the meantime."

"Sounds like a plan," I say, and for the first time, I allow myself to be excited about the move. A head coach. I still can't quite believe it's happening, that all my hard work has paid off, and I'm one step closer to the NHL. The years I had to spend working in the minors, maintaining a long-distance relationship with Andy, were akin to torture, but it has all worked out.

How is this my life? It feels like a dream but so much better because, as Andy squeezes my hand in his, I know that it's real.

"I love you," Andy says, making the reality fifty times better. I'll never get tired of hearing those words from him.

"Love you too," I say with a smile.

We walk down to Andy's desk, and he throws his bag over his shoulder.

"Now all we have to do is tell your parents," Andy says.

Our gazes connect, and at the exact same moment, we both say, "Not it."

Andy laughs. "Take two on the erection game?" he suggests with a snicker. "Loser tells your parents about Chicago."

I slide my hand behind Andy's back and squeeze his ass. "You're on, professor."

In the end, Andy wins again.

But I get to spend the rest of my life with him, so really, I'm the winner here.

The End

# ACKNOWLEDGMENTS

A big thank you to my family for their continued support and for being my biggest cheerleaders.

I'd also liked to thank Jill Wexler for beta reading, proofreading and encouraging me from the first e-mail we exchanged. And Louisa Keller for editing and fixing all those pesky commas and prepositions.

And lastly, thank you, LesCourt Author Services. I don't think I would have gone through with publishing this book without your help.

# ABOUT THE AUTHOR

Briar Prescott is a work in progress. She swears too much, doesn't eat enough leafy greens and binge watches too much television. It's okay, though. One of these days she'll get a hang of that adulting thing.

Probably.

Maybe.

She hopes.

You can contact Briar by email at prescottbriar@gmail.com. Seriously, she'd be so happy to hear from you.

You can also visit Briar's webpage at briarprescott.com.

And, you know, there's always Facebook.